Stuart Neville's debut novel, *The Twelve* (published in the US as *The Ghosts of Belfast*), won the Mystery/Thriller category of the *Los Angeles Times* Book Prize, and was picked as one of the top crime novels of 2009 by both the *New York Times* and the *LA Times*. He has been shortlisted for various awards, including the MWA Edgar, CWA Dagger, Theakstons Old Peculier Novel of the Year, Barry, Macavity and Dilys awards, as well as the Irish Book Awards Crime Novel of the Year.

He has since published nine more critically acclaimed books, two of which were under the pen name Haylen Beck, as well as a short story collection, *The Traveller and Other Stories*.

Stuart's novels have been translated into numerous languages, including German, Japanese, Korean, Polish, Swedish, Greek and more. The French edition of *The Twelve* won Le Prix Mystère de la Critique du Meilleur Roman Étranger and Grand Prix du Roman Noir Étranger.

Also by Stuart Neville

The Twelve (published in the US as *The Ghosts of Belfast*)
Collusion
Stolen Souls
The Final Silence
Those We Left Behind
So Say the Fallen
The Traveller and Other Stories

THE
HOUSE
OF
ASHES

Stuart Neville

ZAFFRE

First published in the UK in 2022
This paperback edition published in 2022 by
ZAFFRE
An imprint of Bonnier Books UK
4th Floor, Victoria House, Bloomsbury Square, London WC1B 4DA
Owned by Bonnier Books
Sveavägen 56, Stockholm, Sweden

A CIP catalogue record for this book is
available from the British Library.

ISBN: 978-1-83877-533-9

Also available as an ebook and an audiobook

1 3 5 7 9 10 8 6 4 2

Typeset by IDSUK (Data Connection) Ltd
Printed and bound in Great Britain by Clays Ltd, Elcograf S.p.A.

Zaffre is an imprint of Bonnier Books UK
www.bonnierbooks.co.uk

To Jo, Issy and Ezra, for giving me a reason

Fire

GLASS BREAKS DOWNSTAIRS AND SHE freezes in her bed, the blankets tight around her. Then a low noise, not quite a thump, but she feels it rise up through the floor, into the bedstead. Outside, a car door slams, then its engine rattles and fades.

She lies still for a time, listening, frightened. People come to her door sometimes. Not often, but sometimes. Children from the village, mostly, daring to walk all the way out here and knock on the mad old woman's door and run into the trees. This is different. She can't tell the time, but she knows it's near dawn from the milky grey that covers everything.

She listens. Something hums down below, as if the house has come awake along with her. A crackling, then one of the cats yowls, things knocked down and scattered. She sits up, the blankets falling away, and the damp chill of the air creeps beneath her nightdress. The smell reaches her, the dark, bitter smell, and she looks to the door, sees the glowing red and orange and the black swirling fingers reaching through the gaps.

Oh, no, she whispers. Oh, no, no, no.

Another cat howls, screams, she hears its pain.

Please God and Jesus, no.

1

She pushes the blankets back and pulls her legs from under them, ignoring the aches that come along with the movement. Lowering her feet to the floor, her lower back spasms, and she whines. The air has thickened now, the milky-grey light giving way to a greater darkness that reaches inside of her, scratching at her lungs.

She gets to her feet, her hips and knees protesting. The floor seems to tilt beneath her and she staggers to the door, reaching for the old ceramic handle. As she turns it, she feels the presence of heat, but too late. The door is already opening inward, pushed by some mighty force, and she falls back as scorching air blasts through.

As the floor connects with the rear of her head, something fiery streaks through the doorway and into the room, screaming, hitting the far wall, leaping, turning, trying to escape the flames that swarm it. She doesn't know which of the cats it is, but she covers her ears, trying to blot out its torment until it falls silent.

A thick black fog now covers the ceiling, like a roiling sky above her. Her eyes sting, and she coughs so hard she sees dark constellations.

Out, she says. Get out.

She rolls onto her stomach. She knows the stairs are aflame and offer no escape, that the landing will soon be engulfed. The heat is already unbearable. The window above the dresser: she gets her knees beneath her and crawls towards it, gasping and coughing. Items scatter from the surface of the dresser as she pulls herself upright. A hairbrush, a Bible, a perfume bottle that has been empty for decades. She reaches for the sash window, tries to pull it up and open. It will not move, and she cries out in anger and sorrow, knowing that she will die here.

No, she will not. Not now, not like this. Not after everything she's lived through. Not while the children still need her.

Oh, the children.

Are they burning with the wood and floors and walls? She can't hear them, only the cats trapped downstairs. But the children never speak, never make a sound, even when she was a girl, playing with them in the shaded corners of the secret room below the house. They were always silent. But will they burn?

She pulls at the window once more, and this time it moves, if only an inch or two. Enough to get her fingers underneath, to haul upwards with what little strength she has. She tastes the air from outside, clean, so clean. Up onto the top of the dresser, her head and shoulders out and through, and she sees the drop. How far to the ground? She can't tell. It might kill her. Better than burning. Anything is better than that.

Then she's falling.

She is not conscious of climbing through the window, of hanging by her hands from the frame, or the decision to let herself drop. First she is there, dangling by her fingertips, looking down at the ground, the overgrown bushes below the window, the past autumn's leaves, old gravel. Then the ground is rushing up to her and she cries out.

She turns in the air and catches a glimpse of them, the children, watching her fall. Then she lands in the bushes, branches clawing at her, then rolling away into a drift of leaves and twigs, her shoulder hitting the ground, and the pain is immense, exploding from her arm. Things go black for a moment, and when she opens her eyes again, the children are all around, and she sees the worry on their faces. She goes to speak to them, though she knows not what, and instead screams.

The little boy she knows is Matthew, the boy she has known for so many years, kneels down beside her and takes her hand.

Help me, she says.

The bigger children gather around, watching. The pain comes in waves, in torrents, screaming from the bones of her. She screams too.

From inside the house, she hears walls and ceilings collapse. The children wander away from her vision, towards the flames and smoke. She turns her head to see them return to the house, through the collapsed front door, to where they belong, where they have always been, where they will always be.

There, in the doorway, the girl she knows best of all, looking back at her. The girl in the plain white dress, dark hair falling around her shoulders, clutching a tangled bundle of scarlet ribbons to her belly. She does not burn. The flames do not touch her.

Nothing can touch her.

1

Sara

Sara Keane was kneeling on the kitchen floor not long after six thirty in the morning, scrubbing the flagstones, when the old woman hammered on the front door.

The stains. The brownish-red stains that were so faint she couldn't be sure they were there at all. Was this the third or fourth morning she had woken in the house? Time had become diaphanous, slipping by without her noticing. Days became weeks as she looked the other way, weeks turning to months before she knew they'd been lost to her.

She had not slept since they moved in. Not real sleep, not the warm dark that brings light, but the dim hinterland where bitter memories surfaced to torment her. Each morning, the chattering of birds outside the window banished the last hope of sleep before dawn. Each morning, she came downstairs in the milky-blue early light, passing the stacks of unpacked boxes.

The house had stood for more than a hundred and twenty years, so she was told. It rested behind a cluster of ash trees, taking its name from them: The Ashes, carved in one of the stone pillars at the gate. Her father-in-law, Francis – Francie, as he preferred – had found the house. Bought it for a song and gifted it to Sara and her husband Damien. A fire had left the place a shell, but it had been rebuilt. The original stone flooring remained intact, worn smooth by a century and more of footfall, dark and glossy like the skin of some ancient creature. It felt sinful to walk on it with bare feet, and all the better for it, the stone cooling her soles.

The first morning, however many days ago that was, Sara had come down here at dawn and made coffee while Damien snored upstairs. She noticed the stains over by the alcove that used to be a fireplace. An Aga cooker had been fitted where a wood-burning stove had once been. The stone in front of it was mottled with a deep red, as if something had spilled there years before. Clean it, she had thought. Damien would not tolerate mess. She had fetched a surface-cleaning wipe from a packet by the sink and got down on her knees. The stains seemed to fade as she rubbed the stone, though no residue was apparent on the wipe when she was done. Still, they were gone, and she thought no more about them until the following morning, when Damien was eating toast at the island in the centre of the room. She saw the stains, returned, as morning light brightened the kitchen.

'Look,' she had said, touching them with her bare toe, seeking a change in texture against her skin but finding none.

'Hmm?' He did not look up from his phone, one thumb scrolling while he sucked melted butter from the other.

'Those stains are back,' she said. 'I cleaned them yesterday morning, and now they've come back.'

'Yeah?' He took another bite of toast, a sip of coffee, kept his eyes on the phone.

'Look,' she said, 'here.'

Damien huffed out an impatient breath and put his slice of toast on the plate, leaned over on his stool, tilting his head one way, then the other.

'*Here,*' she said again, tapping the stain with her toe.

'I don't see it. It's just the pattern of the stone, no?'

Damien wore his good Hugo Boss jeans with a striped shirt tucked in at the waist, brown Grenson brogues, his Canali blazer on a hanger, suspended from a cupboard door. He was starting work today, the new in-house architect at his father's property development firm.

Things had come together quickly after what had happened back home — she still thought of it as back home — in Bath. She had been raised there in the West Country of England, had met Damien at the University of Bath, he a postgrad architecture student, she in her second year of studying for a social work degree. She never imagined, even after they married, that she would come to live in the place he never ever called Northern Ireland. Always the North, the North of Ireland, sometimes the Six Counties, but never Northern Ireland. As if to speak its name would shame him. She accepted his reasons, even if she never fully understood them. Not that it mattered, she had thought, because they would never move there, not to that place. But then things went bad, she had come so close to that most wretched sin, and they had decided to start over. Here, where he came from.

And it all fell into place, just like that, as if some unknown god had been waiting for her to take the overdose, as if the job for Damien had been here all along, as if this house had been biding its time until their arrival.

'It's there, *look,*' Sara said.

Damien pulled a sheet of kitchen paper from the roll on the island and wiped his hands clean before balling it up and leaving it by his plate. He reached for his jacket, slipped it on, and came to her side.

Looking down, he said, 'No, I don't see it. It's just the colour of the stone.'

'No, it's—'

'It's your imagination. I need to get going. You'll get some stuff unpacked, won't you? I don't want Da to be tripping over boxes when he comes round. You don't want the place to be a tip, do you?'

Francie Keane was due to visit this week to see how the work on the house was coming along. The parts the electrician needed hadn't turned up, and half the light switches remained uninstalled, clusters of wires snaking from the holes in the walls, ready to bite.

Damien didn't wait for a response, and Sara heard the front door close as she toed the stain. When the sound of his car had receded, she went to the sink, filled the plastic basin with warm water and washing-up liquid, and took the dish scrubbing brush from the windowsill. On her knees, she cleaned the floor, the deep red blotches fading into the smooth darkness of the stone.

She knew they would come back.

This morning, as the world lightened, she had listened to the birds for a while before finally giving up on sleep. Some of their calls had become familiar, and she wondered what kinds they might be. Maybe she would buy a book, some sort of guide to the different breeds. Another item on the list of things she would do one day, when she got around to it.

Sara wore a light cardigan over her pyjamas when she tiptoed downstairs, always soft in her step so as not to wake Damien. He didn't like being woken early, and he would be sullen and irritable for the rest of the day if she disturbed him. Half a dozen boxes remained in the hall, filled with books and DVDs and CDs, waiting for the joiner to shelve out the alcoves around the fireplace in the living room. None of them were hers. The hall's chill was deepened by the darkness there with no switches yet fitted for the lights.

In the kitchen, Sara filled the kettle and flicked it on. When it had boiled, she warmed the cafetière – Damien insisted that it be warmed first – then spooned in the coffee grounds. As she allowed it to stand, she gazed out of the window over the sink, towards the front of the property. She watched the ash trees, looking for the birds she'd been listening to these last few mornings. Brown earth stretched away from either side of the driveway, dotted by green shoots of new grass, freshly seeded a few weeks ago. The early autumn's first fallen leaves drifted and gathered in the sheltered spots. A river lay beyond the trees and the lane, down a steep bank. Perhaps she would go for a walk along there later; she had intended to yesterday but somehow the hours had gotten away from her, as was their habit.

The warm and earthy smell of coffee reminded her it would be ready now. As she went back to the island where the cafetière waited, she glanced at the floor in front of the Aga and stopped.

Those stains, returned. Of course they had.

She got down on her hands and knees, scratched at the largest one with the nail of her forefinger. The nail was bitten blunt, but she thought she might be able to scratch some of

9

the stain away. She rubbed the tip of her finger against her thumb, looking for residue, even a speck of some crumbling matter. There was nothing.

Sara cursed and got to her feet. She went to the door at the opposite side of the kitchen, the one that opened onto a staircase leading down into the dark. Inside, she found the light switch, one of the few that had been fitted. The space below illuminated. She held the railing as she stepped down, ducking beneath the low ceiling.

She did not like this room, finding it oppressive, the darkness of its corners unleavened no matter how many ceiling lights were installed. Not many houses here had basements, Damien had explained, due to the high water table. But this house had one, dug out decades ago and reinforced with wooden beams, reaching under the hall and part way beneath the living room. His father's tradesmen had modernised the basement, put in waterproof membranes, a new floor, and walls all freshly plastered, ready for painting. It had been plumbed and ventilated and fitted with a washer and dryer, along with shelves for cleaning items. She fetched a mop and bucket from one of the dim corners, and a stout brush from a shelf, along with a bottle of floor detergent.

As she climbed the stairs, Sara did not look back, feeling that she might see someone return her gaze. An irrational thought, but Damien said she was given to those.

In the kitchen, she half filled the bucket with hot water, along with a generous splash of the detergent. She brought the bucket to the space in front of the Aga, and once again got to her knees. Sara soaked the bristles of the brush and sloshed water onto the stained floor. She worked the brush hard into the stone, the detergent foaming. Her temples and jaw ached, and she realised how hard she had been grinding her teeth together.

After a few minutes of scrubbing, she wiped the suds away with her hand, showing clean stone, no stains left. Gone, finally.

'Thank—'

Before the second word could form in her mouth, a thunderous hammering boomed through the house, causing her to cry out. She remained on her knees for a moment, her mind scrambling to make sense of the noise, what it was, where it had come from.

Again, the rattling, booming thunder. Again, she startled.

Damien. Don't wake Damien.

As that thought flitted through her head, she realised it was the new front door. Someone banging hard on the PVC. She looked to the window over the sink. The sky still bluish grey, barely dawn. A pealing fear sounded in her. No one knocked on doors at dawn unless they brought terrible news. Sara got to her feet and went to the sink, leaned over it, peered through the window.

There, an elderly woman, impossibly small.

She wore a nightdress, a dressing gown pulled loosely over it, one foot bare, the other with a slipper half on. The woman's eyes darted here and there, across the front of the house, window to window. Her face twisted with fright and confusion. It occurred to Sara that she should go to the door and open it, ask this woman what she was doing here, help her.

Don't wake Damien, she thought, the words pushing to the front of her mind.

As she remained frozen in place, staring, the old woman noticed her. The woman stepped towards the window, limping. Only inches between their faces now, separated by glass, the old woman's eyes wild and piercing. Her mouth moved, and Sara heard her voice, weak and wavering, but she could not discern her words.

The old woman formed her right hand into a fist and hammered on the windowpane, wrenching Sara from her paralysis. Sara stepped back, retreating from the woman's stare. The woman pounded on the glass once more.

Help her, Sara thought. For God's sake, help her.

Finally, she moved, went to the hall and the front door. She pulled the lever handle, but it remained solidly in place. Locked, she remembered, and she ran back to the kitchen, to the bowl on the island, and grabbed the keys. Returning to the hall, she unlocked the door and opened it. The old woman was already there, pushing, pushing, stronger than Sara could have imagined, her voice rising as she forced her way inside, past Sara and into the hall. A trail of bloody footprints followed her. The insane idea to get the mop from the kitchen and clean the floor flashed in Sara's mind.

The woman turned in a circle, her burning gaze moving from floor to wall to doorway to Sara, her voice a panicked shriek.

'Who are you?' the woman asked. 'Why are you in my house?'

Sara backed against the wall, her hands up and out, as if to defend herself. 'I live here,' she said. 'We just moved—'

'Get out!' The woman bent double with the force of her own voice. 'Get out of my house!'

Sara shook her head. 'I don't—'

'Where are the children? What did you do with the children?'

Damien appeared on the stairs, eyes puffy, hair tousled, fastening the belt on his jeans, still wearing the T-shirt he'd slept in. The woman heard his footsteps, turned to stare up at him.

'What are you doing in my house?' she shouted at him.

'Oh, Jesus,' he said. He paused for a moment, then rushed down the remaining stairs.

'Damien,' Sara said, 'what's going—'

Before she could finish the question, the woman turned back to her.

'Get out of my house! Get—'

She fell to the floor like a bundle of twigs. While Sara remained against the wall, her back pressed to it, Damien rushed to the old woman, crouched down beside her. The woman cowered on the stone floor, her hands up to shield herself.

'You're all right, love, let's get you back.' He turned to speak to Sara. 'Grab my car key from the kitchen.'

Sara didn't move. 'We need to call the police.'

'No police,' he said, his voice hardening. 'I'll take her back. Just get the key, will you?'

'Take her back where? She's bleeding. She needs a hospital. We should call—'

'Just get the fucking key!'

His anger stirred her into motion, and she knew not to argue any further. She hurried to the kitchen, avoiding the woman's bloody footprints. When she returned with the key, fat and black in her palm, he snatched it from her and hauled the woman to her feet. The woman cried out as he pushed her towards Sara.

13

'Keep a hold of her,' he said as he went to the mat by the front door where his trainers sat beside hers.

Sara took the woman in her arms, felt her quivering, felt the chill of her skin through the dressing gown.

'My God, she's freezing,' Sara said, wrapping her open cardigan around the woman, hoping to share some warmth with her. 'She needs to go to hospital.'

Damien pulled each shoe on, yanking on the toggled cord to fasten them. 'The care home can sort that out.'

Sara felt anger drag her into the moment, time and reality connecting for the first time in months.

'What care home? Damien, who is she?'

'It's not my home,' the woman said. '*This* is my home. Where are the children? They need me. Where are they?'

Sara bent down to the woman's eye level. 'What children? What's your name?'

Damien took the woman from Sara's arms, his eyes flashing a warning. She did not drop her gaze.

'Never mind her name, she's away in the head. Just get that floor cleaned.'

As he carried her to the front door, still open, the woman said, 'Mary. My name's Mary, and this is my house.'

Damien slammed the door behind him.

Sara looked down at her bare feet and saw she stood in the woman's blood.

2

Mary

HERE, NOW, TILL I TELL you.

I always lived in the house. I never knew any different. Underneath, in the room down the stairs. In the dark. That's what I remember the most, when we were telt to put the lamps out. They locked the door at the top of the stairs and that was that. Dark until they opened it again. I still don't like the dark.

As far as I know, I was born there. Nobody ever telt me any different, and I don't mind any different. From I was wee, that's all I remembered. Always. Thon room under the house, then the rest of the place when I was allowed up.

The only light down there was the couple of oil lamps they allowed us to have. It was always cold and wet. They'd made a floor out of wooden boards, and a ceiling, with posts to holt it up. The floor was always damp. Sometimes, if it rained hard outside, mucky water would come up through the cracks.

I don't mind what age I was the first time they let me up the stairs by my own self. Five, maybe, or six. Old enough that I could do a lock of wee things about the place. Sweeping up the floors or dunging out the ashes from the fireplaces. Mummy Noreen telt me what to do. Says she, when the Daddies is around, you don't look at them, just you get on with your work. Just you pretend you aren't there, and they'll not bother with you. Unless they *do* bother with you, then you be polite and don't give them any cheek.

So that's what I did. I just bate on with what I had to do, and if Daddy George or Daddy Ivan came in, I just put my head down and said nothing. And that wasn't hard to do, either. I was wild afeart of them. They weren't slow about giving beatings, them boys. Many's a time Mummy Noreen or Mummy Joy would have a black eye or a sore back from a kicking.

Daddy Tam was the worst of them. He was a cribb'd auld skitter, so he was. He'd slap you soon as look at you. And them big hands of his. If he hit you, you knew you were hit.

I mind the first time he hit me. I'd finished sweeping up the ashes around the hearth in the living room. It was the wintertime because it would've foundered you in the house, but I remember the sun was out, and it was shining between the bare branches of the trees outside, and through the windows. Mummy Joy had just cleaned them, and you'd hardly know the glass was there she'd cleaned them that well. And I was there in the room all by myself and the sun was shining in and it felt warm on my arms, so here, didn't I start dancing? I don't know what notion I took, but I started twirling around like I don't know what. Just spinning around and tittering away.

Then something slammed into my head, bang, and I didn't know what it was. I thought the roof had fallen on me. Then here's me on the floor, didn't know what way up I was, and Daddy Tam's standing over me.

Says he, What do you think you're at?

16

I was that afeart I couldn't answer him. I just stared up at him. Then he kicked me in the backside, awful hard, I'd never felt the like of it. I'd been hurt before, I'd had the odd wee bump or scrape, but no one had ever *hurt* me before. Not like that.

I don't mind too well, but I suppose I must've cried or screamed because Mummy Joy came running in and she got down beside me, between me and Daddy Tam, and says she, Get you away from her.

No one ever talked back to Daddy Tam. Never, never, never. I could see the anger in him. He was always angry, that man, they all were, but this was not the same. He was raging so much he went all quiet. And pale, except for the red blotches on his cheeks. I remember his big hands opening and closing. I remember feeling Mummy Joy starting to shake.

Then he points at me, and says he, Get thon child out of my sight, then you get back up here.

Mummy Joy didn't argue with him. She picked me up and she carried me out into the hall, then into the kitchen, and through the door and down the stairs. She put me on the wee bed I had in the corner and put a blanket around me.

I suppose I must've been crying, and Mummy Joy was too, and says I, Don't go up there, but says she, I have to, and away she went. She left me holding one of the wee dollies I'd made from tying sticks together with twine, the ones I kept hidden under my mattress so Daddy Ivan wouldn't take them from me.

I heard all of it, Daddy Tam shouting and raging, the banging and the thumping, her screaming. It sounded like he was dragging her across the floor, back into the kitchen, and the way she was squealing, I suppose he must've been dragging her by the hair. Then I heard Daddy George telling him to quit it, he was going to kill her if he kept on.

So what if I do, says he.

Then I'll kill you, says Daddy George.

Then them two went at it. Mummy Joy closed the door behind her and came down the stairs in the dark. She found her way to me and got into the bed and we cuddled up in the dark, under the blanket. All the time, from upstairs, banging and thumping and shouting. Then we heard Daddy Ivan come along and that was the end of it. As afeart as I was of Daddy Tam, him and Daddy George were more afeart of Daddy Ivan.

A wee while later, I don't mind how long, Mummy Noreen came down and she lit the lamps and said we should stay down there for the rest of the day, just till things calm down. Things is bad, says she. Daddy Tam's thran, he's in a terrible twist, and he's on the drink again. Don't show yourself, either of yous, not till tomorrow, not till he's sobered up.

What age was I then? I don't know. Six, maybe. I never had a great notion what age I was. Tell you the God's honest truth, I don't know what age I am now.

But that was our days and nights. Up early in the morning, up into the house, cleaning and tidying, Mummy Noreen sometimes doing the cooking for the Daddies, other times Mummy Joy. Then downstairs in the evening to ate whatever leftovers there was. Whoever did the cooking always made sure there was just enough. Then when it was time to go to sleep, one of the Daddies would call down to us to put the lamps out, and he'd close the door and lock us in for the night.

It was always like that. Sure, I never knew any different.

3

Sara

SARA WAS CLEANING THE HALL floor with the mop and bucket she'd fetched from the basement when Francie arrived, letting himself in. He stood in the doorway for a moment, studying her. It wasn't the first time he'd looked at her that way, his gaze travelling over her, pausing where it shouldn't. She pulled her cardigan tight around herself with her one free hand.

'Not dressed yet?' he said.

'I haven't had the chance,' she said, wondering what the time was. It couldn't be much past seven fifteen, and yet here he was, letting himself into her house.

Her house?

An uncomfortable thought flickered at the edge of her mind. She ignored it.

'Any danger of a cup of tea?' Francie asked.

His voice was deep and rasping, roughened by a lifetime of shouting at other men. Sara knew a little of his past, including the six years he'd spent in the Maze prison before getting an early release as part of the Good Friday Agreement. A builder by trade, he'd established his property development business not long after getting out, and it had flourished in the twenty years since. Damien had never told her what offence his father had been sent away for, only that he had been wrongly convicted. When she looked his name up on Google, archived news stories said it had been for possession of explosives. He was not a tall man, but he was wide at the shoulders, and the belly, and he seemed to take up the entire hall. Standing with his hands in his pockets, he ran his gaze over the boxes stacked against the wall.

'Let me just finish up with this,' Sara said.

'Sure, I'll get it myself,' he said.

He stepped past her into the kitchen, and she listened to him hum and whistle to himself while he filled the kettle. The water in the bucket had grown dim and murky, but the floor was now clear of blood. Yet she felt it lingering on her soles, warm and slick, as if it was her own.

Her own.

Sara became aware of the air around her, the pressure and weight of it, and the bar of sunlight that cut through the glass panel in the door to fall on her skin. The heat of it. She inhaled, her lungs filling, and reached out a hand to steady herself against the wall. Her heart rate accelerated and she felt her pulse in her throat, resonating up through her head.

She recognised this sensation, the alignment of time and reality. It had come upon her once before, and she had drowned it with sleeping pills.

'You all right?'

Francie's voice startled her. He stood in the kitchen doorway, watching her.

She had to force the words out of her mouth.

'I'm fine,' she said. 'A bit dizzy, that's all.'

Francie grunted, nodded, and returned to the kitchen.

Sara inhaled through her nose, exhaled through her mouth, deep breaths until her heart rate slowed. Balance restored, she brought the bucket and mop to the small bathroom off the back hall and emptied the dirty water into the toilet. When she returned to the kitchen, Francie sat on one of the stools at the island, nursing his mug of tea. He hadn't made one for her.

'I'm fine,' Sara said again, without being asked.

Francie looked at her over his steaming tea. 'Mm-hm.'

'Did Damien call you?' she asked.

'Aye,' he said. 'Crazy woman.'

Sara stood at the far end of the island, blocking his view of the window. 'She said this was her house.'

'Mm-hm?' he said.

'Was it?'

His shoulders slumped as if he were dealing with a child who had asked one question too many. 'She started a fire. Lucky to get out alive. The local health trust ruled she wasn't fit to look after herself. She was put in that care home on the other side of Morganstown. The house had to be sold to pay for it.'

'Why didn't you tell us that?'

'I told Damien.'

'He didn't tell me.'

Francie set down his tea. 'Look, don't you worry about it. Happens all the time, people losing their homes like that. If I hadn't bought this house, someone else would've. Worse than that, another developer probably would've took a bulldozer to the place and put up a dozen three- and four-bedroom houses. Isn't it better it was left standing so a family could make a home of it?'

21

'I'd just like to have been told, that's all,' she said.

'I told Damien,' he repeated.

'She kept talking about children. She asked where they were.'

'She didn't have any children, unless you count all the cats she had about the place. Maybe that's what she meant. God knows how many of the bloody things she had. Look, she's just a crazy old woman. Don't worry yourself about it.'

Before she could argue, she heard her husband's car outside, tyres crunching on the loose stone. She turned to the window over the sink and saw his BMW pull up alongside his father's Range Rover. Sara's first thought was of the floor in the hall, was it clean enough? Damien was particular about such things. She watched through the open kitchen door as he entered, examining the floor as he wiped his feet on the mat. He appeared to be satisfied, and she felt a quiet relief.

As he came into the kitchen, Damien noted the tea in front of his father. 'Any for me?' he asked.

'I got it myself,' Francie said.

'You made him get his own tea?' Damien asked, his eyes hard on Sara.

'Well, she was busy,' Francie said.

The need to know about the woman defeated the need to defend herself, and the fear of doing so.

'You told me to clean the floor,' she said, her fingers twining together. She forced them apart. 'Why did that woman come here? What did she want?'

'You could've stopped to make him a cup of tea,' Damien said, ignoring her question.

'Why was she here?'

He became still, his gaze fixed on her. Francie kept his attention on his tea.

'We'll talk about it later,' Damien said. He spoke to his father. 'You wanted to look at the extension?'

'Aye,' Francie said, easing himself off the stool. 'Come on, we'll do it now.'

Damien followed his father into the back hall, out into the shell of the new wing that had been added to the house, the structure eventually turning it from a three- to a six-bedroom dwelling, along with two more receptions. When the plans were being drawn up, Sara had asked about a space for herself, perhaps a room with good light where she could paint, a passion she had allowed to drift away since before they married. We'll see, Damien had said.

She went to the island, lifted the mug Francie had left there, and brought it to the sink. As the tea swirled around the plughole, the idea flashed in her mind to smash the mug into the enamel. How satisfying it would be to hear it shatter, to watch the fragments fly. Then she imagined having to explain it to her husband, and the idea drained away like the drink she had just poured out.

Damien and Francie would be a while, she knew, examining the work on the extension, taking stock of what had been done and what needed doing. Time to have a shower, get dressed. She climbed the stairs to the small bedroom she and her husband shared. Once the extension was completed, they would move into a new room with an en suite and a walk-in wardrobe. For now, they made do.

Her phone sat on the wireless charging dock by the bed. She lifted it and checked for messages, even though she knew there would be none. Hadn't been for months. Not since before she had taken those pills. Damien had asked her friends, the few she'd had left, to give her some space. He had told her so after she had regained consciousness on the emergency ward. They were no good for her anyway, he'd said. Poisoning her mind with their gossip. They were jealous, he'd said, envying what she and Damien had together. They'd ruin things if she let them. Better to keep them at a distance, just for now. Just until things were more settled.

The phone was three generations out of date, but she had no need to upgrade it. The only person who ever called or texted these days was her husband.

A thought occurred to her, and she hesitated for a moment. Should she? She should.

Sara sat on the edge of the bed and opened the phone's web browser. She searched for the words 'care home' and 'Morganstown'. They still lacked an internet connection at the house, and the 4G signal was patchy at best out here, so it took some time for the results to load.

The first was Greenway Care and Convalescence Home, Morganstown. Next to it, a blue icon of a telephone handset, with the word 'Call' beneath it. Without considering her actions, she thumbed the icon and brought the phone to her ear. The dial tone chimed twice.

'Good morning, Greenway, Margaret speaking, how can I help?'

Hang up, Sara thought. Hang up now.

Instead, she asked, 'Do you have a resident called Mary?'

The question felt blunt in her mouth, tumbling gracelessly out.

A pause, then, 'Who's calling, please?'

Sara closed her eyes tight, swallowed, gathered her words. 'Sorry, my name is Sara Keane. A woman came to our house this morning. She'd wandered off from a care home nearby, and my husband brought her back. He didn't tell me which one, and I wondered if it was yours?'

'Mary Jackson,' Margaret said, her voice officious. 'Yes, we must apologise again. We're still looking into how she managed to find her way out during the night. We're very grateful to Mr Keane for bringing her back. I can assure you, this sort of incident is very rare. We take the security of our residents very—'

'Is she all right?' Sara asked. 'She had a cut. And she was so cold. I just wanted to make sure she was okay.'

'She's fine,' Margaret said. 'One of the nurses on staff is looking at the cut, and we've a doctor coming out to check on her later.'

'Good,' Sara said. 'It's just, I was worried for her.'

She heard Margaret's exhalation, an easing in her tone.

'We were worried too,' Margaret said. 'The police were out looking for her. I'm sure they would have tried your place before too long, but we didn't think she could have got that far. It's what, two, three miles away?'

Sara pictured Mary's bloody foot.

'She must be exhausted.'

'God love her,' Margaret said. 'We're very fond of Mary here. She gets confused sometimes, but she's an awful sweet soul. Wee Mary, everyone calls her. It's a wonder that woman has any sanity left, everything she's been through.'

'What do you mean?' Sara asked.

'Well, the fire for one, but all that business when she was a child. Such a thing to go through.'

Sara's throat tightened.

'What business? What happened?'

A pause, then Margaret asked, 'You don't know?'

'No,' Sara said.

'Oh. When I heard someone had taken over the house, I wondered. I thought you would've known.'

'Please tell me,' Sara said.

'The killings. It's more than sixty years ago now, maybe sixty-five, long before my time, but it was a terrible thing. Her just a child and all. I don't remember how many died, four or five, maybe, the whole family wiped out. A terrible thing. You really didn't—?'

Damien's footsteps on the stairs.

Sara hung up, found the call-history list, the care home at the top. She swiped left with her thumb, hit the red delete button, returned to the home screen as Damien entered the room.

He stopped in the doorway. 'Who were you talking to?'

'No one,' she said. 'I was just reading the news.'

Damien approached the bed and held out his hand. He didn't have to ask. Sara gave him the phone. He studied the screen, as he thumbed through menus.

'I thought I heard you talking,' he said.

'Just to myself,' she said.

He stared down at her for a moment before handing back the phone.

'You embarrassed me in front of my father.'

'I was just asking a question.'

'Don't do it again,' he said. 'Time you were dressed, no?'

Sara nodded as she took the phone from him, cradled it in her lap. She held back the tremors until he left the room.

4

Mary

I F THE WEATHER WAS GOOD, and if they were in decent form, the Daddies would let us all out into the yard on a Sunday afternoon. Behind the house, with the auld cowshed at the far end, the stone buildings on either side. The lane cut down the back to the fields, with a gate across. I wasn't allowed over to the gate, none of us were, we had to stay near to the house.

Sometimes, not often, but sometimes, if Daddy George was watching us, he'd let me go over to the cows and say hello to them. I liked that. The way they'd all crowd together when they saw me coming. The way they'd sniff at my hand and lick my fingers, their tongues rough like wet sandpaper. The way their heads felt all hard and warm under their coats.

Daddy George was better than the other two, I suppose. He never struck me nor the Mummies. Not like Daddy Ivan, he'd give you a hiding for no reason at all. And Daddy Tam, he was the worst when he was thran. Most cribb'd auld hoor you ever met. But Daddy George wasn't as bad.

Anyway, some Sundays, after the Daddies came back from church and they'd let us upstairs, we'd be allowed out into the yard. Mummy Joy and Mummy Noreen would just walk in circles around it, sometimes not even talking much to each other. They could talk all they wanted downstairs in the house, but outside, they just walked and walked. And I just ran and leapt about the place. Sometimes I chased the chickens. I had to be quiet, though. There was no shouting and getting on, oh, no, Daddy Ivan would never tolerate that.

I used to wonder what was outside the yard. I could see the hills and the fields and the trees and the sky, but that was all. I knew there was roads and towns and cars and other people, even if I'd never seen them. Mummy Joy telt me about them. Her and Mummy Noreen weren't born in the house, not like me, they hadn't always lived there. Mummy Joy was from Armagh, and Mummy Noreen was from Belfast. I've still never been to them places. I've never been anywhere. No call to, I suppose.

I'm not sure, but I think Mummy Joy was my real mummy. Both of them were awful good to me, but Mummy Joy was the one who coddled me the most. She was the one who looked after me if one of the Daddies gave me a hiding. Aye, I think she was my real mummy.

You know, I don't mind awful well, but sometimes I think there was another mummy about the place, older than the others, but sometimes I think that was just a notion I had. But I do know there was a wee boy at one time. It must've been when I was very wee because I can't mind what he looked like, just that he was small, and he didn't be well. He stayed in bed near the whole time. Then he wasn't there any more, and Mummy Noreen wasn't at herself for a long time after. I mind that more than I mind him. Her staying quiet for weeks and weeks and her crying at night after the lamps went out. And there was the time Mummy Joy's belly got big like she had a baby in her and then she got a hiding from Daddy Tam and she got awful sick and was bleeding and I had to stay downstairs while Mummy Noreen looked after her upstairs.

Things like that all run together in my head. I couldn't tell you which was when, what came first or came last. Not really. Time doesn't work the same way when you're older than it did when you were a wee'un. And every day was like the other, no difference between them at all, except for Sundays, if the weather was good.

I mind this one Sunday we were out in the yard, I was maybe nine or ten at that time, I don't know, but it was me and the Mummies, and Daddy George, and I was skipping and dancing around and the Mummies were walking in circles, their heads together, talking. I mind the sun was out, and it was warm in the yard. I could hear the birds all around us. Daddy Ivan used to put food out for the birds and I watched them whenever I could. I never learnt the names of many of them, except the crows and the magpies, and the big fat wood pigeons. Daddy Tam would go hunting the wood pigeons and bring them back for us to pluck for his tea.

But here, this one Sunday, we all heard something. Me first. An engine. Except it wasn't all rattly like the tractor Daddy Tam drove around the farm. This was different. Not as loud, not as hard sounding. It was a nice sound, even if it wasn't natural. I stopped skipping and froze to the spot. I saw the birds, over the roof of the house, all flutter up into the high branches of the trees. Then the Mummies heard it too, and they froze as well. Daddy George just stood there, looking at us. He hadn't heard it, I don't know for why.

29

Next thing, the back door flies open, and Daddy Ivan's there telling us to come on, get inside, now, now, now, come on! Nobody moved, so he comes out into the yard and grabs me by the arm, and Daddy George gets a holt of the Mummies, one hand each, and we're all dragged inside.

When we were in the kitchen, on our way to the door downstairs, I looked out the window to the front, and I saw the car. I'd seen a car before, Daddy Ivan had one, but this wasn't like his auld thing. This one was new and shiny. And here, didn't a man get out of it? Right in front of the window where we could all see him. He had this uniform on him, dark green, and a tie. And he lifted a hat out of the car and put it on his head. I mind it had a peak to it. I'd never seen a policeman before, but I knew that's what he was. And he was awful handsome. The only men I'd ever laid eyes on before was the Daddies, and they was all big auld lumps, but this man, he was beautiful. I thought he was, anyway, and here I froze to the spot and I wouldn't move because I wanted to watch this man.

And Mummy Joy, she wanted to see him too. That's what I thought at the time. I know that's not true now, but sure, I didn't know any better. I mind she opened her mouth and breathed in like she was going to shout hello to him, only Daddy George took holt of her and put his hand over her mouth. She tried to shout anyway, but he helt her so tight she couldn't make a sound.

And he leans in, and he says to her, They'll kill you. They'll kill him and they'll kill you and the wee girl, they'll kill all of yous, so, for God's sake, be quiet. And she was. She went still and quiet and she took me by the hand and we all went downstairs into the dark and Daddy George closed the door behind us.

That wasn't the last time I saw thon policeman. I wish it was the last time, for I still have dreams about thon man. About what they did to him.

5

Sara

AFTER SHE'D SHOWERED, WHILE SHE dressed in the newly fitted bathroom, Sara heard a raised, angry voice from outside. She knew it belonged to Francie. In the bedroom, she went to the window and looked down at the front of the property. A man stood by a van, his head down, looking at his feet. Francie, a good six inches shorter, stood so close his belly pressed against him, his forefinger stabbing at the air an inch from the man's face. The man wore a tool belt. The electrician, she thought.

She could hear snatches of Francie's words now.

'A week ago . . . get the fuck in there . . . get it finished . . . I'll knock the shite out of you.'

Sara went to the top of the stairs. From there, she could see the open front door. The electrician stepped through, carrying a toolbox. He noticed her watching and froze for a moment. She saw the shame on him, knowing she'd witnessed his humiliation. He got himself moving and disappeared from her view. She had the urge to call after him, but Damien entered and jogged up the stairs. He brushed past her on his way to the bedroom. She followed him.

'Your father told me about that woman,' Sara said.

Damien peeled off his T-shirt and selected a fresh shirt from the wardrobe. 'Aye?'

'Why didn't you tell me?'

'I thought I had,' he said, feigning a thoughtful look. 'Yeah, I'm sure I did.'

'No, you didn't.'

'Yeah, I did,' he said, his voice firmer now. 'When I first told you Da had bought this place. I mentioned it then. Remember, I told you, that's why it was so cheap.'

'I don't remember,' Sara said.

That conversation seemed clear in her mind. A fortnight after she'd got out of hospital. There's this house, Damien had said over dinner. And he told her about it, out in the country, by a river, peaceful and quiet, just what we need to get things back to normal. To get your head straight. There had been a fire, yes, she remembered him saying that, but she couldn't recall mention of the woman having to go to a care home.

But maybe she was mistaken. Certainty had become a stranger to her. Damien often remembered things she didn't. Things that had happened or hadn't happened. Words spoken or unspoken. She had learnt to distrust her own memories.

'Was there anything else?' she asked.

He paused buttoning his shirt and studied her more intently. 'What do you mean?'

'About this house,' she said, holding his gaze.

'What are you getting at?'

'It's an old house. It must have a history. I just wondered about it.'

'Is that what you're wearing?' he asked.

She looked down at the top she wore, simple, short-sleeved, light cotton, with a V-neck. 'What's wrong with it?' she asked, aware that he'd sidestepped her previous question.

'Just, with the electrician around the house . . .'

He let his words trail away, knowing his meaning was clear. He reached into the wardrobe, found a faded old hoodie. She took it from him and slipped it on, went to ask him once more about the house, but he was already heading to the door.

'I need to go,' he said, nudging her out of his way. 'I'm running late.'

The idea of being alone in the house, even with the electrician, caused unease in her.

'Can I have the car?' Sara asked, knowing she was on the edge of angering him.

He paused at the top of the stairs. 'What for?'

'Just so I can get out for a while,' she said, scrabbling for a reason to give him. 'Your father can give you a lift, can't he? I don't want to hang around the house all day while the electrician's working, and besides, we need some bits and pieces. I could go into the village to that little grocer's shop we saw.'

'No, he's already away,' Damien said. 'We'll see about a car of your own once we're settled. I need to get going.'

He descended the stairs and closed the front door behind him. Sara hesitated, considered locking herself into the bedroom and remaining there for the day, but she would not let cowardice guide her. She went downstairs and found the electrician in the living room, on his knees, working on a power outlet. He did not acknowledge her presence, though she knew he was aware of it. It was her natural inclination to leave him, pretend he wasn't there, but she decided to attempt an interaction.

'Can I get you anything?' she asked.

He didn't look up. 'No, ta.'

'It's no trouble. The kettle's not long boiled.'

Keeping his attention on his work, he said, 'Look, I just want to get my work done and get out of this house, all right?'

'Okay,' she said. 'Sorry.'

He glanced up at her, and she sensed his shame at having snapped at her. She left him alone and entered the kitchen. The emptiness of the space surrounded her, and she felt small in this room, engulfed by it. She went to the island at its centre and placed her hand on its polished granite surface. The cool stone against her palms, the chill rising up through her arms.

The killings, the receptionist at the care home had said. Four or five dead.

Sara felt the hollowness of the basement below, felt it like a vacuum that wanted to swallow her whole, a bottomless pit waiting for her to stumble into its mouth. The urge to leave, to get out of the house, grew stronger. She went to the back hall, through to the door that opened out onto the yard. Opening it, she stepped outside onto the loose stones and gravel. The warmth of the autumn sun touched her, washed the chill away.

The shell of the extension stood to her left, larger than the original house, all glass and stone cladding. The sliding patio doors opened out onto what would some day be an impressive expanse of garden. For now, it looked like a battlefield. The old concrete yard had been dug up, rubble piled at the far end where a cowshed had once stood. Topsoil would be laid over the exposed earth at some point, with paths making channels through it. Damien had promised her flower beds and herb patches to look after, despite her having no interest in gardening.

Not mine, she thought. I shouldn't be here.

I'm walking on graves.

That idea formed in her mind, unbidden, and it swept away any warmth she had found out here. She tried to push it back down, but it lingered like a shameful memory.

'Stop it,' Sara said aloud, and she stepped back inside the house, closing the door and locking it. She walked through the back hall towards the kitchen, arms wrapped around herself. In the kitchen, the shape of a man startled her, and she gasped.

'Sorry,' the electrician said, his hands up and out. 'I didn't mean to scare you.'

Sara placed her palm against her stomach to quell the fluttering things the fright had stirred. 'It's okay,' she said.

The electrician shuffled his feet, looked at the floor, looked at her. She sensed the fear in him, though why he should be afraid of her, she could not fathom.

'I came in to apologise,' he said. 'I shouldn't have snapped at you. I was out of order. I'm sorry.'

Sara shook her head, forced a smile. 'It's fine. No need to apologise.'

'If Francie knew I'd done that, he'd . . .'

The words faltered as he spoke, and he looked at the floor once more. She realised then the man wasn't afraid of her, but of her father-in-law.

'He'd do what?' she asked.

He searched for an answer. 'I don't know,' he said. 'He wouldn't be happy, anyway.'

'I won't tell him,' Sara said, truthfully.

'Thanks,' he said, and turned to leave, then changed his mind. 'You know, I'd take that tea if it's still going.'

A smile broke on Sara's face, a real one, and for a moment it felt alien to her. She wondered when she'd last felt one on her lips. Too long.

'Sure,' she said and went to the kettle. She filled it at the sink, returned it to its base, and flicked it on.

'How are you settling in?' the electrician asked.

It occurred to Sara that she didn't know his name, so she asked him.

'Tony,' he said, ducking his head as if embarrassed. 'Tony Rossi.'

'Italian?' she asked, her surprise genuine.

'Aye,' he said. 'Tony, as in Antonio, but no one calls me that except my mother when she's annoyed at me.'

'Are there many Italians in Ireland? I'm Sara, by the way.'

'I know who you are,' he said, taking a seat at the island. 'Aye, there's a few of us. A lot came over in the eighteen hundreds, working on the churches and the big houses, stucco work, stained glass, that sort of thing. My grandparents on my father's side came over after the Second World War, rebuilding after the Belfast Blitz. My people were all tradesmen. But, here, you don't need the history of the Rossi clan.'

She set a mug of steaming tea in front of him, offered him milk and sugar. He took both. She noted the small scars on his hands as he spooned sugar into the tea, the definition of his forearms.

'I'm sorry,' she said, 'I'd give you something to eat, but we don't have much in.'

'Never worry, this'll do me all right,' he said. He dipped his head, thumbing the lip of the mug. 'I heard you earlier, asking Damien for the car. If you need anything in the village, I could give you a lift in. I'd have to finish my work first or Francie will kick my arse up and down the driveway, but this afternoon, I could run you in. If you want.'

For no reason she could grasp, Sara felt heat on her throat and face. Without thinking, she put a hand to her cheek, as if to cool it. She caught herself and dropped her hand to slap against the granite top of the island, almost knocking over the mug of tea she'd made for herself.

'Maybe,' she said.

A question had been lingering on her tongue since she'd found him in the kitchen. She summoned the nerve to ask it.

'Earlier, you said you just wanted to get out of this house. Why?'

His face darkened. He shook his head. 'I don't know. I was in bad form after Francie had a go at me, that's all.'

Sara remembered her time as a social worker, sessions with youngsters, coaxing their most fiercely guarded secrets from them. They always left crumbs to follow, whether they intended to or not.

'That's all?' she echoed.

He shifted his balance on the stool, kept his gaze on the mug in front of him. 'I mean, it's your house, so I can't say anything against it.'

'Yes, you can,' she said.

Tony glanced up at her and away, scratched at the back of his neck.

'Say it.'

He took a breath, then his shoulders slumped.

'It's just . . . there's a bad vibe about the place.' He looked at her now. 'I can't tell you what it is, exactly, just a bad feeling.

39

Not all of it, not all the time. But it's there. The basement more than anywhere else. I did the wiring down there, and it was . . .'

His gaze dropped once more.

'It was what?' she asked.

'I didn't see anything down there, nothing like that. But it would get cold sometimes, all of a sudden, for no reason. I'd feel like there was someone looking over my shoulder, and I'd look up from my work and turn to see, and there'd be nothing there. And there was this thing my mate told me.'

'What did he tell you?'

He scratched at the back of his head then spread his hands out in the air, as if giving something up. 'My mate John Joe. He's a plasterer. He told me he was upstairs, not in your bedroom, one of the others, working late. It had gotten dark. He told me he looked through the door and he saw a wee boy playing on the landing up there. Just a wee lad running and jumping about. John Joe went out onto the landing and there was no one there. Mind you, John Joe likes a wee puff on the weed, so I don't know. It was probably his imagination.'

He gave a breathy laugh, dismissing his own words. 'It was my imagination too, I know, but with everything that happened here, it puts things in your head.'

'What happened here?' she asked.

Tony stared at her now, as if he couldn't understand the question.

After a moment, he said, 'What, you mean you don't know?'

'I heard there was a killing,' Sara said, 'but that's all. I don't know what happened.'

'Neither do I. Not really. It was a long time ago. Sixty years, maybe more, I'm not sure. Before the Troubles started up, anyway. The whole lot of them was killed, except the woman who had this house, she was the only survivor. That's as much as I know about it. I tell you who might know more, though.'

'Who?'

'Mr Buchanan, he has the grocer's shop on the way into Morganstown. I think he used to bring food out here for her. Might be worth asking him about it.' Tony pushed his stool back and stood. 'Anyway, thanks for the tea. I should get back to my work. But, when I'm done, do you want me to run you into the village?'

'Yes, please,' Sara said. 'I'd like that.'

6

Mary

EVERYTHING STAYED THE SAME FOR a long time.
Could have been a lock of weeks or months, or maybe
years, I don't know. I mind I got some new clothes.
One of the Daddies would go away for a day or two and come
back with new clothes for us all. Well, I say new, but I suppose
some of them was worn before. But I was always glad of them,
whether they fit me or not. Dresses and knickers and socks
and shoes. We all had a paper bag each full of things, and we
tried them on downstairs.

I mind Daddy Tam standing on the stairs, watching us while
we changed, with his hands in his pockets. He did that sometimes. Just stand and watch you with his hands in his pockets,
moving about inside them. Sometimes he'd start breathing
hard. I didn't know then what he was at, but I know now.
Dirty auld hoor. Anyway, Mummy Joy moved me so I was
behind her, so he couldn't see me when I got changed into
the new clothes.

When we'd tried everything on, and we knew what fit and
what didn't, Daddy Tam spake up. He pointed over at the wall
where the extra bed was leaned up agin it. Get that made up,

says he. We'll maybe have someone joining yous in a day or two.

Mummy Joy and Mummy Noreen looked at each other. Daddy Tam turned and went back up the stairs, said he'd be back in a while to lock up for the night, and we'd better have that bed sorted.

Mummy Joy pulled the bed away from the wall. It was one of those wee ones with the metal frame, like a soldier would sleep on, with a wee thin mattress. Like we all had. I unfolded the sheets and blankets and the Mummies spread them out on the bed, tucked the ends in. It was like a, what you call it, a ritual, yes, like a ritual. I'd never been in a church, but I thought that was what it must be like. People doing these rituals together, all quiet.

When they were done, the Mummies sat down on their own beds, and they whispered. Not so quiet I couldn't hear them, but quiet enough they wouldn't be heard upstairs.

Who do you think it'll be?

What age will she be?

God, I hope she's not too young.

I was fourteen when I came here. What age were you?

Fifteen.

How long have we been here?

Fifteen winters.

Thirteen winters.

I don't mind what age I was then, I suppose ten or eleven or so, but that was the first time the thought entered my head that the Mummies weren't much more than wee girls themselves. I'd no notion of it then, but when I think of them now, I suppose they were only in their twenties.

Mummy Noreen, she started to cry awful hard, like I never seen her cry before. Wrapping her arms around her middle, hugging herself. Then Mummy Joy starts crying too.

We'll never get out of here, Mummy Joy says.

Yes, we will, Mummy Noreen says, yes, we bloody will.

I should be married now, Mummy Joy says, I should have a family of my own. I wanted to be a schoolteacher. My big sister, she had a job in a bank. She used to go to the dances. I used to watch her get ready, doing her hair and putting on her make-up. I used to pretend it was me getting ready to go to the town hall, going to meet my friends, and the boys would be asking me to dance with them. I should've done that. I never got to go to a dance. That's not fair, is it?

No, it's not, Mummy Noreen says.

She crossed over to Mummy Joy's bed and put her arm around her, helt her tight.

It's not bloody fair, says she, and them bastards up there thieved that from us. But we'll get it back, I swear to God we will.

What's all this?

I mind I near jumped out of my skin at the sound of his voice. The Mummies let each other go and Mummy Noreen went back to her own bed.

Daddy Tam came down the stairs, them creaking under his weight. Says he, What's going on here?

Everybody kept whisht, so he roars, Answer me when I ask you a question!

Mummy Noreen spake up. Says she, Joy was upset and I was comforting her, that's all.

What's she gurning about? says he.

45

And, here, doesn't Mummy Noreen look him in the eye and says, What do *you* bloody think?

I didn't see it happen. As soon as she said that, I looked down at the floor, and so did Mummy Joy. I heard his boots on the stairs and across the floor, and I could feel the weight of him through the mattress I was sitting on, and I could feel the anger of him, I could hear it. And Mummy Noreen says, I'm sorry, I didn't mean it, I'm sorry.

I heard his hand agin her head. I felt it.

She landed in a heap on the floor, by my feet, her eyes all far away, and she was trying to say something. Then he kicked her hard in the back, and she twisted and turned, trying to reach there with her hands, and he kicked her again, and he caught her fingers, and she screamed awful hard.

I couldn't see terrible clear for I was crying now and I daren't have moved to wipe my eyes. I just wanted him to stop, but I daren't have said anything, for I'd have got it too. I do know he reached down and grabbed her by the hair, and he dragged her away across the floor, and she was screaming, and she reached for Mummy Joy, but Mummy Joy could do nothing for her.

I thought he was going to kill her, honest to God. I think he might have done if Daddy Ivan hadn't appeared at the top of the stairs.

Let her alone, says he.

Did you hear what she said to me? asks Daddy Tam.

I don't care what she said to you, just you let her go.

And Daddy Tam did as he was bid. That's one thing always struck me. As afeart of Daddy Tam as I was, as afeart of him as we all were, he was more afeart of Daddy Ivan. He was the one said what was what. Nobody argued with him. Never ever.

They left us alone then, put out the lamp at the top of the stairs. Mummy Joy and me, we helped Mummy Noreen up onto her bed. The fingers of her left hand were all swole up and purple, I think maybe some of them were broke. Mummy Joy tore up some material from her old dress and made bandages out of them. She reached under my mattress and took out one of the wee dollies I'd made for myself out of sticks and twine. I didn't whinge when she pulled it apart and wrapped Mummy Noreen's fingers to one of the sticks, to holt them steady. I mind the veins on Mummy Noreen's forehead when she helt the screams in.

When all that was done we put the last lamp out and went to bed. I didn't sleep much that night. I was too het up. There was the shock of what happened, aye, but it was more than that. There was someone new coming. I was ashamed of the way I felt, after what had happened, but I couldn't help it. Sure, I was only a wee girl. How else would I feel about someone new coming along?

I was excited.

7

Sara

AS THE VAN RATTLED AROUND her, and the hedgerows whipped past, Sara wondered when she'd last sat alone in a vehicle with a man other than her husband. She searched her memory and could not recall a single occasion since their wedding. Not even a taxi. They had been married a little over two years, been a couple twice as long before that. Damien had overwhelmed her with his charm, his love, the intensity of that first year of their relationship seeming now like a strange dream. She had never known anything like it, nor anyone like him. They moved in together when she graduated university and started work for Bath Community Health and Care Services as a child protection officer. And for another year, she was happy. They both were.

Their first real argument came after a dinner party they had attended, a reunion of Damien's university friends. They seemed to regard Damien as somehow exotic, not just because of his accent, but because they knew his father had been imprisoned. Oliver, the host, the son of a Labour MP, found him particularly fascinating, enraptured by tales of the armed struggle back in Ireland. They had been seated around the table, boy-girl-boy-girl, separated from their respective partners. Damien sat diagonally across from Sara. By the end of the evening, she couldn't remember the name of the man who had been seated next to her, only that he had been drunk and she'd had to remove his hand from her thigh at least three times.

She had noticed Damien was quiet on the taxi ride back to their flat, and that he barely spoke as they readied for bed. Asking him what was wrong had been her mistake.

'You really don't know?' he had said, sitting on the edge of their bed, watching her slip into her pyjamas.

'No,' she had replied, truthfully, feeling the haze of alcohol lift as her senses sharpened to the danger. She pulled a cleansing wipe from the packet on the dressing table, sat on the opposite side of the bed, and began removing her make-up.

'You and Craig were all over each other,' he said, his back to her.

'Ah, Craig, that's it, I couldn't remember his name. Wasn't he in your—'

'You let him feel you up all evening.'

'What? I didn't let him do anything. He was a bit handsy, but I—'

'A bit handsy? You might as well have fucked him on the table.'

The cold blades of his words cut at her. 'That's not fair,' she said. 'It was nothing like that. He was drunk, and his hands were wandering, but I kept them off.'

'What do you expect, tarted up like that?' he asked, turning to leer at her.

Sara looked down at the wipe in her hand, the make-up smeared on it. 'You can't blame me for his behaviour.'

'He's a man and he'll behave like a man. You lead him on like that, what do you think he's going to do?'

'Is that what you really think of me?' she asked, taking hold of her anger.

'What am I supposed to think of you? Letting him touch you like that, embarrassing me in front of my friends.'

'I'm an embarrassment,' Sara echoed. 'Okay.'

She got up from the bed and went to the wardrobe, grabbing a backpack from the floor, pulling clothes from the hangers.

'What are you doing?' Damien asked, his angry tone now tainted with fear.

'I'm going to Amanda's place,' she said. 'I'll sleep on her couch.'

He rose from the bed, crossed the room to her, arms outstretched.

'No, no, I didn't mean it like that.'

'I know what you meant,' Sara said, stuffing clothes into the backpack.

His hands gripped her upper arms, and she shrugged them off.

'Don't,' she said.

He forced his body between hers and the wardrobe, his arms around her, pulling her in close. She tried to struggle, but he was too strong, too heavy to push away.

'I'm sorry,' he said, his lips pressed against her ear, his voice dropping low and whispery, thickening with sadness and regret. 'I didn't mean it. I swear to God, I didn't. It's just I love you so much. Seeing another man touching you, it's . . . I couldn't bear to lose you. I'm nothing without you.'

He rocked her from side to side, taking her balance, taking her anger.

'I'm sorry,' he said. 'Forgive me. Please.'

And he whispered into her ear how much he loved her, needed her, couldn't be without her. She believed him, and she stayed.

The following morning, a bouquet arrived for her at the office, and everyone asked what the occasion was before she could read the note. Forgive me, the note had said. When her workmates pressed her, she had said, Nothing, just some flowers, feeling the sting of defeat, the humiliation of surrender.

So that became the way of things. An innocent act turned sinful, his anger pouring on her until she went to leave, then apologies and love and flowers and promises. It might have been a male workmate of hers who texted too often, or a friend of his who leaned in too close to her at a party. Another explosion of anger and accusations, another attempt to leave, another gush of love and apology. Each time his explosion was more fierce than the last, her threat to leave more half-hearted, the apology and love more shrill. And each time, another friend lost, the circle of people she knew by name diminishing little by little, their orbits drifting from hers almost without her noticing.

Amanda noticed. Sara wished she hadn't. They had been friends since their first year at university. The kind of friend Sara had never had before and would never have again. The kind of friend who doesn't know the meaning of secrets, who knows your soul, who can fill the cracks in your heart. A friend who will tell you things you don't want to hear.

But still, for all her good intentions, Amanda had only made things worse. Some things are better left alone. No good can come from digging under the stones of someone else's life. None at all. Amanda should have known that.

Sara closed her eyes and listened to the rattle of the van, let it pull her back to the here and now. Tony didn't speak much as he drove, and Sara was glad. He had a calm stillness about him that seemed catching, his presence soothing the jangling nerves that had become a constant in her existence. The unending awareness of Damien's temper, his mood swings, how her smallest transgressions could bring that rage out of him. But here, with this man, the static of fear seemed to fade.

She had a sense of a haze lifting, a clarity of sight she hadn't experienced for months, maybe years, and she supposed it should have frightened her. But it didn't. The very idea of being alone with another man should have terrified her. But it didn't.

Sara turned her attention back to the world outside the van as the first homes on the edge of Morganstown came into view. The village was not much more than a main street with a scattering of housing developments branching away from it. It had been named after the owner of the linen mill who had built rows of small homes to house his workers. The mill was long gone, but his name and some of the houses remained. Damien had told her this when he described their new home to her, but he had definitely not mentioned the old woman or her troubled past. She was sure about that, or as sure as she could be. And she desired to know more about that woman and what brought her to the doorstep of the house that had been taken from her.

As they approached the main street, Tony pulled the van over to the kerb. He nodded to the other side of the road, and the shop on the corner. A table stood outside, laden with potted plants, flowers and herbs. Bags of coal and firewood were stacked underneath.

'That's it,' Tony said. 'I'll wait for you.'

'Thank you,' she said, wondering if he understood how grateful she truly was.

Sara reached down for the shopping bag at her feet, got out of the van, and crossed the road. She glanced back over her shoulder and saw Tony watching her. He looked away a full second after their eyes met.

8

Esther

ESTHER MOONEY SHOOK WITH NERVES as she waited in the Lido Café on Belfast's Great Victoria Street. He had said ten in the morning. It was now five past and she feared he wouldn't come, that it had been some sort of strange and cruel joke. She wore her best clothes, the modest dress her mother had bought for her two summers ago, just a week before she died, leaving Esther an orphan. It wasn't an expensive dress, but it had cost every last penny her mother had. Her father's passing two years before had left them close to destitute, but her mother insisted she would have a decent dress for going to church on a Sunday. She wouldn't be looked down upon by the others in the congregation. Her mother couldn't bear to be pitied, to be seen to have been brought so low by their bad luck.

So low?

Her mother had no idea how deep and bottomless low can be. Esther knew. She had found out in the back of a strange man's car and was paid a pound for the humiliation. If it were possible for a person to die twice, then her mother would have done so at the knowledge of what Esther allowed that man to do to her. As she staggered from the car, the pound note in one hand, her torn underwear in the other, she swore she would never do that again. She would starve first. When the money was spent, she chose a different degradation: she stole a roll of silk from a draper's shop with the intention of trying to sell it to one of the traders at Smithfield Market. The shop's owner had caught her halfway through the door, dragged her back in by her wrist, and held her down on the floor while his young assistant called the police. Esther had kicked and screamed and cursed but it did no good.

She did not go to prison, for which she supposed she should have been glad. Instead she was sent to live at the workhouse, given a bed in a dormitory full of other girls and women. All of them knew what she was as soon as she entered, that she was not from their world, that she had fallen from a greater height than them. She did not sleep those first nights, the thin blanket pulled over her head, hearing the whispers of the others. Posh girl, they called her. Stuck-up bitch.

As she hid there, nothing but coarse material between her and them, she realised that she didn't believe in God. No loving God could treat her this way, could take so much away from her, could abandon her here in this place.

Less than four years ago she had lived in a grand house on Belfast's Malone Road, a short walk from Methodist College, the school she had been attending since she was eleven. Her father ran a linen brokerage, buying and selling the locally produced material. He was not as rich as those who owned the mills, but he made enough to buy a very presentable home for his wife and only child, and he drove an expensive car. Neither Esther nor her mother had any inkling of his financial worries arising from the decline of the worldwide linen trade.

Not, that is, until Esther heard a gunshot as she walked up the drive to her front door on a sunny May afternoon, then heard her mother's frantic screaming.

They never ruled it a suicide, but rather a tragic accident caused by carelessness while cleaning his legally owned pistol. As Mrs Mooney struggled to gather the pieces over the following weeks, she discovered correspondence between Mr Mooney and the bank that had provided the mortgage for the house. He had been three months in arrears. There was also a notice from another lender that they intended to seize his car.

Nothing was left. All savings burned up in vain attempts to keep the business alive. Creditors circled, debtors fled. Esther and her mother moved to a small rented house closer to the university. Mrs Mooney would not go to the council to ask for a house in one of those dreadful streets in the west of the city. She covered the rent with the small funds she had put away, and she fed and clothed them both with the meagre salary she earned in the receptionist's post she had been forced to accept from a friend of her late husband.

Esther went back to Methody, but things were not the same. Her school friends looked at her differently. She was no longer one of them. Not only was she marked by bereavement, but by near poverty. When she asked her mother if she could leave that school and go to another, Mrs Mooney refused. And they would continue to attend the same church. They had lost a husband and father, and she'd be damned if they would also lose their standing in the area. Esther pointed out that their standing was already lost, and her mother slapped her hard across the cheek and sent her to bed. She wailed for an hour while Esther covered her ears.

They scraped by like that for two years, keeping up the appearance of managing. Then on another sunny May afternoon, Mrs Mooney told her daughter that she'd been to the doctor. That there had been blood in the toilet for some weeks now, but she had been afraid to seek help. And now it was too late. The cancer had gotten the better of her. She had two, perhaps three, months. She told Esther not to be afraid; she had an aunt and uncle in Canada who had promised to take her in. Once she was gone, they would send a ticket for Esther, and she would have a new life across the ocean. Imagine, getting to grow up in Canada, what a wonderful time she would have.

Eleven weeks and three days later, Mrs Mooney was in the ground and the ticket hadn't arrived. It never did.

Reverend Clarke invited her to stay with his family, at least for a while, until she found her feet. At fifteen, she was too young to stay on her own. Reverend Clarke had always been kind and had been at her mother's side when she passed. He and his wife had three young children of their own.

On the first night, he showed Esther to her room, which was small but comfortable. Cosy, even. He sat wordlessly on the chair in the corner, waiting as Esther unpacked her things. When she laid her nightdress out on the bed, she paused, and looked at him.

'Don't mind me,' he said, his voice soft and slithering.

Esther turned her back and undressed, hunched over, guarding as much of herself as she could. She climbed in and under the covers, pulled them up to her chin. Reverend Clarke remained in the corner, watching, as if she would forget his presence if he stayed still.

'I'd like to go to sleep now,' she said.

Reverend Clarke smiled and said, 'Of course.'

He stood and came to the bedside, reached down, and touched his thumb to her lips.

'Poor girl,' he said. 'Such an awful time you've had of it. Just let me know if you need anything. Anything at all.'

He left her there, turning out the light before closing the door.

For the next six nights, the ritual continued. Each night he stayed a little longer. Each night, he touched her somewhere else. On the seventh evening, he suggested she take a bath before dinner. Esther gratefully accepted. She had been washing at the handbasin in her room, but her hair felt lank and greasy, and the idea of a good soak seemed the most wonderful thing.

Reverend Clarke's wife ran the bath for her, even tossed in a handful of salts. The bathroom filled with steam, and Esther could already feel the hot water on her skin. Mrs Clarke shut off the taps and left her to it.

Esther closed the door behind her and reached for the lock. But there was none. She froze, struck with a sudden awareness of hinges and handles, of in here, and out there, and how little stood between the two.

Foolishness, she told herself. No one in this house means you harm.

She undressed and stepped over the side of the bath, plunging one foot in, gasping at the heat. Then the other, then lowering herself, inching in, letting the water creep like vines over her body. Slowly, slowly, until she was able to sit and rest her back against the enamel. She inhaled, felt the steam fill her lungs, cleansing her inside and out. The overflow drain gurgled as she sank further down, the water rising.

Esther lay there, quite still, until she lost track of time. As if she were floating in an exotic ocean on the other side of the world, far away from everything. Her mind drifted on the sea, leaving strange images in its wake. Faces and hands, old friends, playmates, teachers, her father. All of them whispering to her as she drifted, untethered from—

The knock on the door startled her into a jangling alertness. A soft knock, as if whoever stood on the other side of the door didn't fully intend it to be heard. The water splashed around her as she sat upright, masking all other sound. She listened hard as the water settled.

Another knock, as gentle as the first.

'Yes?' Esther said, her voice wavering.

'It's Godfrey,' he said.

His Christian name sounded strange through the closed door. In her mind, he had always been Reverend Clarke. She had always known his name, of course, but hearing it spoken aloud felt wrong. It felt too intimate.

'Yes?' she said again.

'Do you have everything you need? Towels? Soap? Shampoo?'

'Yes, everything,' she said. 'Thank you.'

'Good,' he said.

Quiet for a time, and Esther wondered if he had gone. Then he spoke once more.

'Can I come in?'

Esther turned her head to see the door with no lock.

'No,' she said.

Silence again, then, 'I'd like to come in.'

'I don't want you to,' she said.

'Esther,' he said, 'this is my house. It's my bathroom. I don't think you—'

His words were lost in the sound of churning water as she hauled herself out of the bath, almost falling over the side. The handle turned as she found her feet, and she threw herself at the door, pushing it back into its frame. The handle turned again, and she felt pressure from the other side. She pushed back, forcing the door closed.

A shove from the other side, and her bare wet feet slid on the polished wooden floorboards. She put her shoulder against the door, put her weight behind her shoulder, and it slammed closed. Silence from the other side. She pressed her ear to the wood, listened, heard short, cutting breaths.

'Please go away,' she said.

He kept his silence.

'Please,' she said.

'I just thought a little gratitude wouldn't be too much to ask,' he said, 'after all we've done for you.'

'Please leave me alone,' Esther said, 'or I'll tell Mrs Clarke.'

'Tell her what?'

'That you tried to come in here while I was in the bath.'

'All I did was knock on the door to see if you needed anything. That's not a crime, is it?'

'I don't need anything.'

'All right, then,' he said. 'Dinner on the table in half an hour.'

She heard his footsteps on the stairs, descending, fading.

At the table, dried and dressed, Esther closed her eyes and clasped her hands together as Reverend Clarke said grace, emphasising the importance of gratitude for all the blessings of life. The tangy smell of liver rose from Esther's plate, merging with the low dun odour of boiled things. When he'd finished, she spoke up.

'I'm going to leave in the morning,' she said. 'Thank you for everything you've done for me, but it's time I moved on.'

'Where will you go?' Mrs Clarke asked.

'Oh, I'll sort something out,' Esther said, smiling, feigning certainty.

It was then that she noticed the eldest Clarke child, Jennifer, who was thirteen and small for her age. Her face had drained of colour, her eyes gone distant, and welling, glistening. Something cold touched Esther's heart, a knowledge that her presence in this house had spared Jennifer something, and her absence would allow it to return.

The idea of taking it back flashed in her mind, sparing this girl whatever haunted her. But Esther could not do that. She had endured too much to take on someone else's torment. Instead she ate her food and did not look at the girl.

Esther did not sleep that night. For the first time since she'd arrived at this house, Reverend Clarke did not show her to her room at bedtime. Even so, she moved the chair from the corner and wedged its back beneath the door handle. She had seen this in a film once, and she doubted if it would do any good, but it gave her a small amount of comfort, nonetheless.

As the night's quiet fell all around, she packed her things ready for the morning, then turned out the light and went to bed. She supposed an hour had passed, perhaps two, when she became aware of a presence on the other side of the bedroom door. She did not hear it there, saw no movement of shadow on the sill, but she could feel it. A cold and dark thing whose being drew all light and oxygen and good from the air around it.

Esther sat up in bed and stared at the door, or rather, beyond it to where the presence stood, staring back. She could feel the hate from here. He wanted her, she knew that, in the way that men want women, but there was no love in his desire. His desire was made of anger and pain, and he hated her for it, she knew this, and he hated himself also. He loathed himself more than anything, she thought, but she did not pity him.

She drew a breath and commanded, 'Go away.'

Holding the air in her lungs, she heard nothing but her own heart, and one creak as his weight shifted, and then the presence was gone.

In the morning, Esther waited in her room and listened until she was certain the children had left for school and Reverend Clarke had gone to take morning prayers. She carried her bag downstairs and went to the kitchen where Mrs Clarke washed the breakfast things in the sink.

From the doorway, Esther said, 'Before I go . . .'

Mrs Clarke lifted a tea towel from the dish rack and turned to Esther as she dried her hands. 'Yes, love?'

Esther had spent most of the night searching for a way to say what needed to be said and still she had nothing.

'Your husband, Reverend Clarke. He's not right. He tried to—'

'Well, you look after yourself, love,' Mrs Clarke said, turning back to the sink and the dishes and the greasy water. Not hearing, Esther's words closed out, ignored.

'What about Jennifer?' Esther asked. 'Your wee girl, she—'

Mrs Clarke spun around, a small knife in her hand, pointed it at Esther, the blade an accusation, a warning.

'Don't,' she said. 'Don't you dare.'

Hate in her eyes, sparking and flaring.

Esther said no more. She lifted her bag from the floor and left the house.

That was the year before last. Now, nearing four years since her father had torn her world asunder, she had the prospect of a home once more. A bed of her own, a room of her own. A kind man had offered them to her. Those and a small wage. All she had to do was help look after him, his father and his brother. They lived on a farm not quite an hour outside of Belfast. It would be hard work, she realised that, but it would be honest work.

Esther checked the clock on the wall. Ten past ten. Perhaps he wasn't coming. Maybe it had been a cruel joke. Give her the hope of a better life then take it away from her.

'He will come,' she said aloud.

A chime sounded as the cafe's door opened. Esther looked in that direction.

Her heart lifted.

9

Mary

I DON'T MIND HOW LONG WENT by, I suppose it was just a couple of days, but it felt like longer. Just waiting and waiting. Mummy Joy and Mummy Noreen were acting odd. They were upset, always whispering one to the other. Always close. And remembering, always remembering things from the outside. I liked that, hearing about out there, hearing about Belfast and Armagh, and all the people they knew.

Things went bad for them, that was what they had in common. Both of them had wound up on the street. Mummy Noreen was born in a workhouse. Born out of wedlock. That was a terrible thing in them days, a terrible shame to hang over you, though I suppose it doesn't matter so much nowadays. Mummy Noreen's mother lived in the workhouse in Belfast because she was a . . . I don't like to use the word. She went with men for money. I suppose it was hard times, right enough, but still. Mummy Noreen always carried that with her, knowing her father was some boy who gave her mother a lock of shillings so he could do his business with her.

But they were upset, and talking more about the outside than they used to, and I was worried and scared too. But I was excited. And you know, I think deep inside them, even though neither of them would say it out loud, I think they were excited too. Maybe they felt ashamed of that. I know I did. Being excited that someone new was coming to suffer the same as us, sure that's nothing to be excited about, is it? But all the same, I was.

That was why they talked so much about the outside. Because the outside was coming in, and they wanted to know what had changed and what had stayed the same. To see someone new from out there.

Two days, maybe, I'm not sure. They dragged on and we kept working, Mummy Noreen doing the best she could with only one good hand, her broken fingers still twined together with the stick Mummy Joy had taken from one of my dollies. The Daddies were acting strange too. You could see the excitement in them, but they felt no shame in it. And they wanted the place shining, top to bottom. They never worked us so hard before or after.

It was maybe the third morning when we were allowed upstairs for a short while, just to get the place sorted, the breakfast things redd up, all that. Then Daddy Tam put on his suit, the one he wore to church on a Sunday, and he went off in the car. Then Daddy Ivan chased us down the stairs and gave us a talking-to. He telt us we had to stay quiet down there, not make a sound, no matter what. He said if we made any noise, we'd be dealt with. And not just a slap or a kick either. He'd really hurt us. He was serious, you could tell to look at him.

So we stayed down there, just the one lamp burning, keeping quiet. The Mummies whispered one to the other, but only now and again. Mostly, we just waited. Mummy Joy had to scold me for fidgeting, but I couldn't help it. I couldn't holt still. I had to keep going to piddle in the bucket in the corner.

It was a long time past before anything happened. I don't know how long, I still don't have a great notion of time, I can hardly tell you the difference between a minute and an hour. But I'd gotten powerful hungry, I know that much, even though Daddy Ivan had sent down some bread and cheese with us. We could hear nothing but our own bellies rumbling. Not a noise from upstairs.

Then all of a sudden, there was footsteps. You could always hear the Daddies clumping about up there, and we could tell them apart, just by the sound of them. This was Daddy Ivan and Daddy George moving about. We all looked at each other because we knew something was happening. And then we heard Daddy Tam come in, and he had someone with him. Someone with hardly anything to them at all. You could hardly hear her footsteps. I say her because we knew it would be a girl. She must have weighed next to nothing, and I imagined in my head it was a fairy up there, just flitting about the place.

We all watched the door at the top of the stairs, waiting for it to open. But it didn't, at least not for a long time yet. But we could smell cooking. A good smell, meat first, then later on, something sweet that made my mouth water. It must have been the evening time before anything happened. I'd fallen asleep on my bed, and so had the Mummies, I think. The noise of the door being unlocked woke me up, and I shot up, all dizzy with that sick feeling you get when you're woken up in a fright. And Mummy Joy and Mummy Noreen were lying cuddled together, staring up at the door. I mind the red creases on Mummy Joy's cheek, from the pillow. I don't know why that sticks in my head.

The door opened, and I couldn't see much through the light from upstairs, just a shape. Then she stepped down onto the stairs and I could see her and I could hardly breathe. I thought she was the most beautiful thing I'd ever seen. I thought she was an angel, I did, I believed she'd come down from heaven to take us away. She had on her the most beautiful dress I'd ever seen, a deep blue colour, not like the auld rags we had to wear. And her hair was lovely, all clean and smooth, not wild like mine. Her face, her skin, everything about her.

We all stayed there for a while, us staring up at her, her staring down at us. Then Daddy Tam steps down behind her, gives her a nudge. But she didn't move, just stood there, her eyes all big and wide.

Says she, Who are they?

10

Sara

A BELL OVER THE SHOP DOOR chimed as Sara entered. She paused there for a moment, her eyes adjusting to the gloom, and realised some of the lights had been switched off. Checking her watch, she saw it was close to five thirty.

'Here, now, you just caught me,' a voice called from the back of the shop.

Sara stepped around a refrigerated unit full of fruit and vegetables and saw a man behind the counter, standing at the open cash register. She guessed him to be in his mid-seventies, well past retirement age, a slight man but possessing a strong build. He wore a shirt and tie underneath his white overcoat, and she imagined him straightening the knot before he opened his door each morning.

'I was about to start redding up the place. What can I do for you?'

'Sorry, I just need a few things, is that okay?'

'Course it is,' he said, closing the drawer. 'There's no rush.'

She returned his smile and lifted a basket from a stack by the door. Browsing the shelves and chillers, she selected milk, butter, a half-dozen eggs, then came to the rows of bread. She chose a wheaten loaf, which she knew Damien liked, along with something called Irwin's Nutty Krust, which came wrapped in waxy orange and white paper. She added a bag of apples to her basket, some oranges, plums, and then browsed the vegetables. Peppers, onions, courgettes; there was some dried pasta at home, and tinned tomatoes. Perhaps she could make up a ragu for dinner. It seemed an age since she had really cooked anything.

As she brought her items to the counter, the man winked and said, 'That's not a local accent.'

'No,' she said. 'I'm from just outside Bath, originally.'

'Ah, an English girl.'

She almost bristled at being called a girl, but his easy manner disarmed any offence he could have caused.

'My husband's from Lurgan,' she said, placing the basket on the counter. 'We just moved into an old farmhouse out the road. The Ashes, it's called, because of the trees around it. It still needs a lot of work, but it's getting there.'

He looked more closely at her now, as if he hadn't really seen her before.

'The old Jackson place?' he asked.

His friendly manner had cooled, and the urge came upon her to leave the basket and exit the shop. She gave him her warmest smile as she searched her memory for the name Tony had given her.

'You're Mr Buchanan, aren't you?'

'Aye,' he said, his expression drawn and tight.

His scrutiny burned her, as if she had done him some wrong by coming here. She should say nothing more, pay for the groceries and go. But she wanted to know.

'Someone told me you know Mary, the woman who lived there before us.'

'Aye, I do. In fact, I was about to take a spin over to the care home and see how she's doing. I was told she wandered off early this morning.'

'Yes,' Sara said, a defensive feeling rising in her. 'She came to the house around six, knocked on the door. She was confused. My husband brought her back.'

'Well,' Mr Buchanan said, lifting the first item from her basket and ringing it up on the till. 'So long as she's safe, that's the main thing.'

'I wondered about her,' Sara said.

'Aye?'

He seemed to have no desire to discuss Mary further, but Sara's time working with vulnerable children had taught her that such apparent reticence is often deceptive. Coax him a little and he might open up.

'About what happened to her. About what happened out at the house all those years ago. I tried searching online but I couldn't find much.'

Mr Buchanan looked up from the till, studied her, his eyes watchful.

'Maybe you shouldn't know too much about that place,' he said. 'Not if you're going to live in it.'

'I'd like to know. I heard you were close to Mary.'

He let out an exhalation as his expression softened. 'As close as anybody could be, I suppose.'

'How did you get to know her?' Sara asked.

Mr Buchanan gave a sorrowful smile and lowered himself onto a stool behind the counter, his movements stiffened by age.

71

'It was this shop she walked into that morning,' he said. 'After the killings out there at the farm. My father opened the door to her. Me and my mother were in the back having breakfast, and he called my mother out. We used to live above the shop in them days, with the kitchen just through the storeroom.' He pointed over his shoulder to the open door. 'I followed after my mother, came out here, and here was this wee girl, not much younger than me, standing right where you are now. She was spattered in blood, wasn't saying anything, no matter what my father asked her. Not even her name. She wouldn't talk to my mother either. Just stood there, not even shaking. Completely still.

'I don't know how long that went on. My mother knelt down in front of her, holding her hands, trying to get something out of her. My father was pacing up and down, asking what to do. Then I remember she looked at me. I was here, behind the counter. Mary looked me in the eye, just for a second, then she fell to the floor. My mother screamed like the wee girl had dropped dead, but she hadn't. My father dragged me out from behind the counter and told me to run up the street and get Dr James, wake him up if I had to. So, here's me running up Morganstown Main Street in my pyjamas at the scrake of dawn. Dr James – James Cardwell was his name – he was at his breakfast when I got to his house, up by the church there. He came huffing and puffing behind me, and the wee girl was still lying in a heap on the floor when we got back.

'Dr James turned her over on her side, arranged her arms and legs, said it was to stop her from choking. He reckoned she was in shock and we had to get an ambulance out for her, and the police. They took her away to hospital, and the police took my father into the back to talk to them about it.

'It was a few days before she said a word to anyone. Nobody knew where she'd come from, who she was, or what had happened to her. I mind the newspapermen coming by here, and my mother telling me not to say a word to them. I think it was the third or the fourth day before she told the doctors anything, and from what I heard, all she could say was they're all dead, they're all dead. It wasn't till she said the names of them that a policeman from the village here figured out who she was talking about. Big Ivan Jackson, and his two sons, George and Tam, or Thomas to give him his proper name.'

'Who were they?' Sara asked.

'Farmers,' he said. He frowned before continuing. 'Big ignorant lumps of men, they were. Reared cattle out there, for beef, not for milking. I mind I would see them in church on a Sunday morning, the three of them together taking up about six people's worth of the pew. They weren't pleasant men. My father never liked dealing with them. Big Ivan would come in once or twice a week, and he'd always crib over the price of everything, no matter how cheap it was. If you gave him a ha'penny off, he'd look a shilling. And he'd get in an awful twist if you didn't give it to him. There's times I remember him shouting at my father, telling him he was a thief for looking the full price of things.'

'Why didn't your father kick him out?' Sara asked.

'I wondered that myself plenty of times,' Mr Buchanan said. 'It wasn't till I was older that I realised the truth. It was because he was scared of him. And well he should have been, knowing what happened out there.'

'What did happen?' Sara asked, fearing the answer. 'All I know is the family was killed.'

'Family,' Mr Buchanan echoed, distaste in his voice and on his face. 'Seems an odd word for it. No one really knows what the situation was out there. What led up to it. What I do know is, five of them died. Big Ivan, the two sons, and the two women who'd been living there. No one knew who they were till later on, and no one really knew what they were doing there. Whether they were wives to the Jackson boys or what. Tell you the truth, I can't even mind their names now. Either way, they all died. They reckon George, the younger brother, lost the head and did them all in before he shot himself. At least, that's what the inquiry decided. Mary went and hid in the cattle shed till the morning, then she walked into the village here and knocked on that door.'

Sara thought of the red stains on the stone kitchen floor. She remembered picking at them with her fingernail. Without meaning to, she wiped her fingertips on her jeans, hard enough to hurt.

'When did you see Mary again?' she asked.

'It was a few years. My father gave his testimony at the hearings, and that was that for a while. All the fuss died down after a few months. The newspapermen stopped calling. That was around the time things were starting to go bad here. It was before the shooting and the bombing, a good few years before the army was out on the streets, but there was trouble brewing in Belfast and Londonderry, or Derry, or whatever you want to call it. What happened out the road was soon forgotten about. Wee Mary was in care until she was sixteen, then she was turned out. She had nowhere to go but back to that house. It was hers by right, seeing as she was the last survivor of that family, if you could call it a family. No one ever knew for sure which one of them was her father.

'Anyway, when my father found out she was living out there, him and me filled a box with bits and pieces, whatever fruit and veg was about to turn, and we drove out there in his wee van. The place was wild, all overgrown, weeds everywhere, half the windows broken. My father knocked on the door for a good five or ten minutes and there was no answer, but we knew she was there. You know the way you can tell if someone's in or not? You can feel them there. I knew in my bones she was watching us.

'My father calls out, says he, we'll just leave this here for you. We'll come back in a lock of days and see what you need.'

'He sounds like he was a good man,' Sara said.

Mr Buchanan's gaze became distant, a warm smile on his mouth.

'He was. My father was a proper Christian man. Not like these auld hoors who just pretend to be Christians so they can excuse their own hatred. He knew what it meant, what Jesus said on the mount. He never refused anyone in need, no matter who they were. And that wee girl was in need.

'So, we came back three or four days later, and the empty box was on the doorstep waiting for us. We had another one with us, along with a few rashers of bacon and some eggs we'd got from Herron's Butchers, they were just across the street from here. My father knocked on the door again, and here, this time, didn't it open? I still remember the sight of her in the doorway. She can't have been even five foot tall, as thin as my wee finger, and pale. And she was awful pretty, even with the filth of her. Like a doll. She was like a doll someone had

75

found on the street. I was seventeen at the time, I think. A couple of years out of school, anyway. My father told me to quit staring, then he turned to her and asked if she was all right, if she needed anything. She just took the box of food from him and closed the door.

'But that was the start of it. Over the next lock of months, my father got boys out to tidy the place up for her, to fix the windows, patch up the roof and whatnot. Paid them out of his own pocket. He got her some hens and a rooster and put up a wee house for them so she could have eggs. He helped her arrange renting out the fields she owned so she'd have a few shillings of her own, and she could pay him for the food. It was never as much as it really cost him, but he wanted her to feel like she was paying her way. That's how things went on for fifteen years or so, then a stroke did for my father, and I took over. I've been going out there twice a week for forty-odd years. I've gotten to know her about as well as anybody could. People about the town here would say she's mad in the head. Some of the children used to call her Scary Mary. And fair enough, she might be a wee bit touched, but who wouldn't be after what she went through?'

He had finished ringing up her items and told Sara the price. She fished her purse from the bottom of the shopping bag, opened it, and sorted through the few notes and coins. For a horrifying moment, she feared she might not have enough, and Damien kept her bank cards. He had done since they married, when he insisted on joint finances, and she agreed. She wasn't good with money. He often told her that. After digging in the folds of the purse, she found the last few pence she needed and felt a wash of relief. She handed over the money in exact change, and Mr Buchanan thanked her.

Sara packed her bag of groceries, lifted it from the counter, and said, 'Thank you for taking the time to talk to me. I appreciate it.'

'I'm sorry it wasn't a happier topic,' he said.

She had reached the door when he called after her.

'There's one thing.'

Sara stopped and turned to look back at him, passing the bag from one hand to the other.

'You seem like a decent young woman, so I don't know if I should say this or not. Francie Keane would be your father-in-law, wouldn't he?'

She felt the fine hairs on her arms ripple and stand. 'Yes,' she said.

'About a fortnight before the fire at Mary Jackson's house, he came in here. He asked me about Mary, if she was fit to keep that place, and did I think she'd ever sell it if someone offered the right money. I told him Mary didn't have any sense of money, what it was and what it was for, but I could ask her if he wanted me to. So I did, and she said, no, she wasn't for selling. I called your father-in-law's solicitor, like he told me to, and passed it on. Two weeks later, there was a fire.'

He dropped his gaze and ran his fingertips over the counter's surface, sweeping away some detritus that only he could see.

'I never told anyone else about that, and I never will, it's none of my business. But I thought if you didn't know, then maybe you should.'

She searched for a response, anything, but found none. She turned and left the shop.

11

Esther

ESTHER HAD GRATEFULLY ACCEPTED THOMAS'S offer of another cup of tea, and he'd bought one for himself, but they didn't finish them. 'We should get down the road,' he'd said, and Esther had agreed as butterflies and small birds flittered around inside her.

He wore a suit. The same one he'd worn the first day he'd approached her in the cafe. She had been trying to hide her tears, weeping behind her hand as she wondered how long the owners would let her sit there without buying anything more than the tea that had gone cold an hour before. He was a big man, tall and broad, with blunt and meaty fingers and dirt under his nails. He had the odour of the farm about him, manure and earth and sweat.

But he was kind, and Esther had found kindness hard to come by in recent times. He had bought her tea, and a slice of cake, and told her about his farm where he lived with his father and brother. How his mother had died some time ago and they found it terrible hard to manage the house, they could barely boil an egg between them, the place was an awful state, and they needed a housekeeper, but it was desperate hard to find one. And anyway, it was nice talking to her, and maybe he'd see her again, he was in Belfast on business, and he'd be back the next day.

So was she. And when he came in and found her there, he smiled, showing his yellow teeth. He sat with her again, bought her tea, and a chocolate eclair, and she told him she knew how to sew, and could cook a decent meal, and clean, and could she please be his housekeeper?

Now they drove in Thomas's car, Esther noting the road signs as they travelled south-west. Lisburn, where her mother's family had been from, then on to Moira. Esther had read in a newspaper about the building work on a new motorway that would cut the journey time to Belfast by half, but for now the road seemed wide enough. The car rattled and juddered all around them and seemed to travel at a fierce speed. Even in her father's expensive car, Esther had never gone so fast, and she felt the bright thrill of adventure.

Soon they travelled along small country roads, passing tractors and little else. Cattle grazed the fields, and sheep with newborn lambs. Esther couldn't remember the last time she'd left the city. The world seemed to throb with green life, from the grass in the fields to the budding leaves on the trees that whipped past.

They didn't talk much until Thomas turned at a sign for Morganstown, when Esther cleared her throat to signal her intention to speak.

Thomas turned his head towards her for a moment.

'Which church do you go to?' she asked.

'Church of Ireland, in the village. Every Sunday morning.'

'I was raised Methodist,' Esther said, 'but it's all the same, really, isn't it?'

'Well, some people think that,' Thomas said.

His answer confused her, and she felt her cheeks redden with heat, fearing she had said something wrong. A battle erupted within her: to speak or keep her silence? She chose to be brave.

'It's good to go to church,' she said, knowing herself to be a hypocrite. She did not believe, would not believe, not any more. 'It's good to hear the word of the Lord. I'm glad that you're churchgoers.'

'Nearly there,' he said, and she turned her attention to the road ahead.

The car turned onto a single-track lane, a river visible through the hedgerow and down a steep bank to her left. She asked what it was called, but he didn't answer as they approached a walled entrance with an open gateway on the right. One of the stone pillars bore an engraved name.

'The Ashes,' Esther said. 'Like the trees?'

Thomas grunted, which she took as a yes.

They drove through, beneath the branches, onto a short gravel driveway, and she saw the house. A good-size place, neater than she expected, pebble-dash walls, small sash windows, the front door painted green with a single frosted glass pane at the centre.

'It looks nice,' she said, surprised by the lightness of her own voice.

'It's not bad,' he said as the car came to a shuddering halt. The handbrake creaked, and he shut off the engine. The car rocked, relieved of his weight as he climbed out. Esther remained where she was, unsure if he intended to open the passenger door for her. He did not. She watched through the window as he walked around the front of the car and towards the house. He paused, looked back at her, and indicated that she should follow him. She opened the door, climbed out, and reached into the back for her bag. By the time she closed the passenger door and went after him, he had already disappeared inside.

She paused there, by the car, in front of the house. The smell enveloped her. Of animals and earth, rich and deep and dark, and not entirely unpleasant. Birds called all around, full of spring and mischief. She looked up, saw clouds rolling across a wide blue sky. Turning in a circle, she took it in, the expanse of it all. Then she looked towards the door.

A warning bell rang in the distant reaches of her mind, but she dismissed it.

Esther stepped into the hall, her shoes echoing on the stone floor. A stairway in front of her, a sitting room to the right, and what she guessed was the kitchen to the left. A jangle of fear sounded inside her, bright and piercing. The urge rose to turn and flee from this place, and she forced it away, told herself to be grateful for God's mercy in bringing her here.

But I don't believe in God, she thought. Not really.

Before another thought could follow, Thomas's voice rang out from the kitchen. 'In here,' he called.

Esther followed the voice into the kitchen and found the three men standing there, in a line, as if presenting themselves to her. Thomas, then the younger brother, George, and the father, Ivan. All in their Sunday suits, like it was a special occasion. Thomas introduced the other two, but no one offered to shake her hand, the other two standing awkwardly straight with their arms by their sides. Big men, all of them, tall and wide. All shoulders and belly, red skinned and hard.

Thomas took her bag and set it against the wall, near a door with a stout lock, then said, 'I suppose you should get started. There's spuds and beef for a roast in the larder.'

She remained still for a moment, then moved toward the door with the stout lock.

'Not that one,' Thomas said, and pointed to another on the far side of the kitchen. 'That one there.'

She crossed to the larder, opened it, and found a sack of potatoes on the floor, a crate with carrots and turnips on a shelf, and a joint of beef resting on a slab of marble to keep it cool. Her hands shook, so she clasped them together. I don't know what to do, she thought, and fear threatened to become panic. What do I do?

'Here,' a gentle voice said. She turned her head and saw Ivan next to her. He reached past and dragged the sack of potatoes out of the larder. They gave off the smell of dark soil as they rolled against each other.

Ivan pointed a thick finger. 'There's a knife in thon drawer, and get the two big bowls out from the sideboard. Put the peelings into one, wash the spuds in the sink, and then put them in water in the other.'

Of course. Peel them. Everyone knows how to do that. Esther exhaled her relief and set to work.

An hour later, under Ivan's guidance, she had peeled and cut a generous batch of potatoes for boiling over the wood stove, seared the beef in a pan, and placed it into the oven to roast. The kitchen hummed like all kitchens should, and the smells fetched up memories of her own home, before her father had left them, when her mother would happily spend a Sunday afternoon preparing food for their small family.

Thomas and George had disappeared, she didn't know where to. Ivan remained, sitting at the table, packing tobacco into a pipe, toying with it, but never lighting it. He watched her with a cool stillness that seemed to crawl beneath her clothing, next to her skin. She fought the urge to brush her fingertips across the back of her neck, to shoo away some imaginary touch.

When she went back to the larder to fetch the carrots, she noticed a bag of fat, ugly apples, and an idea occurred to her, a memory of the home economics classes she'd taken at Methody. She searched through the other shelves and found caster sugar, flour and butter wrapped in paper. A smile broke on her mouth. What about eggs? They had chickens, so they were bound to have eggs. There, on the middle shelf, in a wicker basket, still speckled with straw and droppings. Cream? No, but there was a pint and a half of milk. That would do, wouldn't it? The smile turned to a grin and she felt so light inside that her feet might have floated an inch from the stone floor.

She turned to Ivan, breathless with joy, and said, 'I can do an apple crumble. All the makings are there. And I can do custard to go with it. There's no cream, but there's milk, and that's almost as good.'

Ivan sat back in his chair with something close to a smile on his lips. 'Lovely,' he said. 'Aye, that'll be lovely.'

Esther couldn't help but clap her hands and giggle like she was a child again in her mother's kitchen, allowed to lick the whipped cream from the whisk.

While the beef roasted and the potatoes boiled, she cored and sliced the apples and worked the flour, sugar and butter together to make the crumble, all ready for the oven. Two hours after entering the house, she carved the beef and drained the potatoes. As the men took their seats, she laid out cutlery for them. It was then that she noticed there were only three chairs at the table. The fourth had been set against the wall, turned in to face the corner.

'Should I get that chair?' she asked.

None of them answered.

'Or maybe I should just take mine later?'

'Aye,' Ivan said, 'just you take yours later.'

The light feeling inside lost its buoyancy, her feet suddenly heavier on the floor. 'Oh,' she said. 'That's all right.'

She fetched the dinnerware from the sideboard and plated up the beef, potato and carrots, and placed one in front of each of the men. They leaned in, smelled, examined.

'No gravy?' George asked.

Esther's stomach dropped. 'Oh . . . I . . . I forgot. I'm sorry.'

Tears threatened. She inhaled, drawing them back in.

'Sure, never worry,' Ivan said. He reached out, patted her arm.

'It'll be awful dry,' George said.

'It'll be grand,' Ivan said, his voice sharper than before. 'Won't it, boys?'

Thomas and George both said, aye, sure it'll be grand, lowering their gaze to their plates.

'Come on, now,' Ivan said, 'this girl's worked awful hard to make this meal, so quit your gurning and eat it up.'

As Esther retreated back to the stove, she heard the clinking of forks and knives on china. She placed the apple crumble into the oven and set about making the custard.

Their plates were bare when she lifted them away. She placed a bowl of steaming hot apple crumble in front of each of them and poured custard from a chipped jug. The smell, thick and eggy and sweet, made her stomach grumble.

'Oh, now,' Thomas said, examining his bowl. 'Now, now, now.'

She left them to eat, listening to their contented huffing and chewing. Some might have thought them ignorant, unmannered, but she felt a warm satisfaction at their pleasure.

When they'd finished, as she washed the dishes, and Ivan finally lit his pipe, she heard them talk in low voices. What do you think? Will she do? Aye, she can cook all right, and she'll learn better. And she's biddable. Aye, she'll do all right.

The dishes dried and put away, her calves aching, Esther could focus her mind on only two things: the leftover food, and a warm bed. She cleared her throat to get the men's attention. Thomas looked irritated at her interruption, but Ivan said, 'Yes, love?'

'I wondered,' she said, 'where will I be sleeping?'

Ivan looked to Thomas, who got to his feet. He walked to the door with the lock and searched his trouser pocket until he retrieved a set of jangling keys. He undid the padlock and beckoned her over. Even though she didn't want to, even though she again wanted to flee this house, she did as she was told. He held open the door. She saw the dimness inside and took a step back. He took her arm, guided her to the top step.

She looked down into the weak lamplight.

She saw the young women and the girl looking back.

'Who are they?' she asked.

Thomas gave her a nudge and said, 'It's all right, go on down, they'll look after you.'

Alarm clamoured inside her like a firehouse bell. 'Who are they?' she asked again. 'What's going on?'

'Just go on down,' Thomas said, and he gave her another push, harder than the last.

She tripped down three or four steps before she could stop herself, her hand grabbing the crude handrail made of raw wood, splinters biting into her palm. Ignoring the fiery sting, she turned and looked back up to him.

'I want to go,' she said. 'Take me back to Belfast.'

'Whisht, now,' Thomas said, 'don't be thran, just get down them stairs. The girls'll look after you.'

Fear threatened to steal the words from her tongue, the reason from her mind. She held it back, though it pressed hard on her.

'You don't have to take me,' she said, 'I'll get a bus.'

She climbed the few steps up to him, and she was suddenly aware of his size, the breadth of him, the height.

'Come on, now,' he said, 'let's not be making trouble.'

Anger rose in her, breaking through the fear.

'Let me past,' she said, her voice shaking along with every other part of her.

She tried to push past him, between his body and the wall, but there was too much of him and too little of her. Nothing she could do would move him, like a rock, no, a mountain, a cliff face of a man, and she nothing but a breeze to him.

Then he pushed her.

His hand flat on her chest, almost as wide as her torso, and she teetered on the edge of the step, her heels betraying her. Her arms spinning as if she could save herself from falling, as if she could fly if she tried hard enough.

But she couldn't save herself. She fell down, down into the pit.

12

Mary

I MIND THE SOUND SHE MADE when she tilted back.
That was the worst of it, the cry she let out of her. A
desperate sound. I think that's the sound a soul makes
when it goes to hell.

She landed on her back and slid down a few steps, her head
clattering off the wood, then her legs went up and over her,
so she was on her front, and she rolled the rest of the way
until she landed in a heap at the bottom. I mind the way she
landed, her dress was all bunched up, and we could see her
underthings. The first thought came into my head was I wanted
to fix the dress for her. It wasn't right to be showing herself
like that.

We all stayed still and quiet for a while, me, the Mummies,
and Daddy Tam, all looking at each other. Then Daddy Tam
nodded his head, and the Mummies dived off the bed they'd
been cuddled up on and went to her, knelt down beside her.

Says Daddy Tam, Is she all right?

She's cut her head, says Mummy Noreen, but she's all right.

Look after her, says Daddy Tam, and he went back up the
stairs and locked the door behind him. Mummy Noreen telt
me to get the jug of water from the corner, and a dress or a

nightie, anything, so long as it was clean. They helped her over to her bed, laid her down on it. I found a white dress that didn't fit me any more and brought it and the water over. Mummy Noreen tore strips off the dress and dipped them in the water, then cleaned the cut on the back of the girl's head.

Her eyes were wide, and she kept staring at us, one then the other, then the other. Her mouth opening and closing like she was looking for a word to say but couldn't get a holt of it. The Mummies clucking and soothing her.

After a while, she found her words. Says she, What is this? What's going on here?

Not a one of us had the heart to tell her.

*　*　*

Time's an awful funny thing. The way it stretches and shrinks, gets bigger and smaller, thinner and fatter. How some things seem like the size of the whole wide world when you're in the middle of them, and all these years later, they feel like nothing at all. And the wee things stay with you and they're all you really remember.

I mind Daddy Ivan brought down two big bowls of food. One was full of beef and spuds and the other had sweet things I'd never seen nor tasted before. Mummy Noreen telt me they were apple crumble and custard. I'd never had the like of it in my mouth before. I would've ate the whole bowl myself if they'd let me.

The three of us took into thon food while that poor girl lay on the bed and cried her heart out. I suppose we should've felt bad about that, eating like pigs with the spoons Daddy Ivan gave us, with her only just knowing what was happening to her. That's what I really mind about that night. Not her cowping down the stairs, not her tears, but thon food.

After it was gone, we all sat quiet for a long time. The only sound was her crying. We found out her name was Esther, and she was from Belfast, but I don't mind if she said it then or later. She was different from Mummy Joy and Mummy Noreen. She was softer in the way of her, and how she spake. Mummy Joy thought maybe she was a posh girl, from a rich house, not like either of them.

I don't think she understood where she was for a day or two. That she was there to stay, that there was no going home. I don't think she knew the men upstairs wanted more from her than cooking and cleaning. Daddy Tam especially. She belonged to him now, whether she wanted to be his or she didn't. I didn't know myself what they really wanted with us, not then. The Mummies never telt me. I suppose they wanted to spare me from it for as long as they could.

None of us slept right that night, not a real sleep. Listening to her crying and getting on. She climbed the steps a lock of times, tried to push the door open, shoving it and kicking it, and the Mummies telt her it would do her no good at all, but she wouldn't listen to them. One time, Daddy Tam clattered the door from the other side, guldered at her to hould her whisht, everyone was trying to sleep.

The next morning, the Mummies had to go upstairs and get on with the housework, but Daddy Tam telt me to stay down there with Esther and look after her. She was laid on her bed, facing the wall, quivering and sniffling. Now and then she'd pick a splinter out of her hand, leaving wee spots of blood on her skin, or put her finger to the cut on her head, which wasn't as bad as it looked the night before.

Even just looking at the back of her, I thought she was beautiful. That dress she had on her, the colour of it. I'd never seen a dress like that. Not like the auld drab things me and the Mummies wore. And her shoes. I'd only ever worn boots that never fit me proper, but she had on these shoes that were shiny and hardly even covered her toes. I wanted to touch them and feel them and I imagined what they'd be like agin my fingers and on my feet. I imagined wearing that dress.

I didn't say anything for a long time, and neither did she, till she spake up.

Says she, What's your name?

Mary, I telt her.

What age are you?

Ten, says I. I think so, anyway. Maybe eleven.

Says she, You think so? Do you not know for certain? Everyone knows how old they are.

She rolled over and looked at me, and I saw her face. It was dirty with tears and sweat, but still she was the most beautiful thing I'd ever seen. I mind her teeth, how clean they were, how white. And her skin, under the dirt. Like the china cups upstairs, the ones with the roses painted on them.

Says I, How old are you?

Sixteen, says she, nearly seventeen.

Then she started crying again. She cried terrible hard. I don't know why, but I felt like I should get on the bed beside her and put my arms around her, the way Mummy Noreen did for Mummy Joy, and the way Mummy Joy did for me. She went awful stiff when I lay beside her, and then she went all soft, and I could feel the bones of her.

I started to sing to her. No song in particular, because I didn't know any, just words I could remember from hearing the Mummies sing to each other. Esther must've minded something I sang, because she started then, too.

The Lord's my shepherd, I'll not want. He makes me down to lie.

She couldn't mind much more of the words, so she hummed them instead. I could feel her voice, my chest agin her back. Like it was my voice too, and we lay there a long time until we both fell asleep.

Her crying out woke me up. She had tried to sit up, and the pain must have grabbed her awful hard, the way she was trying to claw at her back. I helped her get upright and she rested herself agin the wall. I went to my own bed and watched her, her face all twisted, breathing through her teeth. After a time, she got loose of the pain, and she looked back at me.

Says she, How long have you been here?

Always, says I.

Were you born here?

I think so, says I.

Where's your mummy?

I pointed up the stairs.

Says she, Which one?

I shook my head.

You don't know?

No, says I. I think maybe Mummy Joy, but I don't know. Not for sure.

I have to get out of here, says she.

You can't, says I.

Says she, Why not? There has to be a way.

They'll kill us, says I.

She went quiet, then, staring at me. After a time, she says, There has to be a way. I'll get out and I'll get the police and they'll take you away from those men. You and the others.

Says I, I saw a policeman one time. He came to the house. We had to be quiet till he went away.

Says she, Why was he here?

I don't know, says I, he talked to Daddy Ivan for a minute then he went away. He had a big car. I liked the noise it made.

She said it again. There has to be a way. And again, and again, she said it over and over like it would come true if she said it enough times.

And here till I tell you, it did come true. I wish it hadn't, but it did.

13

Sara

SARA FELT HER PHONE VIBRATE in her hip pocket. She shifted in the van's passenger seat and reached behind to retrieve it. Checking the display, she saw it was Damien calling. Who else would it be? Past six o'clock, he'd be home by now, wondering where she'd gone. Even though she knew she would regret it, she refused the call.

'When we get back,' she said, 'I'll get out on the lane. No need to come all the way in.'

'No, sure I'll drop you at the door,' Tony said. 'That'll be easier than trying to turn in the lane. I'd wind up in the river if I wasn't careful.'

She wanted to argue, but she couldn't admit the reason she didn't want him to bring her to the house. Not even to herself.

'You know,' Tony said, 'my granda used to collect local newspapers. The *Irish News* and the *Belfast Telegraph*, some of the smaller ones too. We found stacks of them after he died and we had to clear his house. There's still a load of them in my mother's attic. I could look and see if there's any from around the time of the killings.'

Sara wondered if she truly wanted to know more. She already knew she would not sleep tonight; she hadn't slept since they'd moved in, not properly, and she doubted she ever would find rest in that house. As Tony turned the van into the lane that ran alongside the river, leading to the house, she imagined telling Damien she wanted them to sell the place and move.

Walking on graves, she thought. The second time that day the idea had come to her mind, again unbidden. The van grew cold around her.

'Should I?' Tony asked.

Sara shivered and said, 'Sorry?'

'Dig out those old papers,' Tony said, steering between the gateposts, onto the drive, through the ash trees with their thinning leaves.

Damien waited on the doorstep, watching them approach.

'I asked you,' she said. 'You didn't offer.'

'What?'

'Tell him I asked you to take me into the village. You didn't offer to take me.'

She saw Tony from the corner of her eye, turning to look at her, and she knew she had revealed too much of herself. Too much of her marriage. More than she wanted to admit to herself. Shame withered her.

As the van halted, Damien walked towards it, his right hand outstretched. He grabbed the passenger door handle, yanked it, but the door did not open. Sara saw the anger in his eyes. He gritted his teeth and pulled the handle once more, and again, making the van rock on its suspension.

'Hang on,' Tony called, turning the ignition off. When the engine died, he pulled the key out, and the locks clunked.

Damien opened the door and reached for Sara. 'Come on,' he said, the smooth calm of his voice sparking fear in her.

'Wait,' she said, grappling with the seat belt.

Damien gripped her upper arm and dug his fingers into her flesh. A warning.

'Here,' Tony said, releasing the seat belt's clasp.

Damien kept hold of Sara's arm, his grip tightening, as she climbed down from the van. 'Go on in the house,' he said, lifting the shopping bag from the footwell and placing it in her arms. His eyes met hers. 'I'll see you in there.'

Sara made no attempt to argue and walked towards the open front door, her head down. She paused once, glanced back, and saw Tony looking back at her, the muscles in his jaw working. Inside, she left the door open a few inches and listened.

'What the fuck do you think you're at?' Damien asked, his voice rasping.

Tell him I asked you, she thought, willing Tony to somehow hear the words.

'Mrs Keane asked me for a lift into the village,' Tony said, and Sara exhaled. 'She said she needed a few things. It was no trouble.'

'Your work's not done,' Damien said. 'There's still wiring hanging from the walls.'

'I've done all I can today,' Tony said. 'I'm picking up the switch plates for the upstairs lights at the suppliers in the morning, and we're still waiting on—'

'Get the fuck out of here,' Damien said, and Sara heard the van door slam.

She hurried into the kitchen and set the bag on the island and began unpacking. The front door closed, and she turned to see Damien on the kitchen's threshold.

'Does your phone not work?' he asked, his voice low in his chest.

She kept her own voice light, as if nothing was the matter, as if she could soothe him with reason. 'Sorry I didn't answer, we were just at the end of the road, so I knew I'd be back in a minute or—'

'What are you doing, disappearing like that? I come home, you're not here, what am I supposed to think?'

'I told you we needed some things,' Sara said. 'You wouldn't let me have the car, so I asked—'

'That fucking toerag?' Damien crossed the kitchen to her in three strides, and she backed into the island, her hands instinctively up. 'You got into that piece of shit's van so you could go for a wee ride?'

'You wouldn't let me have the car,' she said, fighting the quiver in her throat, 'and we needed some things.'

Less than an inch between them. She felt the heat of him. Smelled his breath.

'What for?' he asked.

'I wanted to make us dinner. For you. I wanted to cook for you.'

He remained there, frozen in his anger, as seconds dragged by. Then he exhaled, the muscles in his jaws relaxing. The sliver of air between them expanded.

'I'm going to Ma's for dinner,' he said, taking a step back. 'I need to go over some stuff with my da.'

It crossed her mind to argue, point to the food she'd bought, but she knew better. Instead, she folded her arms around herself, nodded, and turned her gaze to the floor.

'Don't disappear like that on me again,' he said, placing his hands on her upper arms. He bent at the knees so he could look up at her. 'I was worried, that's all. You could've fallen in the river for all I knew. Just let me know next time. All right?'

'Yeah,' she said. 'Sorry.'

'It's okay. I'll see you later.'

He kissed her forehead and left her there.

Sara closed her eyes and listened to the front door close, the BMW's ignition, the tyres on the gravel. Then screeching silence. The fingers of her left hand crept inside her right sleeve, found the bare, smooth flesh of her forearm.

She knew she shouldn't. She had promised she wouldn't do it again.

But she had to.

Her nails dug into the skin. Bitten and stubbed as they were, they gripped and scratched. Brilliant pain flooded her mind, forcing out all else. The nails travelled along her skin, leaving bright streaks behind like comet trails. She scratched and dug until she could stand it no more.

But it was not enough.

She rolled up the sleeve of the hoodie Damien had given her that morning, brought her forearm to her mouth, and closed the flesh between her teeth. Lightning-bright pain, scorching and beautiful, a firebrand on her skin. She held the flesh there between her teeth for as long as she could bear, until the tears streamed from her eyes and damped her forearm.

But it was not enough.

Before the idea had fully formed, she reached for the plastic milk bottle on the island. It exploded on the floor, white liquid blooming across the stonework in firework patterns, splashing on her legs. Then she lifted the box of eggs, raised them over her head, cried out as she hurled it at the floor. Shell and yolk and white scattered through the milk. Finally, she swept the bag along with the rest of the groceries from the island's worktop. Loose peppers and apples rolled against the cupboards.

When it was done, and reason had returned, Sara wept.

* * *

It took her two hours to clean the floor, the walls of the island, the cupboard doors, first mopping up the milk and egg yolks, then sweeping up the shells, and finally scrubbing the cracks in the stone. She had salvaged what she could of the food, cleaning whatever had been in contact with the floor, and stored it all away. She paused now and then, the hard edge of reality coming into view. The madness of what she'd done.

She couldn't let Damien know. He would say he was right about her, about the state of her mind. That she was coming undone again. He would talk about doctors and pills, ways to dull the blades that cut at her. She couldn't face that. Not again.

By the time the floor and cupboards were clean, her shoulders and back ached, and her knees felt as if a hammer had been taken to them. The kitchen had darkened around her, the sun low in the sky outside. She had to use the island to haul herself up on her feet, and her lower back complained at the effort. A deep quiet had settled over the house, and she imagined Damien at his parents' home on the outskirts of Lurgan, his mother feeding him and tut-tutting about his own wife not putting a decent meal on the table for him.

The quiet pressed in on her, and her own breathing seemed thunderous. Even the birds outside had fallen silent. She turned in a circle, her gaze moving from corner to corner, not lingering for fear of what she might catch a glimpse of. Nowhere in the living world could be so quiet.

Walking on graves.

The idea presented itself again, and she became aware of her own weight on the floor, and what lay beneath. She realised then that she had not wandered more than a few yards from this house since she had arrived here, the lanes and fields unexplored. Now the walls seemed too thick, the ceilings too low, the air inside too dense to breathe.

A walk. Hadn't she thought of that earlier? Yes, a walk.

She went to the hall and the front door beyond, outside, feeling the chilled wet fabric of her jeans cling to her legs. Loose stones and gravel slipped beneath her feet as she headed for the gateway that led to the lane. She didn't look back towards the house, and she knew she had left the front door open. Doesn't matter, she thought. Just go.

Cold out here. Sara shivered as she walked along the lane, avoiding the potholes and the seam of stubbled grass that ran along the centre. Through the hedgerow to her right, she saw the bank leading down to the river, the low evening sun reflecting gold on the sluggish water. She imagined wading in, letting the water swallow her. Letting it enter her, fill her up and drag her down to the bottom to rest in the silt and rocks.

A heron glided along the river's path, silent as the breeze, before dipping beyond her view. She wondered where it had landed. Ahead, a gap in the hedge. She pushed her way through and found herself at the top of the bank, a slope of thick grass and weeds dropping away below her. Another shiver coursed through her as the sun sank lower in the sky and the temperature fell along with it. She took a cautious step down, the soles of her trainers struggling for purchase. Then another, and then her feet slipped away from her and she slid down and down until she reached the bare, stony earth at the water's edge.

Mud and grass stains coated her jeans, grazes stung the heels of her hands. She cursed and got up on her hands and knees, her body still aching from cleaning the kitchen. If she stretched out her hand, she could touch the water. So she did, let the cold soothe the abrasions on her skin.

Would it be so bad? Just crawl in, let the slow current take her.

A sinful idea, a sin she had committed once before.

The low sun's reflection on the water pierced Sara's vision, and she shaded her eyes with her free hand, looking out across the surface.

There, a girl, looking back at her.

A cry escaped Sara's throat and she fell back against the earth and grass.

The girl, aching beauty, fixed her stare on Sara. Submerged to her waist, she wore a plain white dress, her dark hair falling around her shoulders. In her hands, pressed to her belly, a tangle of scarlet ribbons. They trailed into the water, red tendrils threading out to Sara, inviting her.

Reach out, Sara thought, take hold of one.

But the water is so cold. Dark down there. The sun can't reach.

The girl did not shiver, showed no sign of the water's chill.

But Sara knew, she could feel it from here, the cold darkness, had felt it before.

She got to her feet and took a step back, stones and earth shifting beneath her shoes. Shook her head, no.

The girl stared, the calm on her face giving way to sorrow, fathoms deep. She lay back in the water, turning her face to the dimming sky. The water reclaimed her, pulling her down, no disruption on the surface save for the swirling scarlet ribbons, and soon they too were gone, leaving only the dying sun's glare.

Sara remained on the bank, the world darkening around her. She heard the river now, the whisper and sigh of it, and the birds in the trees and the hedges. Her breath quickened, her lungs pulling in air faster than she could expel it, filling her chest.

'God,' she whispered. 'Oh, God.'

She turned and scrambled up the bank, slipping, sliding back, before finding her feet again. When she'd struggled to the top, her hands and knees wet with mud and grass stains, she dared one glance back down at the river. She saw only golden light on slow water, the heron wading in the shallows.

Get away, she thought. Back to the house? She didn't know, was only sure that she needed to be gone from here. She pushed through the hedge, stumbled onto the lane.

Sara heard the hiss of tyres, the whine of brakes. She saw only an impression of the car, a wall of colour, and held her hands out as if they could stop it.

Damien's BMW halted, its grille inches from her knees, and her legs betrayed her. She fell forward, her hands on the car's bonnet, hot on her skin. Through the windscreen, she saw her husband stare back at her, eyes wide, lips moving. She heard his voice, muted, but the anger cut through. He threw off his seat belt and opened the door, climbed out, already shouting.

'. . . the fuck's going on? What are you doing out here? I could've killed you.'

She tried to speak but there wasn't enough air. All she could do was open her mouth and watch as he walked around the car to her. He seized her arm and dragged her to the passenger door, opened it, and bundled her inside.

His questions continued as he climbed into the driver's seat and set off towards the house. She had no answers, only the image of ribbons reaching out across the water to her, inviting her into their tangles and swirls of scarlet.

14

Esther

ESTHER SPENT HOURS IN THOUGHT, sometimes drifting on sluggish tides of sleep, but more often awake. She wondered about the two women, their ratty hair and dirty faces and fingers. Their missing teeth. The smell of them, their low and stale odours mingling with the damp and rot of the cellar. Sweat and urine, excrement and worse. Their dull and thready clothes. She watched them that first morning as they lit the lamps with thin and grubby fingers, made their toilet, went about their ablutions. All of it had the banality of routine and the urgency of ritual. The men summoning them from above, like heathen gods, taking the women up into the light.

How did they come to be here? How long ago? She wondered if their stories were like hers, grasping for a handful of kindness, and being dragged into this. And the strange little girl, so small, so watchful. Even after she had left her side, Esther still felt the girl's eyes on her back, seeking. A girl who had never known any place but this.

It was still daylight up above when the door opened, and the two women descended the steps. One carried a jug, the other a bowl. The girl took the jug, drank from it, leaving a white film of milk on her upper lip. The bowl was set on the middle bed, and Esther turned to see what it contained: scraps of bread and cheese, and leftover beef from the night before. The two women and the girl dipped their hands in, brought food to their hungry mouths.

'Take some,' one of the women said.

Esther shook her head and turned back to the wall.

'You need to eat.'

'Don't want to,' Esther said.

She felt the weight of another person on her bed. A hand on her back.

'Come on. No sense starving yourself. It'll do you no good. Sit up. Eat.'

Esther closed her eyes and wished herself away from here, knowing it was futile. But then her belly grumbled with want. She turned and pushed herself upright.

'Here,' the woman on the other bed said, and reached out a piece of cheese rolled in bread.

Esther took it, saying nothing, and as she bit into the food, tasted the salt, her stomach growled again. She shoved the rest into her mouth, barely chewing, swallowed it down.

'More,' she said.

This time, the woman wrapped some beef in the bread. Esther snatched it from her and palmed it into her mouth. The little girl passed her the jug of milk, and Esther took a long swallow. It was warm and sweet, thick with cream, and now her stomach threatened rebellion. She covered her mouth and burped, then swallowed again.

'It's fresh from the cow,' one of the women said.

They had told Esther their names the night before, but she could not pick them out from the tangle of images and emotions in her mind. It was as if the woman had read her thoughts.

'I'm Noreen,' she said.

'I'm Joy,' the other said.

'Esther. Esther Mooney. What is this place?'

Noreen and Joy exchanged a look, an ache of sadness passing between them.

'It's a farm,' Noreen said. 'Cattle, for beef, mostly. They keep a couple of cows for milk, but just for the house.'

'How long have you been here?'

'I don't know,' Joy said. 'Twelve or thirteen years, maybe. I'm not sure.'

'A bit longer,' Noreen said.

Noreen was missing at least one tooth, and her scalp showed pink through her hair. Two fingers of her left hand were bound together with a piece of wood, their flesh puffy and bruised. It crossed Esther's mind to tell her she should see a doctor, but she caught herself.

She became conscious of the smell once again, the entwined murky odours of this place and these women. Her stomach lurched, and she swallowed bile.

'How can you live like this?' she asked. 'Like animals.'

Noreen's face darkened. 'We didn't choose this. No more than you did. You wait, give it a few weeks, you'll be as filthy as we are.'

Esther realised she had found the hard nub of pride that remained in this woman. Good, she thought, glad of anything at all she could grasp to. That meant she hadn't been broken. Not yet.

'Who are the men upstairs?' she asked.

'My Daddies,' the little girl, Mary, said.

Esther looked at her now, once again shocked at how small she was, how dark her eyes. 'They can't all be your father.'

'We don't talk about that,' Noreen said. 'We don't want her to know too much. To get attached to anyone in particular.'

Joy cast her eyes down, hugging her own elbows. Esther noticed, and understood.

'How did you get here?'

'Probably same as you,' Noreen said. 'I was desperate. I needed a place to go, and I took what I was offered. I didn't know what was happening till it was too late.'

'George told me they needed a housekeeper,' Joy said. 'I had nowhere else to go.'

'Have you tried to get out?' Esther asked.

'What do you think?' Noreen said, her voice sharp. 'Course we have. I don't know how many times. And I don't know how many times I've been dragged back by my hair, or worse. There's been others here. Others that tried to get away. They died. We're the lucky ones.'

'Died?'

'Aye. They died. But we're alive.'

Esther felt her anger ebb, dampened by the fear.

'There has to be a way,' she said. 'There's more of us than them.'

'And they're stronger than us.'

'There's knives upstairs, I used one yesterday. We just need to get one and—'

'They have guns,' Noreen said. 'A knife's no good against a gun.'

'We have to try,' Esther said. 'What else can we do?'

'We can live,' Noreen said, leaning forward, her voice rising. 'We can bloody well stay alive, and maybe we'll outlive them. That's what we can do. Just get by, just try to get through the day without making them angry. And they're always angry. All we can do is survive, one day after another. Stay quiet, keep our heads down. You try to do anything else, and they'll kill you. They'll kill us. They've done it before, and they'll do it again. We're no better to them than the cattle in the fields. We're less than that to them. You're right, we live like animals, because that's what we are to them. The best we can do is cook for them, clean for them, and please them when they want pleasing.'

Noreen got to her feet and marched in circles around the floor, her fists and her jaw clenched, her nostrils flaring. Esther played the words over in her mind.

'What do you mean, please them?'

Noreen stopped, stared at her. 'You know what I mean.'

Joy glanced at Mary. 'We don't like to talk out loud about it.'

Esther remembered the man in the car, his sticky hands, his tainted breath. Her walking away with her underwear in her hand, swearing to herself that she'd never allow such a thing to happen again.

'No,' she said. 'They won't touch me. I won't have it.'

Noreen sat down again on the bed opposite. 'They don't care what you'll have or you won't. They'll take what they want.'

'Not from me,' Esther said, meaning it. 'And I won't die here. I swear on my mother and my father's grave, I will not die here.'

Noreen and Joy could not look at her. But Mary could. Her eyes deep and black and seeing into Esther's very soul. Esther could stand to hold her gaze for no more than a moment, then she had to look away.

15
Mary

I WAS DOTING ON THAT GIRL from the moment she came down them stairs. Or fell down them, I suppose. Most of the time I couldn't wait to get upstairs into the light, even if I had to work like a dog, it was better than down there in the dark and the damp and the smell. But when she was there, that's where I wanted to stay. The only thing I wanted was to be with her. I near wished she'd cry more so I could cuddle in and comfort her. And it wasn't just that she was awful pretty and that she smelled clean and good and she didn't have the filth under her nails that we did. It was because she was from out there, from the real world, where real people lived.

Sometimes I thought out there was just in my head. A place where people could go wherever they wanted whenever they wanted and no one was bating them and they could eat all the food they could fit in their mouths and they could drive cars and go to the seaside or the big city and all those things. Sometimes I felt like none of that was real, it was just stories Mummy Joy and Mummy Noreen telt me, and there was nothing further away than I could see from the windows or the yard.

And now here, wasn't there someone from out there, and that made it real, and that made her special, and I wanted to know everything about it. So when the Mummies was upstairs working again, I asked her.

Says I, What's it like out there? What's the real world like? Better than this, says she.

Do you live in the city, says I, or by the sea?

The city, says she, Belfast. We had a nice house, I went to a nice school. Before my father died, and then my mother. We lived on a nice road with lots of other big houses. I thought I'd have that forever. And now I'm here.

She cried again, quiet tears, not like before. I knew I shouldn't go to her now. I should let her be.

I asked her about cars and buses. She telt me she got the bus into town sometimes, and other times her daddy took her in his car. I asked her about aeroplanes. She'd never been on one, but she telt me one time her and her mummy and daddy got on a big boat and crossed the sea to the Isle of Man. She said the sea was rough and everyone on the boat was sick. I tried to imagine that, being on a boat on the sea, and it going up and down and up and down. I tried to picture it, but I couldn't. I'd never seen a boat.

I asked her about school, and she telt me she had lots of friends, boys and girls, and they all wore uniforms and they learnt to count and to read and they learnt about things that happened years ago all around the world. And how things work in the world, what makes the wind blow and why rain falls. And I had a terrible feeling inside me just then: I hated her, just for a wee while, but I hated her because she'd had all those things and I never heard tell of them before then. I was jealous of her, and I hated her for it, but I wanted to know more. I wanted to know about televisions and radios and picture houses and all those good things. But she didn't want to talk about it any more, she was getting tired of me asking her things, so she helt her whisht and lay down again.

I don't mind what time of day it was, but the Mummies had been upstairs at their work for a good long while, when Daddy Tam opened the door.

There's cleaning needs doing, says he. Get changed out of thon dress and put on something from the wardrobe. The child'll help you. The fireplaces need cleaning out. The child'll show you what to do.

Says Esther, Let me go. I won't say anything to anybody, just let me go.

Daddy Tam said nothing and closed the door, let us alone.

You should do what he tells you, says I. He'll hurt you if you don't.

I mind she stared at me for a wee moment, then she seemed to get smaller in front of me, like the air had been let out of her. Then she got up and went to the wardrobe. It had no doors, just a rail inside with dresses hanging on it. They were plain auld things, not like the dress Esther had on her. They might have been white at one time, but now they were grey and raggedy. She lifted one down, then another, and helt them agin herself to see which would fit best. She chose one and set it on her bed.

I watched her as she undid a button at the back of her dress, at her neck, then reached up between her shoulders and felt for a zip. I didn't know that was what it was called then. I'd never seen one before. Everything we had was buttons. She pulled it down and the dress fell off her shoulders, and I couldn't breathe. She lowered it down to the floor and she stepped out of it and I couldn't lift my eyes from her. The Mummies, when they got changed, I could see the bones of them, their ribs, their shoulder blades. Not Esther. Her body was full and her skin was white and she had no scars and no sores, only a lock of bruises from falling down the stairs. She was perfect. I don't mind if I knew that word back then, but I know it now, and that's what she was.

Just perfect.

She lifted her dress and she laid it on the bed, smoothed it out all flat, spread out the skirt of it, the arms. She ran her fingers over it, touched the hems and the stitching and the pleats. Like it was a precious thing, like a treasure. And then she noticed me watching her, and she covered herself up, like she was ashamed. I wanted to tell her not to be ashamed, not to hide, because she was perfect, but I didn't have a breath in me. She gathered up the dress she'd taken from the wardrobe and pulled it on over her head. Then she looked down at herself and cried awful hard. I didn't think she could have any tears left in her, but she did.

Says I, We should go up and get started before Daddy Tam comes looking us. He'll be thran if he has to come and get us.

She followed me up the stairs, still wearing her good shoes. The door at the top was open, and we went out into the kitchen. Daddy Ivan sat at the table, writing numbers in his big book, counting money, sorting it into piles. I lifted the shovel, brush and tin bucket from beside the wood stove, which still wasn't lit because it hadn't been cleaned out yet. Mummy Joy was washing clothes in the sink. Mummy Noreen was cleaning the floor.

We start at the top, says I, in the bedrooms.

There were three rooms upstairs, one for each of the Daddies. We went to Daddy Ivan's first. I lifted the fireguard away from the hearth and knelt down. Like this, says I, sweeping the ashes out from under the grate and onto the shovel, and pouring them into the bucket.

Says she, I know how to clean out a fireplace. Where are the others?

The Daddies? says I. They'll be out in the fields or in the cowsheds, doing their work.

So there's only him, says she, the older one.

I was finished cleaning Daddy Ivan's hearth, so I went to the next room, Daddy George's. Esther followed me, and this time she lifted the fireguard away, got down on her knees and did the sweeping out. We didn't talk any more, but I could see she was thinking, thinking, thinking.

When we'd done all the fireplaces upstairs, Esther carried the bucketful of ashes down to the kitchen, and I showed her where to empty it out in the yard. She stood there for a minute and looked around her. The only way out was through the gate at the far side, the one that led to the fields. She stared at it, her hands making fists at her sides.

They'll catch you, says I.

Maybe, says she, maybe not.

They'll hurt you.

Not if I hurt them first.

Come on, says I, we have the stove to do.

I thought for a second she wouldn't follow me back inside, that she'd try to run, but she came ahead. She cleared out the stove, brushing the ashes into the bucket, while I folded old sheets of newspaper into criss-cross shapes, just like Mummy Noreen had showed me how to do. When the stove was emptied, I filled it with wood and newspaper, and then I put a match to the paper. I tended it a while, just to be sure the wood was lit, then I closed the door, opened the vent wide to help it take. I turned my head and saw Esther over by the sink.

I saw what she was looking at: the knives laid out on the draining board. Big ones and wee ones, all of them like razors. Her hand moved to the biggest of them, with its long blade and thick handle made of wood.

I whispered to her, Don't.

She didn't hear me or she didn't listen, I don't know, but she lifted that knife in her hand and my heart dropped down into my stomach. She turned around to face Daddy Ivan, the knife in her hand, helt out in front of her. Mummy Joy stepped away from her, soapy water dripping off her fingers. She put her back into the corner as far as it would go, afraid to look at anybody. Mummy Noreen stayed down on the floor where she'd been scrubbing.

Daddy Ivan looked up from the numbers in his book. He squinted his eyes at her.

Says he, What have you got there?

Esther lifted the knife higher, turned it so the blade shone in the light from the window.

Says she, I'm going. I'll cut you if you try to stop me.

Daddy Ivan sat back in his chair and watched her, his mouth tight shut.

Esther says to Mummy Joy, Come with me.

Mummy Joy shook her head and looked down at the floor.

Esther turned to me. Come on, says she, we'll get help.

I helt my whisht, stayed down by the stove, on my knees. So did Mummy Noreen, with the scrubbing brush in her hands. The safest place to be is on your knees.

Esther started to shake, that blade glittering in the air in front of her. She knew she was on her own, no one was going with her. She took a step closer to Daddy Ivan.

I'm going and you can't stop me, says she.

Daddy Ivan sat still, looking at her like she was nothing.

You'd better go on, then, says he.

16

Sara

S ARA SAT ON A STOOL at the island, her arms wrapped
around her middle, her sleeves damp with mud. The
same mud blended with the milk on her jeans, the
denim pulling at the skin of her thighs and calves. She could
smell the earth on her, a deep and ancient scent that reached
down inside her.

Damien stood at the sink, leaning back on it, the dying day's
light making a silhouette of him against the window. She could
barely make out his features, but she imagined his face blank
like a doll's, his eyes a channel to the empty space at his centre.

'So?' he said.

Sara didn't answer. Words drifted beyond the reach of
her tongue.

'Am I talking to myself?' he asked.

She shook her head.

'Then answer me,' he said, his voice remaining low, like a
stalking dog. 'What were you doing out there?'

She found her own voice, small and weak in her throat.
'I went for a walk.'

'Is that what you call it? Look at the state of you.'

'I fell,' she said. 'I wanted to see the river and I slipped.'

He watched her for a moment, his gaze crawling over her. She hunched her back, curled in on herself. She would not tell him about the girl in the water, the scarlet ribbons she held to her stomach.

'Are we going to have problems?' he asked. 'Like before?'

'No,' she said, too quickly, too sure.

She tried not to flinch when he moved from the sink and crossed the dark kitchen to where she sat. She tried, but she failed. He came to her side, turned her to face him. Rolling up her sleeve, he examined her skin. He ran his thumb along the tracks her fingernails had left there.

'Have you been hurting yourself again?'

'No,' she said, too quickly, too sure.

'How did you get these scratches?'

'When I fell.'

He rolled the sleeve up further, revealing the mirrored crescents of the teeth marks.

'Jesus, love,' he said.

'I'm sorry,' she said, the shame of it threatening to topple her from the stool.

'Look at me.'

When she didn't, he placed a finger beneath her chin and tilted her head back.

'I'm only trying to look after you,' he said, his voice soft now, like his mouth was filled with sugar. 'I don't want you to hurt yourself. I don't want to come home and find you unconscious on the floor. You promise me you won't do that again.'

She dropped her gaze, shook her head.

'Say it.'

'I promise,' she said.

He took her in his arms, and she remembered that she loved him. God help her, she loved him. That needful thought came to her as a forgotten sorrow, a torment long buried and now returned. She still loved him, and it shamed her more than the bite on her arm.

'Don't do that to me again,' he said. 'This isn't Bath. It's not like England. This is such a small place. Everyone knows everything. There's no secrets. You try that here, the whole country finds out. Think of my family.'

'I won't do it again,' she said, unsure if she believed herself. 'I promise.'

He held her tight, his arms strong, pressing hers into her sides, binding, enveloping her until she couldn't see or hear anything but him, no scent in the world but his.

'I know you won't,' he said. 'And you've no call to go wandering off. I can't be going to work and worrying about you, can I? All you have to do is stay here.'

She wanted to tell him something, but she couldn't. It would wound him. Anger him. But it would fester if she didn't say it now.

'I don't want to live here,' she said.

'What?'

His arms loosened enough to allow her to turn her head.

'I don't want to live here,' she said again. 'Not in this house.'

'What are you talking about?'

He released her, took a step back. She felt as if she might topple from the stool, and she placed a hand on the island to steady herself.

'We don't belong here,' she said. 'It's not our house.'

'Yes, it is. My father paid a fair price for it. He bought it for us, and it's ours.'

'Things happened here.'

Damien's shoulders slumped. 'Who've you been talking to? The spark?'

Sara wondered who he meant for a moment, then she remembered it was slang for an electrician. He meant Tony.

'Not him,' she said, searching for a lie. 'I saw something online.'

'It was sixty-odd years ago. You don't have to worry about it.'

'But I do. I can't help it.'

He took a step back. 'All right, this place has a history, all old houses do. But, Jesus, he got it so cheap, and we get to live without a mortgage hanging over us. How many couples our age get to do that? Give me your phone.'

She could feel his anger, restrained, pulsing in him.

'Why?' she asked.

'Because I don't want you getting your head turned by some nonsense you found on the internet.'

'It's not nonsense,' she said, knowing it was a mistake. 'It really happened. People died here.'

'Give me the phone,' he said, holding his hand out.

Sara pulled it from her pocket and handed it over. He unlocked the phone, thumbed through a few menus and lists, then tucked it away in his own pocket. Taking her in his arms, he pressed his lips against her temple.

'I love you,' he said. 'I want us to be happy here. I want us to have kids and make a family. Don't you want that?'

Sara didn't answer.

'You do, don't you?'

His arms snaked around her, tighter, constricting.

'Yes,' she said, her voice so quiet and small it couldn't possibly have been a lie.

Damien released her from his embrace and said, 'Get yourself cleaned up.'

He left her alone in the kitchen where she remained until full dark had fallen.

* * *

Sara did not sleep, lying with her gaze fixed on the ceiling as she listened to the house breathe around her. Its creaks and groans seemed like a voice, cracked and brittle from disuse, trying to warn her of something. Telling her to leave while she could. She tried not to think of the girl in the water, the scarlet ribbons she clutched to her belly. A figment, a distortion of light on the water's surface, twisted through the prism of her cracked mind. But still the girl's sorrowful eyes stared back at her in the darkness.

Leave.

How often that word had floated in her consciousness, useless, like a birthday candle wish. Leave and go where? Home? She had not spoken to her mother since the week after her wedding, had not seen her father since she was six when he had emigrated to New Zealand. Men leave, women stay. Her mother had told her that, a glass in one hand, a cigarette in the other.

There was only one way Sara could leave. She had tried that, and failed, waking on a hospital bed hours later.

Amanda had come to her one evening, after five, when Sara left her office building, heading for the bus stop. Waiting for her on the corner. Sara had stopped when she saw her, considered turning, walking the other way. But Amanda had called her name, and she couldn't ignore her.

They went for coffee. Even though Damien had said she shouldn't drink coffee after lunchtime, that was why she couldn't sleep at night. A new place, big leather-upholstered chairs and small, low tables, the kind of place you had to lean in to hear and be heard.

'We're worried about you,' Amanda said, her elbows on her knees, her thumbnails clicking against each other. Her blonde hair curled on her shoulders, sharp blue eyes revealing the hardness of her, allowing no place to hide.

They had been friends since their first year at the University of Bath. Sara and Amanda, Chloe and Tanya too. So many nights spent drinking, talking, crying, laughing. They had been an army of four, laying waste to the city. Sara had never had friends like that before. Not since she'd been a child.

'Why?' Sara had said, honest in her question.

'When did we last hang out?' Amanda asked. 'Just the four of us. No boyfriends or partners. When?'

Sara thought about it. 'Hallowe'en,' she said. 'We went out for Hallowe'en. Remember, that bloke in the Dracula costume wouldn't stop pestering you.'

'It's March,' Amanda said. 'Nearly April. Six months. And Tanya wasn't there. The four of us. When were we last together?'

'I've been busy,' Sara said.

'We've all been busy,' Amanda said. 'I texted you just last week. I called. You didn't answer.'

'Did you? Sorry, I should have—'

'Did you know that?' Amanda asked. 'Or did Damien delete the messages from your phone?'

'Of course not.'

'Last night, we were chatting on WhatsApp.'

'What? No, we . . .'

Sara closed her mouth. Kept the words trapped.

Amanda leaned forward, took Sara's hand in hers.

'You and I were chatting on WhatsApp last night,' she said, her voice gentler now. 'We were talking about all sorts. Old boyfriends, for the most part. You were asking me questions. Questions you should've known the answers to.'

Sara had gone to bed before ten last night. Damien had sat up. Said he had work to do. She had left her phone in the living room, as Damien insisted she do, because staring at the screen would keep her awake.

'I've been tired lately,' Sara said. 'I've not been sleeping. There's so much going on at the office.'

'It was Damien talking to me last night,' Amanda said. 'He was pretending to be you, wasn't he?'

'I don't remember,' Sara said. 'Like I said, I was tired. I don't know what I was talking about.'

'You don't remember,' Amanda said, her fingers tightening on Sara's hand. 'Do you remember asking me all about Geoff? That guy you went out with for a month in first year?'

'No,' Sara said.

'It's not right,' Amanda said. 'It's not normal. Him going on WhatsApp, pretending to be you. And what else? Twitter? Facebook? Texts? How can I message you and know it's really you?'

'It's not like that,' Sara said. 'I mean, he has my passwords, but it's just—'

'Just what? Just nothing. It's not right. Do you have his passwords?'

When Sara didn't answer, Amanda grabbed both her hands, squeezed them hard. As Sara dropped her gaze to her lap, Amanda dipped her head, looked up at her. Gave her no room to get away.

'And do you know what that means?' Amanda said. 'It means I can't trust you. As a friend, how can I ever send you a text, a message, a DM, how can I ever do any of that knowing it might not be you who's going to read it?'

Sara raised her shoulders, dropped them, shook her head.

'I have nothing to hide from Damien,' she said.

'But I do,' Amanda said. 'If I tell you something, I'm telling *you*, not him. Jesus, you're my friend, Sara. You and me. Not you and me and him. Don't you understand that? And not just me. Tanya and Chloe as well. Tanya hasn't seen you since the wedding. Christ, you live twenty minutes apart. You haven't seen her in more than eighteen months, doesn't that tell you something?'

Damien had never liked Tanya. He said she talked too much, laughed too hard. And she was a slut, he said, more men in her life than any woman should have. He didn't want Sara to be around her and all those hungry, reaching, feeling men.

'Friends drift apart,' Sara said. 'It happens.'

'We're not drifting away,' Amanda said. 'We're being pushed away. Surely you can see that? He's isolating you.'

'No.'

'Apart from work, do you ever go out without him?'

'Of course I do.'

'Where?'

'Places, I don't know, shops and—'

'Where?'

'Don't badger me like that, it's not fair.'

'What about money? Do you have your own or does he keep it?'

Sara wanted to explain the joint bank account her salary was paid into, the weekly allowance that was transferred to her own account each Friday. To help them budget, Damien had said. And if she ever needed anything more, she could always come to him and ask. He had never refused, had he? Not that she asked often. But it was all too complicated to get into. Not here, not now. And besides, what business was it of Amanda's? It was a liberty to ask such questions.

'Damien does the finances,' she said, keeping the irritation from her voice. 'He's better at it, that's all. I'm not good with money, you know that.'

'No, I don't know any such thing. But I do know an abusive relationship when I see one.'

Those words hit Sara like cold water.

'He's never hit me,' she said, the words tumbling out.

'He doesn't have to,' Amanda said. 'It's coercive control. He doesn't have to be violent to be abusive. Look, I deal with this all the time at work. I see so many women trapped like this, always in denial, always fooling themselves that it'll get better if they stick with it just a few more months.'

Sara tried to pull her hands away, but Amanda held them tight.

'It never gets better,' Amanda said. 'Never.'

Sara felt a cruel smile creep onto her lips knowing guilt would follow soon enough. 'You can't stand it, can you?'

Amanda gave her a warning glare. 'Don't. I know what you're going to say, but don't.'

'You can't stand seeing me have what you can't,' Sara said, both shamed and gratified at the hurt on her friend's face.

Amanda took a breath and said, 'You're lashing out. It's a defensive measure, part of the denial, and I won't—'

'You've never been able to keep a relationship for more than a few weeks, have you? So now you're trying to destroy mine.'

'We both know that's not true,' Amanda said.

Sara freed her hands from Amanda's and got to her feet. 'Don't contact me again,' she said.

She left the coffee shop, sparing only a glance through the window as she passed on her way to the bus stop. Amanda sat where she'd left her, her head bowed, a hand over her eyes, shoulders hitching. She hadn't seen or spoken to her best friend since.

That night, Sara lay awake while Damien snored, her mind chasing itself down twisting paths of denial and fear. The feeling of sinking into a deeper and blacker hole, losing herself in it, Amanda's words echoing there. Liar, she thought. Bloody liar. Jealous and bitter and clawing at my happiness, trying to steal it away.

And yet, and yet, and yet, Sara knew. All along, she knew.

The world collapsed in on itself, dragged her down into the pit as Damien dreamed beside her.

At two in the morning she had risen from their bed and gone to the flat's open-plan kitchen. She opened the high cupboard in the corner, stood on her toes, her fingers searching through boxes of paracetamol and ibuprofen, cold and flu remedies, bottles of vitamins. There at the back, one pack of sleeping pills, and another, both prescribed by different doctors at different times, neither of them opened.

She filled a glass with water and sat at the table, spread the pills on the surface, counted them as she swallowed until she couldn't count any more.

17

Esther

ESTHER STOOD THERE, EVERY PART of her frozen except her right hand, which trembled in front of her, the blade taking up the whole of her vision. How could a knife be so heavy? She inhaled, a quivering gasp, then exhaled, a low moan coming from inside her. How could a knife weigh so much? Her arm ached from holding it out and the idea occurred to her to simply place it back from where she'd lifted it.

'Go on, then,' the old man said.

He had not risen from his place at the table, the ledger open in front of him. Cash sorted into piles, notes and coins.

'Don't try to stop me,' Esther said.

He sat back, his arms out and open, showing her his hands. 'Nobody's stopping you,' he said. 'Away you go.'

Mary still knelt on the floor, her gaze moving between them both. Joy backed into the corner, looking at nothing but the floor. Noreen entirely still, the scrubbing brush in her hands. Esther wanted to scream at them, tell them to come with her, for Christ's sake, leave this place. They would not move, she knew. Maybe they were right. It didn't matter now. Esther had made her choice.

She turned away from Ivan and went to the hall. The front door was locked, wouldn't even move in its frame. She moved to the living room and tried to raise the lower pane of the nearest sash window, whined as she strained to lift it, but it would not budge. She realised it had been fixed shut, wedges of wood screwed into place to prevent its movement. Through the glass, she could see the driveway, the walls and a glimpse of the narrow lane beyond. Maybe she could break the glass and climb through. But what with?

There was an easier way.

She marched back into the kitchen where everyone remained as they had been when she had left moments before. Joy whispered to her as she passed.

'Stop,' she said. 'Don't.'

Esther ignored her. Ivan watched as she hurried past him on her way to the back hall, his face unreadable. She knew the back door was not locked; Mary and she had been able to walk out and in again with the ashes. Esther lifted the latch and pulled the door inward. It was heavy, its lower edge scraping on the stone floor.

Cool air met her on the threshold. She glanced back over her shoulder. Through the door to the kitchen, she could see Ivan, still sitting, still watching. She stepped out into the yard, her soles clicking and scraping on the rough concrete, and felt chilled drops of rain on her skin. The sky had greyed, the world blanketed in a dim stillness. Chickens pecked at scattered grain all around, and their silence disturbed Esther. Where had all the noise gone? Drowned in the rushing river in her ears, she realised, and she swallowed as if that might clear them.

She looked around the yard, flanked by stone outbuildings and barns. The cowshed directly in front of her. The gaps between the buildings had been sealed by wire and wooden fencing, some constructed with care, some crude and cobbled together. She walked deeper into the yard, turning in circles. Two cows stood in one of the outbuildings to the side, what might have been stables. Esther remembered the taste of warm, creamy milk, and she felt bile rise in her throat.

Where to run?

The only way she could see was the gate to the rear of the yard, held closed by a length of twine looped around a hook on the wall of the stable block. She crossed the yard to it, casting glances back towards the house as she went. Dark inside the back hall, the kitchen invisible beyond, but she knew Ivan watched her. She could feel his eyes on her back as sure as she could feel the ground beneath her feet.

Esther reached for the twine that bound the gate closed. She picked at the knot around the hook, but it would not be undone. Cursing, she placed her right foot on one of the gate's horizontal bars, her hands gripping the top, the knife handle pressed between her palm and the metal. She hoisted herself up and threw her left leg over, her foot finding purchase on the other side. Holding tight to the top bar, she slid her body over, the blade inches from her nose. As her weight carried her across, her left foot slipped, and she tumbled, her arms flailing. The ground rushed up to meet her, where the concrete crumbled into earth. Her shoulder rammed into a mix of mud and jagged stones, her hip hitting the concrete hard. She rolled away from the gate, crying out in pain and anger.

As she fought to get back the wind that had been knocked out of her, she allowed herself a moment to stare up at the thick cloud above and feel the cold pinpricks of rain on her skin. But no more. She had to move. The knife had fallen not far from her right hand. She reached for it, then got to her hands and knees before pushing herself upright.

One last time, Esther looked back towards the house. Now Ivan stood on the step, his hands in his pockets, as if this were any dull day. She turned back to the lane ahead of her. Clumps of coarse grass between two tracks gouged out of the earth by tractor tyres. Hoof divots pocked the ground, churned it to mud, leading to and from a large door in the side of the cowshed. Hedgerows either side, a barrier between her and the fields all around.

Somewhere, not far away, she heard the diesel grumble of a tractor, the sound rising and falling as the engine worked. The others were around these fields, doing whatever work they did. She needed to find her way back to the road in front of the house, staying out of their sight. Panic churned beneath the surface of her mind, a monster beneath the waves, a shadow ready to break into the now. She had to keep it below or it would surely devour her.

Esther moved along the lane, the mud sucking at her shoes, pulling her balance from under her. She tried to keep to the grassy channel in the middle, where the tractor's tyres had not stripped the turf away. The ground was firmer here, and she was able to move faster, eyeing the fields as she went.

Too late, she saw the tractor crest the rise up ahead and to her right. She ducked down to a crouch, the hedgerow between her and the driver, but she heard the engine rev and grow louder as it steered down towards her. Keeping low, she broke into a run, and had gone only a few steps before the mud pulled her left shoe loose, and soon the right was gone too. Her bare feet slipped in the mire, and she staggered, then fell onto her stomach, the knife held out in front of her. Somewhere behind her, the tractor's engine rattled to its death, and a brittle silence fell over the lane.

Even though she had sworn to herself that she no longer believed, Esther closed her eyes and said, 'Please, God, please help me.'

She clambered to her feet, got moving again, no longer concerned about keeping out of view. Holding to the grass, she pushed hard with her legs, her arms churning. She had no idea where the lane would lead her, but for now it was her only choice. A sweeping turn ahead, perhaps she could find a gap in the hedge and lose herself there. She rounded the corner and skidded to a halt, her feet sliding out from under her, landing on her back.

A few feet in front of her, a dozen or more cattle blocked the lane, brown and white, stout barrel bodies, heavy on their feet. Startled by her appearance, the first few tried to back away, pushing against those behind. A low chorus of mooing and huffing, and a man's voice above.

'Easy, now, easy, easy.'

George, the younger brother, came behind them, a long cane in his hand, swiping at the cows' backsides. He froze when he saw Esther get back to her feet, alarm on his face.

Esther hesitated, staring back, both of them locked in place for a moment before she spun around and sprinted in the opposite direction. Or she would have if not for the wall of a man whose chest she collided with. Once more, she fell back to the earth, winded. Thomas blocked what little sunlight the clouds allowed through, and she felt the deep chill of his shadow.

'What's all this, now?' he asked, his voice gentle.

Esther went to raise her right hand, the knife's handle gripped hard between her fingers, but his boot slammed down on her wrist, grinding it into the earth. She screamed as much from anger as from pain.

'Whisht, now,' he said, reaching down to pluck the knife from her hand. 'Settle yourself.'

He brought the blade to her throat. She felt the cold of it beneath her jaw, the tip pressing into her skin. A hair more pressure and it would draw blood.

'If you're going to give us trouble,' Thomas said, 'it'd be better to just put an end to it now. Save us all a lot of bother, wouldn't it?'

The mooing and shuffling of hooves grew, the cattle becoming agitated. They smelled her fear and wanted to flee, she could tell.

'Just let me go,' Esther said. 'Please, I'll say nothing to—'

Thomas lifted the blade from her throat, brought it to her eye, the flat of it against her cheek. She dared not blink.

'You know,' he said, 'if I blinded you, you could still be some use about the place. What do you think? I could take your eyes. I could take your tongue so you couldn't talk back. How would that do you?'

'Please, no,' Esther said, and her bladder ached for release.

'Or are you going to behave yourself?'

'Yes,' she said, her voice so whispery thin she couldn't hear it herself. 'Yes, I will, I promise.'

'Right, then,' he said. 'I'll let you up, and you'll go straight back to the house. Will you do that?'

'Yes,' she said.

He lifted his boot from her wrist and stepped back, reached a thick hand down to swallow hers. She allowed him to haul her up onto her feet.

'Never try that again,' he said. 'You know what I'll do.'

Esther couldn't meet his gaze. She would break if she did.

'Away you go.'

Her arms at her sides, her head down, she stepped around him and began the walk back to the gate. She took her time, made sure of her footing. Somehow she knew that if she fell now, it would set her mind loose and there would be no getting it back. She concentrated on the sensation of the grass blades beneath her soles, the stones, the bare earth, the mud. These things, the feel of them, kept her mind in place as she walked. She found her shoes on the way, pulled them from sodden ground, and carried them.

When she reached the gate, it stood open, Ivan waiting. He watched her approach, face as expressionless as when she'd passed him on her way out to the yard.

'Look at the state of you,' he said, no anger in his voice. 'Go on and get yourself cleaned up. There's work needs doing.'

Esther did as she was told.

18
Mary

THAT WAS A TERRIBLE LONG night, so it was. Esther lay there all curled up, her hands over her head, while Mummy Noreen lit into her. Me and Mummy Joy stayed quiet, mostly, but I know Mummy Joy was angry too.

Says Mummy Noreen, What were you thinking? You could've got us all killed. Are you mad in the head?

Esther didn't answer. She curled up tighter, so tight I thought she'd turn herself inside out. I wanted to go to her, but I couldn't. Not with the Mummies watching.

Mummy Noreen grabbed her shoulder and shook her. Says she, Do you know what could've happened today? Even if you'd got away, they would've wiped the rest of us out. Did you think about that?

Esther pushed Mummy Noreen's hand away.

Says she, What else am I supposed to do? Just stay here and rot?

You're supposed to survive, says Mummy Noreen. We all are.

Esther sat up, an awful fierce look on her face.

For how long? Do we just wait for one of them to die? Or one of us? I won't spend the rest of my life here. I need to find a way out.

There is no way out, says Mummy Noreen. Do you think we haven't tried? Me and Joy have both been where you are now. We both thought there was a way out. We were both wrong. And so are you.

I don't know why, but I couldn't holt my whisht any longer, so I spake up.

I want to get out, says I. I want to see the real world.

Mummy Joy put her arms around me and pulled me close to her. Says she, Och, darling, I know you do. And some day you will, I promise.

Says I, When?

And Esther said it too. When?

Some day, says Mummy Joy.

Says Esther, What if some day never comes?

Then at least we survive, says Mummy Noreen.

Esther moved forward to the edge of her bed, staring at Mummy Noreen, her eyes all sparkling and hard.

There's a way, says she. I know there is. We just need to think and come up with a plan.

I felt Mummy Joy's arms get tighter around me.

So you come up with a plan, says she. What if it goes wrong? What if someone gets left behind? What about this child? What do you think they'll do to her?

There was a hammering on the door up above, and Daddy Tam shouts down, Put that lamp out and get to bed.

Mummy Joy helped me change into my nightdress and put me to bed, even though I could do it myself. She pulled the blanket up to my chin.

Says she, Don't you worry. We'll keep you safe.

140

She bent down and kissed my cheek, then she went to the lamp and blew it out. I listened to the creaks of the other beds as everyone settled down, then their breathing as they went to sleep. All except Esther. I could hear her on the other side of the room, even though she made no noise at all. I could feel her there, staring into the dark. I know, I used to do that too when I lived in the cellar. It was so black you knew wild things had to be hiding there, watching you. Those things, their eyes can see in the dark. They can see what you're thinking, even if you hide under the blankets. They don't mean you any hurt; they don't care about you. They just watch.

* * *

I woke up in the same dark that I fell asleep in. I don't know how long I'd been away, but I'd been dreaming about walking free of that house. Just walking onto the road outside and away, walking until I reached the big city, and on until I came to the sea. It went on and on forever, the sea, as far as my eyes could reach. The city behind me, the beach under my feet, and the sea stretching away until it reached England and America and France and Africa and all those places that are on the other side of it.

I had that moment when you wake and you think it might have been real, and you wish it was, you wish you could close your eyes and go back to that other place, but you know you can't and it cuts you awful deep. I lay there still for a while, not knowing if my eyes were open or closed. Then I looked up to where I thought the door was, and I could see no light through the cracks, so I knew it was still the night-time.

Dear knows what notion took me, but I pushed the blankets back and I sat up. The floor was terrible cold and damp under my feet and I shivered. I stood and took a step, making a picture in my head of where the beds were. The Mummies were snoring that soft way they did. That helped me find my way. I worked around their beds, feeling the edges of them with my fingertips. When I came around Mummy Noreen's bed, I caught my toe on the leg of it, and I put my hand over my mouth to stop me guldering. I stayed still for as long as it took for the pain to dull. Then I felt my way over to Esther's bed.

I listened for a minute, and I could hear she was awake. I knew by her breathing.

Says she, What is it?

I said nothing. I pulled the blankets back and I got into the bed beside her. She went stiff when I cuddled into her back and pulled the blankets up around us both. I could smell her hair. It still smelled clean. I put my arm around her, and I felt her shoulders bunch up. Then she went loose and I heard her breathe out.

Says she, What do you want?

Says I, You're my sister now.

What?

They're my mummies, says I. You're my sister.

She didn't say anything, but she put her hand on mine and helt it.

Says I, Tell me a good thing about the outside. A thing you did.

One time, says she, my mummy and daddy took me to the theatre. The Grand Opera House in Belfast. We went to a pantomime.

142

Says I, A what?

A pantomime, says she. It's a special kind of play for children. It was *Cinderella*. Do you know that story?

Aye, says I. Mummy Joy telt me it.

It was that story, says she. There were lots of songs, and there was a big fat man dressed as a lady, and they threw sweets to the children. And in the interval, they sold ice cream. Have you ever had ice cream?

No, says I.

I had raspberry ripple. I remember I ate it so quick it made my head hurt. Then we stopped for fish and chips on the way home.

Tell me about the seaside, says I.

Says she, We used to go to Newcastle for our holidays. We'd spend all day on the beach if it was sunny, or we'd go to the amusements if it was raining. I loved going to the amusements. We used to stay in the Slieve Donard Hotel. They have a lovely restaurant there, and dances in the evenings. I got lemonade and sweets while my daddy drank beer. Then he and my mummy would dance. I wish he hadn't done what he did. Everything would be all right if he hadn't done that.

I didn't know what her daddy had done, and it didn't feel right to ask. Instead, says I, I want to go to the seaside some day.

I'll take you, says she. When we get out of here, we can take the bus to Newcastle or Portrush or maybe Portstewart, it has the nicest beach of them all, and we'll go paddling in the sea.

Says I, Do you promise?

I promise, says she. But we have to get out of here.

We will, says I, and I hugged her tighter and she squeezed my hand.

I closed my eyes and imagined a long beach that went on forever and ever. I imagined walking into the water. I imagined Esther was with me and us holding hands like we did in thon bed.

And we fell asleep like that.

* * *

When I woke up, I could see the light through the cracks in the door, still weak, so I knew it was early. The Mummies slept on, but me stirring must have woke Esther up. I heard her breathing change and I felt her body move the tiniest wee bit.

Says I, I know how to do it.

Says she, What?

I know how we get out of here.

She was wide awake now, I could tell. She turned so she faced me.

Says she, How?

Daddy George, says I.

What do you mean?

Daddy George, he's the weakest one of them. He's soft for Mummy Joy and me. Daddy George is the one. He's the way out.

19

Sara

SARA WENT DOWNSTAIRS TO THE kitchen before six, the grinding weight of tiredness behind her eyes. A fog lingered there, clouding her mind. Perhaps she would try to sleep later, even if it was futile. Without thought, she went to the spot in front of the old fireplace, where the Aga now stood. She peered down at the stone floor.

The red stains, returned.

She would not clean them away again. They belonged here more than she did.

As she turned away, a movement caught her eye. Through the open door to the back hall, where the past night's darkness still remained. A vague form, like a child, watching. When she looked back, she saw nothing. Had seen nothing. Like there had been no girl in the river, no reaching scarlet ribbons.

She needed coffee to sweep these figments from her vision. After two strong cupfuls, she forced herself to eat a bowl of dry cereal as she heard Damien moving about upstairs, drawers opening and closing, the shower running. A steaming mug waited for him when he came down, along with two slices of hot toast ready for the softened butter she'd placed in a dish. As he entered the kitchen, she tugged at the cuffs of the cardigan she wore over her pyjamas, keeping the still red, still angry, tracks on her arms hidden from his sight. He did not thank her for the breakfast she'd prepared for him, did not speak until he'd finished eating, when he pulled her phone from his pocket and set it on the worktop.

'Maybe try and stay out of the spark's way today,' he said, not looking at her.

'You mean the electrician?' she asked, retrieving her phone.

'You've no call to be talking to him,' he said. 'Just let him get on with his work.'

'Maybe I could get out of the house for a while,' Sara said, lifting the two cups and the plate, bringing them to the sink. 'If you left me the car, I could—'

'I need the car,' Damien said. He gathered his jacket and laptop case. 'Look, just stay out of his way. There's nothing you need to talk to him about.'

'I'll go for a walk,' she said as he passed her on the way to the hall. 'Actually, I thought I could go to the care home, see how that woman's doing.'

He stopped in the doorway and turned to look at her, his eyes narrow and searching.

'You what?'

'I keep thinking about her. I don't think she has anybody. Maybe it'd be good for her to have a visitor. It's a couple of miles walk, I think, but I could do with the exercise.'

He became still and quiet for a moment, staring at a distant point, his mind working. Then he came back to himself, nodded, a decision made.

'No,' he said. 'I need you here while the work's going on.'

'You said I've to leave the electrician alone. But you want me here. Which is it?'

She held his stare, would not drop her gaze, even as a deeper part of her mind said, danger, beware. Don't push him. But she needed to talk to the woman. Needed to. She let her arms stretch, let the cardigan's sleeves creep up past her wrists, letting the red, angry tracks on one forearm into the light.

'Just do what I've asked you,' he said, his voice sharp and flat like a blade. 'Please.'

Sara swallowed and said, 'I think I'll do what I want.'

Damien stepped out of the doorway, came close to her. As he opened his mouth to speak, there came a knock on the door.

'That'll be Tony,' Sara said.

Damien glared at her for a moment, reached for each of her right sleeve, pulled it back down to her wrist, then went back to the doorway and the hall beyond. He opened the front door, revealing Tony on the step, his toolbox in one hand, a backpack in the other.

'Morning,' Tony said. 'Here, the supplier didn't have those switch plates in yet. He told me he'll have them by lunchtime. I'll go and get them then, all right?'

Damien didn't answer. He brushed past Tony and went to his car. Tony entered the house and closed the front door behind him. He leaned into the kitchen.

'Everything all right?' he asked.

Sara forced a smile, snugged her hands into the cardigan's pockets. 'Yes. Can I get you anything?'

'Maybe later,' he said, setting his toolbox on the floor. 'I need to get on, but I brought you these.'

He carried the backpack over to the island and placed it on the worktop. Sara watched as he unzipped it and pulled out a bundle of yellowed newspapers.

'There wasn't much,' he said. 'A few *Belfast Telegraph*s, a couple of *News Letter*s, and an *Ulster Gazette*.'

She stood confused for a moment before she remembered he'd promised to look in his mother's attic for old newspapers with stories about the house. A sickly chill appeared in her stomach as she realised she wasn't sure how much she really wanted to know.

Tony spread them out in front of her, eight newspapers in all.

'That's them in order of date,' he said.

She read the headlines. Black letters screamed over yellow.

Police Seek Identity of Mystery Child.

Massacre on Family Farm.

Five Dead in Farmhouse Shooting.

Son Suspected of Killing Family, Then Self.

'My God,' Sara whispered, placing a hand on her stomach.

'Maybe you shouldn't read them,' Tony said. 'I can take them away.'

'No,' Sara said. 'I should read them. I should know.'

As Tony left to go about his work, she opened the first newspaper, feeling it dry and decayed against her skin, the words spidering across the pages, spelling out the horror.

She sat on the stool and read.

* * *

Sara spent more than two hours reading through the articles, following the events as best she could. Not only what had happened in this house, but outside, in the streets and towns of this place. A history of which she was only vaguely aware. The turn of the decade, the fifties turning to the sixties, and like the

148

rest of the United Kingdom, Northern Ireland was recovering from the ruination of the Second World War. Austerity was the norm, except for the most wealthy, and even the rich found some luxuries hard to come by. The IRA were active along the border, moving from the Republic into the North, targeting police and military outposts. Headlines spoke of attacks and assassinations, and men interned without trial by both governments.

In the midst of it all, little Mary Jackson, believed to be at most twelve years old, though no one could be entirely sure. A girl who didn't exist until she wandered into a grocer's shop one early morning, dripping in blood.

Sara worked her way through the pieces, stitching together a picture of what had happened. At first, they knew nothing about this child, where she had come from, what she had endured. As Buchanan the grocer had told Sara, it was a few days before the girl spoke, and even then, she gave the doctors and the police nothing coherent. A week passed before she spoke a name, and then an explosion of headlines, each more frantic than the last.

The first piece focused on the child, as if she were some bloodied angel who had appeared from nowhere. Then the bodies were found, and the glee between the lines of the stories was almost tangible.

The men were identified straightaway: Ivan Jackson, sixty-two, and his sons, Thomas, forty-one, and George, thirty-nine. The identity of the two dead women remained a mystery for several more days. Ivan Jackson had been widowed years ago, left to rear his sons on his own. Word around the village was that there'd been a daughter, but no one could say for sure. Neither of the younger Jacksons had ever married, not even courted any of the local girls, as far as anyone knew. The police continued to work with Mary, trying to build a picture of what went on at the farmhouse. Eventually, she gave them two names: Joy and Noreen. Finally, the women were identified.

Joy Turkington, missing for almost thirteen years, since she was fourteen. She had left her parents' Armagh home one evening after a heated argument. Her parents had wanted her to remain in school, but she wanted to leave and get a job. She was last seen talking with a man in a pub in the town centre. She was buried in the graveyard at St Mark's Parish Church. The article had a photograph of her parents in the funeral procession, walking behind her coffin as if to their own graves.

Noreen Weaver, born in the Lisburn Road Workhouse in Belfast. A known thief and a prostitute, already a record of arrests and convictions for minor offences before she disappeared at the age of fifteen. Not being from respectable stock, no one much cared about her absence from the street corners she had frequented. Fifteen years she'd been missing before an aunt identified her corpse in the mortuary at the Royal Victoria Hospital. The aunt refused to take the body, and Noreen was given a pauper's funeral.

A public inquiry was called by the Stormont government. Many people testified, but Mary Jackson did not, as a doctor had deemed her unfit. Instead, the inquiry relied on transcripts of interviews between her and the investigating police officers, along with statements from the medical professionals who had cared for her.

Sara continued to read, the story clarifying.

As far as the police could ascertain, the two women and the child had been living in the dug-out cellar of the farmhouse.

The women had been in reasonable health, given the circumstances. Mary was small for her age, indicating a lack of good-quality nutrition. There were medicines in the home, intended for the farm's livestock, but probably used for the women. Their dental health was poor; they had been given toothbrushes and toothpaste, but a lack of proper care meant cavities and decay had gone untreated.

Investigators speculated that the women and the girl had been used as house slaves, cleaning, tidying and cooking for the men. Post-mortem examinations indicated that both adult women had given birth to at least one child, possibly more, and it was assumed they had also been used for sexual gratification. Whether they were shared among the men or each took a wife, of sorts, was unclear.

Sara looked to the door across the kitchen, the one that led to the basement. She remembered the feeling of walking on graves and could not suppress a shiver. It took some effort to read on.

Mary Jackson had stated that she had always lived in the basement and had no memory of anywhere else. It was logical, therefore, to assume that she was the daughter of one of the captive women, sired by one of the men. There had been other children, but evidently none had survived. One of the inquiry judges asked if Mary had been violated similarly to the adult women; the doctor on the stand stated that he did not know and had felt a physical examination to determine such would be unnecessarily cruel and invasive without being conclusive.

Sara turned to a photograph of the girl and recalled the grocer's words: like a doll. And she was. Small next to the nurse she was pictured with, her face dark with fear and mistrust. Sara wondered, what did she see? What did she know that could never ever be said aloud?

Mary had appeared at the grocer's door at around 6:30 a.m. on the morning of the 17th May. As far as the inquiry could determine, at some point on the evening of the 16th May, an altercation had broken out in the kitchen. Joy Turkington had been severely beaten, her nose, left orbital socket, and jaw all broken, along with two ribs. Her left lung had collapsed, and she would eventually have died without medical treatment. Before that could happen, she was shot once, the bullet passing through her skull. The weapon was a Lee-Enfield rifle, presumed to belong to Thomas Jackson; he had served in World War Two and had most likely brought the weapon home as a souvenir.

The exact sequence of events was never ascertained, only that Thomas Jackson had been shot a total of four times, and Ivan Jackson had been bludgeoned to death with the butt of the rifle, its magazine having been emptied of its five-round capacity.

Noreen Weaver died from a single bullet that entered her back and exited through her chest. The coroner believed that she had been fleeing the kitchen when her murderer, believed to be George Jackson, fired on her with a Webley revolver, killing her almost instantly. George Jackson then went upstairs, where he sat on his bed, pressed the Webley's muzzle to his forehead, and pulled the trigger.

Sara pictured the bed she shared with her husband, upstairs. She pictured the depression of a man's weight on the mattress. The lurch as his body fell.

'Stop it,' she said aloud, and resumed reading.

From beginning to end, the coroner estimated the entire episode lasted no more than a few minutes. Five lives ended in hardly any time at all. Amidst the horror, one detail struck Sara as odd: the Webley revolver had been identified as being issued to an officer of the Royal Ulster Constabulary, Sergeant Ronald Jennings, aged thirty-one. He had gone missing some weeks before and was presumed to have been the victim of an abduction by the IRA. The *Ulster Gazette* seemed to be local to the small city of Armagh, where Sergeant Jennings had lived, and the last article she read outlined how the hopes raised of finding the policeman had been dashed when searches at the farm revealed no trace of him or the car he'd been driving the evening of his disappearance. No explanation was ever offered for how the weapon came into the possession of George Jackson. As far as Sara could tell, the official line remained that Jennings had been taken by the IRA.

And what about little Mary Jackson? According to the police officers who interviewed her, as soon as the gunfire started, she fled the house and hid in the cowshed at the rear of the yard. She did not emerge until morning when she walked into the nearby village.

Walking at dawn, alone on these country roads. Sara imagined the child, terrified in the early light. And as an ageing woman, making the same walk in reverse, coming back here, more than sixty years later. Still terrified. Still alone.

Terrified. Alone.

Sara knew that feeling. And more, she was terrified of being alone. Perhaps she had always known that about herself but could never admit it.

She closed the newspaper and sat still for a time, aware of the cool around her, the spaces between the walls, the empty basement below. She was glad of the occasional noise from Tony's work, the clatter and rattle of tools picked up and put down.

If she turned her head and leaned to the side, she would be able to see the red stains on the floor. But she would not look. She had seen too much, and now she wanted to be gone from here.

She found Tony upstairs in her bedroom, kneeling at a mains socket, the plate suspended from the wall by coloured wires. He looked up at her, eyes questioning. She became aware of the bed between them, the strange indecency of it. He dropped the wire cutters he'd been using and got to his feet.

'You okay?' he asked.

'Can you take me somewhere?' she asked.

20

Esther

IN THE MORNING, ESTHER WASHED and dressed, putting on a pair of old boots she'd found in the bottom of the doorless wardrobe. They were too big, her feet slipping around in them, and the leather was hard and cracked. But they would have to do. When she went upstairs with the others, she found Ivan sitting at the table in the kitchen.

'I'm sorry about yesterday,' she said. 'I won't do it again.'

Ivan didn't look at her. 'Make sure you don't. Get some tea on the brew, we're dying of thirst here.'

Mary fetched the kettle for her, showed her how to pump water at the sink. Esther had never seen a pump like this, let alone used one. Water in her world came from taps. She filled the kettle and brought it to the wood stove.

'We need to clean it out first,' Mary said. 'Then we need to light it.'

Esther lifted the brush and shovel, got to her knees, opened the stove door and set about cleaning out the ashes. That done, she and Mary went out through the back door to fetch wood from the tarpaulin-covered pile. Thomas was there, waiting, no work to hand. He watched as she and Mary gathered wood in their arms.

As they went to return to the kitchen, Thomas said, 'Here.' They both stopped and turned back to him.

He spoke to Mary. 'Away you go.'

Mary hesitated, looked to Esther, then left them alone together in the yard.

They both stood there for a time, Esther's gaze fixed on the concrete-covered ground, Thomas's wandering over her body, from her feet to the top of her head. She suppressed a shiver of revulsion.

Esther cleared her throat and said, 'I'm sorry about what happened yesterday.'

He didn't acknowledge her apology. Instead, he said, 'See this evening? When the tea things are redd up, get some water heated and give yourself a bath.'

Now Esther lifted her gaze from the ground and looked at him. 'Why?'

'Just do what I tell you,' he said, before walking back into the house.

Now she found herself alone in the yard, her arms filled with wood. She looked around. The same outbuildings as yesterday, the same cowshed and stable blocks. The same gate, the same lane and fields beyond it. The same chickens wandering, seeking out morsels in need of pecking.

All the same except she knew that this morning, neither Thomas nor Ivan were working in those fields. No one to stop her, no one to block her way, no one to knock her to the ground and hold a blade to her throat.

But she thought of the others, of wee Mary, and what might befall them if she went. What might befall her if she was caught.

Esther took the wood and went inside, kicking the back door closed behind her.

* * *

They ate scraps for lunch, sitting in the kitchen, soaked in the light from the back window. Crusts of bread, the scrapings from a pot of porridge, a small portion of cheese between them. Like dogs, Esther thought, eating the leavings of the table. George and Tam – they all called him Tam – were out in the fields. Ivan wandered the yard, tossing feed to the chickens.

'Where do we have baths?' Esther asked.

The others stopped eating and looked at her. All except Mary.

'That thing,' Noreen said, pointing to the tin tub in the back hall. 'You don't get a bath unless they tell you to, though.'

Esther could feel the grime coating her body, under her arms, in the small of her back. And the grease in her hair. She imagined soaking in hot water, breathing in the steam, soap slick between her fingers. The decadence of it.

'Tam told me to have one this evening,' she said. 'After tea.'

Noreen and Joy looked at each other, then down at the table, and the last few crumbs of food. Mary chewed on a piece of crust.

'What?' Esther said.

No one answered. Noreen picked at the material that bound her injured fingers together.

'Tell me,' Esther said, even though she knew the answer. Had known since she first saw these women in the dim cellar. A cold weight settled in her gut as she remembered what they'd told her before. Pleasing them, they called it. But she had ignored it, turned her higher mind away, as if that would make it untrue.

Noreen closed her eyes, leaned her head to one side, as if she heard music from some far-off place. A crease appeared in her brow, and Esther knew something pained her. Noreen opened her eyes and spoke.

'It's always the same. Have a bath so you're clean. Then you go upstairs and do what needs doing.'

'Have they done it to you?' Esther asked.

'What do you think?' Noreen asked. She looked away, softened her tone. 'Aye, but only one. Only Ivan.'

Esther turned to Joy.

'George,' Joy said. 'I'm his. You belong to Tam.'

'What about Mary?' Esther asked.

Mary didn't raise her head, even as Joy put an arm around her.

'Not yet,' Joy said.

'But it's only a matter of time,' Esther said, 'isn't it?'

Joy gave her a look so full of hate that she could not hold her gaze.

'We have to do something,' Esther said.

'Don't start,' Noreen said. 'Not again.'

'I won't let him touch me.'

'Then he'll hurt you,' Joy said.

'Let him try.'

'Oh, God and Jesus,' Noreen said, burying her face in her hands, and Esther wondered for a moment if it was truly a prayer, or merely blasphemy. 'You're going to get us all killed.'

Reaching for a strand of hope, Esther spoke to Mary. 'What about the plan?'

'What plan?' Noreen asked. 'What are you talking about?'

'Mary has a plan.' A smile flashed on her lips, wiped away with her hand, the same hand trapping a giggle that tasted of madness. 'Mary, tell them,' she said from behind her palm.

Mary remained silent, pushing crumbs around the table with her fingertips.

'Leave her alone,' Joy said, craning her neck to see out of the back window, to the yard, checking if Ivan was still out there, not listening from the hall. 'Don't get her mixed up in anything.'

'Tell them, Mary,' Esther said. 'Tell them your plan. Tell them about George.'

'George?' Noreen echoed. 'That's enough, now. Shut up before any of them hears.'

Esther got to her feet and leaned across the table, took Mary's hands in hers. 'Please, Mary, tell them. Tell them what you told me. How George is the weakest of them. How he's soft for you and Joy.'

Joy grabbed Esther's wrist with one hand, pulled at her fingers with the other, trying to free Mary from her grasp. But Esther held on.

'Tell them. For Christ's sake, tell them.'

Mary looked up at her, shook her head.

'What's all this, now?'

Esther released Mary's hands at the sound of Ivan's voice in the hall doorway and stepped back from the table. Noreen and Joy stood too, their chairs scraping against the stone floor. Last of all, Mary got to her feet. None of them looked at him.

'Well?' Ivan stepped into the room. 'What's going on?'

'Nothing,' Noreen said, keeping her gaze downward. 'We just had a wee disagreement, that's all.'

Ivan clucked his disapproval. 'We'll have none of that auld nonsense. Not in this house. Come on, now, get all this mess cleaned up and get on.'

They got to work.

* * *

When the men had eaten their tea, beef and potatoes again, and the women had cleaned up, Noreen lifted the bowl of scraps to take downstairs. Esther went to follow her through the door to the stairs beyond, but Tam called her back.

'You can eat something later,' he said, still sat at the table. 'You're having a bath, remember. The child'll help you get it ready.'

The other men left the kitchen, saying nothing. Only Esther, Mary and Tam remained.

He pointed to the tin bath in the back hall and said, 'Go on.'

'I don't want to,' Esther said.

'What's that got to do with it?' Tam asked. 'You'll do as you're told.'

It was Mary who went and got the bath while Esther stood in the centre of the kitchen, her arms folded around her middle, sobbing. Mary dragged it back into the room, the tin scraping on the stone. Tam winced at the noise.

Mary fetched the big pot from beside the stove, brought it to the sink, and worked the pump to fill it with water. She tried to lift it out of the sink again, but it was too heavy.

'Don't make the child do all the work,' Tam said. He got up from the table and bolted closed the door to the cellar, slid the padlock through the loop, but did not fasten it.

Esther helped her hoist it up and back over to the stove and onto one of the two hotplates. Mary lifted a smaller pot and brought it back to the sink, filled it, and carried it to the stove's second hotplate herself. Esther remained by the window as the water heated, watching magpies pick through the gravel on the driveway. It was still light outside and she could see their white flashes clearly as they squabbled. And she could see the open gate at the end of the driveway, the narrow lane beyond. Only the glass between her and it.

An idea came to her then, bright and shining in her mind. Break the glass. With her fist, maybe, then let a jagged edge tear open the veins in her wrist. Bleed to death right here in this kitchen. Or perhaps take a piece and open her throat before Tam could stop her.

Mary touched her hand, pointed to the steaming pots of water.

They took the largest one and emptied it into the bath tub, followed by the second. Then they repeated the action, filling first one pot, then the other, placing them on the stove.

Esther returned to the window. The magpies had gone. The sun hung low over the trees. She thought of Reverend Clarke, his lingering in her bedroom as she changed, behind the door as she bathed. She wondered why men were so wicked. She wondered if her father had been like that too, had he been cruel and she hadn't known? Perhaps if he hadn't died, then he would have shown that side of himself, eventually.

Her brain registered the movement at the gate before she was conscious of seeing anything. A car turning in.

Esther's skin tingled, every cell of her being suddenly crackling and alive. She held her breath. The car's engine rumbled, its tyres crunching gravel as it approached.

'No,' Tam said.

She heard his chair fall to the floor as he stood. She heard the padlock rattle and the bolt slide. The car's handbrake creaked as it came to a standstill, side on to the front of the house. A man inside, barely visible.

'Come on,' Tam said, a hoarse whisper. 'Get down them stairs. Quick.'

The driver's door opened, on the other side of the car, and a man stood upright. He wore a dark green uniform, a tie, silvery buttons.

A policeman. My God, Esther thought, a policeman. She almost wept when he looked right at her through the glass.

Behind her, Tam barked, 'Come on!'

'It's too late,' Esther said, her voice trembling with a giggle. 'He's seen me.'

21
Mary

I T WAS THE SAME POLICEMAN I'd seen before. I knew his face. So handsome. I saw him take a step closer to the window. He looked at Esther, all confused, like he saw a ghost standing there. Esther started to shake. I think she might have been tittering, I'm not sure.

Says Daddy Tam, No, no, no, no, no.

Over and over and over again like if he said it enough times he could magic that policeman away. He grabbed my arm and tried to pull me over to the door, but I did a thing I'd never done before: I stood my ground.

Says I, He'll see you.

Daddy Tam let go of my arm then and just stood there, breathing hard. I never seen him afeart before, but there he was, near in a panic. The policeman came right up to the window, put his nose to the glass, with his hands around his eyes so he could see better. He looked at us a wee moment then he waved and pointed to the front door.

Daddy Tam didn't move, just stood there, panting like a dog. Only I knew he would've hit me a clip, I would've tittered just like Esther.

Daddy Ivan appeared in the kitchen door and says, Oh, Jesus. He looked at Tam, then back at the window. Says he, Pull yourself together, boy, or we're ruined. I'll go to him.

While Daddy Tam bolted and locked the door to the cellar, Daddy Ivan went out to the hall and I heard him unlock the front door. Then I heard voices, low so I couldn't make out the words. I walked closer to Esther so I could see through the door, see what was happening. Daddy Tam tried to grab at my sleeve, but I slapped his hand away. I never would've dared do that before, never ever, but now I did, because here was the policeman and he was going to take us all away from here, me and Esther and Mummy Joy and Mummy Noreen, he was going to take us out of here to a good place where no one would hurt us.

Daddy Ivan let the policeman into the hall, then he followed him into the kitchen. The policeman didn't have his hat on him, and his shirt collar was unbuttoned, and his tie was loose. There was a smell off him that I'd smelled before, a sweet smell on his breath, like Daddy Tam's when he was drunk and thran, and his eyes were red and watery.

Says he, Tam, how are ye? Then he looks at us, the steaming bathtub. Who's this then?

Daddy Ivan was behind him. Says he, These are my sister's grandchildren. They're just here to visit for a lock o' days.

Daddy Tam came between me and Esther and took us each by the hand.

Says he, Just here for a lock o' days to help out about the place.

Says the policeman, Oh, aye? Nice to meet you, girls. Here, I was supposed to pick up some beef from the butcher's for the missus, but I sort of didn't get around to it. Would yous have a wee joint you could spare? I'll pay for it, like. Not even a good cut, just something she can stick in the pot for the Sunday dinner.

I felt Daddy Tam's fingers squeezing mine awful hard, and I knew he was doing the same to Esther. I thought she was going to say nothing. Nobody said anything. We all stood there not making a sound, the policeman looking from one to the other.

No worries if you can't, like, says he.

Help us, Esther says.

Behind the policeman, Daddy Ivan looked at the floor, his shoulders dropped, and he shook his head. I saw Daddy George, then, in the hall, coming up behind them.

Says the policeman, What, love?

I looked at the policeman's belt, the gun he had in a pocket there. I didn't know it was called a holster or a pistol, but I knew what it was.

Help us, Esther says. They're keeping us prisoners here. Us and two others. They're locked in the cellar.

The policeman stared at her a wee moment, this look on his face like he didn't know if she was codding or not. His eyes were darting about all over the place, from one of us to the other, like he was waiting for someone to explain what was going on.

It was Daddy Ivan who spake up next.

She's playing a joke, says he, patting the policeman's shoulder. She's a bold girl. That's why the two of them was sent here. Their granny thought some farm work would put some manners into them.

It's not a joke, says Esther. Help us.

There was a quake in her voice now. I could see the tears ready to fall from her eyes. She looked down at me, and I swear, my voice was gone. I wanted to speak. I wanted awful badly to ask that policeman to take me away from that house, to take me anywhere but there. But I could only open my mouth.

Says Daddy Ivan, She's having you on. My sister sent them down to me from Ballymena, says they're getting their heads turned living in the town, staying out, talking back, tailing around after the boys, getting up to all sorts. Aye, they don't like it here, but that's only 'cause they're not used to hard work. Sure, you know yourself. You know the sort of them.

The policeman stood there like a mouse caught in a trap. He didn't know what to do, I could tell. He spake to me then.

What do you say, love?

I opened my mouth again, but nothing came out.

Tell him, says Esther. Mary, tell him. This is our chance.

My voice came back, small like a mouse in my throat, but it was there.

I want to go with you, says I to the policeman.

He looked to Esther. You say there's others?

Esther nodded over to the door with the bolt and the closed padlock. Down there, says she.

She's making a cod of you, says Daddy Ivan, laughing like nothing was wrong. Ah, dear-oh, wait till the rest of the boys in Lurgan station hear about this.

Says Esther, Go and look. You'll see.

The policeman looked around at the men once more, and this time he noticed George at his back. He walked further into the kitchen, over to the door to the cellar. Ivan and George followed him. He leaned close to the door and he called, Hello?

Not loud. Weak, like a man who isn't sure of anything.

But there was no mistaking about what happened next. There was thunder on the stairs on the other side of the door, then banging and thumping, and the door shook on its hinges, the bolt rattling.

Who's there? Help! Help us!

It was both of them, Mummy Joy and Mummy Noreen, shouting. There was a moment, hardly even a second, hardly any time at all, where I had this feeling in my chest. A light feeling, like everything was going to be all right. Like we were saved.

And then the policeman turned to look at Daddy Ivan and Daddy George, and he looked more afeart than I've ever seen any man look in my life. He reached for that gun at his hip, but he wasn't quick enough. Daddy Ivan grabbed his wrist. The policeman went for it with his other hand, but Daddy Ivan grabbed that wrist too. He pushed him back agin the door, pinned his hands agin the wood.

Get the pistol, says Daddy Ivan.

Daddy George reached through Daddy Ivan's arms and pulled the gun away from the holster.

Shoot him, says Daddy Ivan.

Says Daddy George, What?

I said, shoot him, for God's sake.

The policeman was fighting now, trying to push away from the door, but Daddy Ivan was too strong. He turned his hips when the policeman tried to kick him between his legs; he ducked to the side when the policeman tried to slam his forehead agin his nose.

I can't, says Daddy George. I can't.

I felt Daddy Tam's hand loosen on my wrist.

Here, I'll do it, says he.

And he let go of Esther's wrist, and mine, and he went to the others and he grabbed the gun from George's hand.

Then Esther near pulled me off my feet.

She dragged me out to the hall, to the front door, and I saw it was open a crack and then I knew what was happening. She threw the door open and pulled me through, and I mind the sun hanging over the trees, just touching the tops of them, lighting the leaves up bright green. Birds scattering out of the branches. And the gate at the end of the drive.

We ran around the car, me trailing behind, and along the drive.

The others, says I, the Mummies.

We can't help them, says Esther. Run. Just run.

And we did, my hand in hers, our feet grinding on the gravel.

There was an awful bang from behind, and something cut through the air between us. I felt it pass even if I couldn't see it. Then another bang, and this time something passed above us, and I heard Daddy Tam curse.

We were almost at the gate, and the lane beyond it. And I was tittering and laughing like it was the best game I'd ever played.

A third bang, and it went wide, the branches of the trees ahead of us turning into splinters. Daddy Tam cursed again and shouted something about his rifle. And now we were through the gate, and says Esther, This way, this is the way we came.

We were on the lane and we were running, Esther in front, pulling me behind and I was laughing and laughing and now Esther was laughing too, and I thought we would really do it. I thought we could really get away.

22

Sara

GREENWAY CARE AND CONVALESCENCE HOME stood at the centre of Morgan Demesne, an expanse of gardens and woodland on the far side of Morganstown. It had once been a grand house, built by the Morgan family who had established the village around its linen mill. The mansion's two wings had been converted into a mix of small assisted-living apartments and single bedrooms. A gentle exercise class was being held on the lawn in front of the house; some of the residents paused and watched as Tony's van passed along the driveway, and he parked in one of the bays in the shadow of the building, facing the expanse of lush green lawn.

'You sure you don't want me to come in with you?' Tony asked as he shut off the engine.

'I'm sure,' Sara said.

'You sure you should be going in there at all?' he asked, his voice dropping. 'Is there anything she can tell you that'd make you feel better?'

'I don't know. But I want to see her.'

Sara undid her seat belt and opened the passenger door.

'You don't need to wait,' she said. 'It's not that far to walk home. I can do it in forty, fifty minutes.'

'I don't mind,' he said. 'I'd enjoy the . . .'

His words faltered, and his skin bloomed red. His hand, raised mid-gesture, fell to the steering wheel. He looked straight ahead, across the grounds to the trees beyond.

'I don't mind,' Tony said again.

'I know,' Sara said. 'But you have to go and fetch those switch plates from the supplier, right?'

He exhaled, smiled, as if released from a trap. 'Yeah, I do. And then I've to get back to the house and get them fitted. So long as you're sure.'

Sara climbed down from the passenger seat, her shoes crunching on fine gravel. 'I'm sure. And Damien doesn't need to know I came here. He doesn't need to know you brought me. Even if he comes home early, for all you know, I went for a walk.'

He turned his gaze to her for a moment, then away, his fingers flexing on the wheel. 'Aye,' he said. 'A walk would do you good.'

'Thank you,' she said, and closed the passenger door.

Sara walked to the steps leading to the open front doors of the house and turned to watch as Tony put the van in gear. As he turned in the small car park, he glanced at her once, and once again, each look seeming like a small theft through the glass. She wondered about him, the scars on his hands, the length of his fingers. The space between his jaw and his ear, the stubble on his throat. She wondered if it would be warm against her lips.

'Stop it,' she whispered.

She hesitated at the doors, questioning why she had come here. Why did she want to see Mary, this woman she didn't know at all, had only met for a few frightening moments the day before? Something had happened in the hallway of the house as Mary screamed and Sara cowered against the wall. A change, a shift, not so much an awakening as a return. Yes, that was it. Sara had the sense of returning to herself having been absent all those months. And it was Mary who had summoned her back. And she needed to know why.

Sara stepped through the doors. Inside, the entrance hall had been turned into a reception area. The desk hosted stacks of brochures, a guestbook and a large bowl of fresh fruit with a sign inviting passers-by to help themselves. It reminded Sara of a hotel she had once stayed in, a place in the Scottish Highlands, where snow still dusted the ground in April and cold draughts haunted the corridors.

A woman got up from her seat behind the desk and leaned over, smiling. 'Can I help you?' she chirped.

Sara approached the desk, feeling a pulse of uncertainty. What if they turned her away? Why would they let her in? What business did she have bothering one of their residents?

'I was hoping to see Mary Jackson?'

She hadn't intended it to be a question, but it was birthed from her mouth as such nonetheless. The receptionist's face switched from open to closed, her eyes studying harder. Sara searched her memory for the name of the woman she had spoken to the morning before when she had phoned this place.

'Are you a relative?' the receptionist asked.

Sara looked at the name tag on her breast. It said: MARGARET SPENCE. She remembered.

'Margaret,' she said. 'I spoke with you on the phone yesterday morning. My name's Sara Keane. Mary came to my house and my husband brought her back here.'

Margaret's face went slack, then brightened, then darkened, all within the space of a second. Finally, she gave a smile that ached with effort, her hands spreading on the desk as if thrown down in supplication.

'Oh, yes, of course. I must apologise again for the upset.'

'It's fine, honestly,' Sara said. 'But I'd like to see Mary, if that's all right? I just want to see if she's okay, see if she needs anything.'

Margaret stared for a moment before her smile brightened again, and she called to another staff member to take over the desk. She came around to Sara and signalled her to follow. They climbed the grand flight of stairs up to the first floor before taking a left along a series of corridors.

'The nurse dressed the cut on Mary's foot, and the doctor came out to see her yesterday afternoon. He said she's fine, just a bit worn out from the walking. She's been resting since then. We brought her meals to her room, just so she could recover in peace.'

Most of the passing doors stood open, each room much the same as the next, plain functional furnishing, few personal touches. Odours laced together, triggering memories in Sara's mind. Schoolrooms, dentists' chairs, libraries, hospitals. She remembered her grandmother's withering years, one stroke after another until there was nothing left of her.

Margaret came to a halt before the second door from the end. Sara couldn't see inside from here. The receptionist fidgeted on the spot for a few agonising seconds before she spoke.

'Like I said yesterday, we take the utmost care over the security of our residents. We're still trying to figure out how Mary managed to find her way out of the grounds, and I can promise you, this will never—'

'I just want to see her,' Sara said.

Margaret squeezed her two fists together to form a ball at her stomach. She hummed with worry.

'I don't want to pry,' Margaret said, 'but have you spoken to anyone else about what happened? I mean, I must be clear, if you want to talk to someone at the health trust about this incident, we won't stand in your way, absolutely not, but if there was any way we could—'

'I haven't spoken to anyone,' Sara said. 'I don't plan to. I'd really just like to see Mary. Is that all right?'

Margaret's hands unclenched as she exhaled through thinned lips.

'Yes,' she said. 'Yes, of course. But I do need to check it's okay with Mary. Just wait here a wee second.'

Alone in the corridor, Sara felt a wave of uncertainty, strong enough to make her hand rest against the wood-panelled wall to steady her. An urge to turn, flee from the home, and back to the house that wasn't hers. She resisted it.

'Come on,' Margaret said, her head appearing from the doorway, as if suspended there, unattached to her body.

Sara approached the open door, saw the room beyond, bright with sunlight. Mary sat in a chair in the corner, her feet resting on a padded stool. One wrapped in a bandage, gauze wadded on her sole.

'Mary, this is Mrs Keane,' Margaret said, moving aside.

As Sara stepped inside, Mary looked away from the window and examined her. Her eyes narrowed as she leaned forward in the chair.

'I know you,' she said.

Sara went to the chair at the far corner of the room. 'Do you mind if I sit?'

Mary shook her head, still staring. Sara brought the chair close and sat down.

'Let me know if you need anything,' Margaret said before disappearing.

She left the door open. The sound of birds and wind in trees bustled in through the sash window. Net curtains billowed in the breeze that whispered against Sara's ankles and wrists, cool and gentle.

'I know you,' Mary said again, her eyes hard like flint.

'You came to my house yesterday,' Sara said.

'No,' Mary said. 'No.'

'Yes, it was early in the morning.'

Mary's eyes widened and her hand came to her mouth. She let out a high, breathy laugh.

'Esther?' she said.

Sara felt an uncertain smile on her lips. 'No. My name's Sara. Sara Keane.'

Mary's smile faded. 'You said you'd take me to the seaside. You promised. You telt me, when we got out, you'd take me to the beach. I've still never been to the sea. You said you'd take me.'

Sara shifted forward in her seat, leaned in closer. 'Mary, I'm not Esther. My name's Sara. I live in the house you used to own.'

Mary's hand dropped from her mouth into her lap. She stared hard at Sara, letting her gaze travel from her face down to her stomach, then she reached out, placed her hand on Sara's belly. It rested there for a moment, a small hand like a child's, then Mary looked back up into her eyes.

'No,' Mary said, withdrawing her hand. 'It's not you.'

'Who's Esther?' Sara asked.

'My sister,' Mary said, her eyes growing distant, staring at some long-ago memory.

'I didn't know you had a sister.'

'Aye, I did.' Mary nodded once, her eyes glistening. 'I had a sister.'

'Where is she now?'

Mary turned her gaze back to the window. 'She's lost. I tried to reach her but I couldn't. That's why I should be at home, not here. So she can find her way back to me. But they say I can't go back home.'

'Because of the fire,' Sara said.

'Aye. They say I started it. They say I can't take care of my own self. But I lived there by my own self for sixty years, and I did all right. And I'll tell you this, I didn't start that fire. Some bad hoor did it in the middle of the night.'

'You think someone else started it?'

Mary leaned forward, the forefinger of her small hand jabbing each word home. 'I don't think it. I know it. It was the glass breaking that woke me. I mind lying there, listening. I thought one of the cats had maybe cowped something over and broke it. Then there was this thump, I felt it more than I heard it, and then there was a car engine started up and I heard it drive away. Then the cats screaming.'

Mary's quivering hand went to her mouth, her eyes brimming.

'I opened my bedroom door and the heat knocked me off my feet. I mind looking up at the ceiling, and it was black, like there was a sea up there made out of night. One of the cats, I don't know which one it was, it came running in and it was on fire and I could do nothing for it. I couldn't get down the stairs, so I crawled to the window and I opened it. I mind falling, but that's all. They tell me I was lucky I wasn't killed. The police wouldn't listen to me. Nobody would. But I telt them, and I'll tell you, I didn't start that fire.'

Sara thought of what Mr Buchanan, the grocer, had said about her father-in-law.

'Did someone want to buy your house?' she asked.

'Aye,' Mary said. 'There was a man came round the house one day, hoking about the place. I telt him to get away wi'that, I wasn't for selling no matter how much he wanted to give me for it.'

'How much did he offer?'

'Och, I don't know. Maybe a hundred pounds.'

Sara couldn't help but smile. 'I think it might have been more than that.'

'Well, whatever it was, I'd no use for it, so I telt him to get away on back to wherever he'd come from and not to come near my house again.'

'How did he take that?'

'He was annoyed, I think. But men are like that. They think everything's theirs and nothing's ours except what they give us. This man was the same. I don't say bad words, but I near said some to him.'

Mary tilted her head and examined Sara. Sara knew then that she was present, here with her now. She might not have been when Sara first entered the room, but at this moment, Mary was here, fierce and alive. She glanced at the rings on Sara's finger.

'You're married,' she said.

'Yes. It was my husband who brought you back here yesterday morning.'

'Oh, aye.' Mary nodded, remembering. 'He was awful cross at me, so he was.'

'I'm sorry.'

'Don't say sorry for him. You didn't do anything. Anyway, I'm the one who should be sorry. And I am. Barging in on you like that. Sometimes I'm not at myself.'

'It's all right. Are you—'

'Is he good to you?' Mary asked, cutting off Sara's question.

Sara searched for an answer. She felt this woman would know a lie when it was uttered.

'He's not,' Mary said, answering for her.

'We have good days and bad days,' Sara said, a small and resentful anger building in her. 'Like all couples do.'

She felt Mary's gaze on her, piercing her skin, drilling into the heart of her. Like Amanda's had done all those months ago, in that other place, that other life.

'Really,' Sara said, her tongue driven by the need to defend herself. To defend Damien, to lie for him. 'We're happy. We had a rough spell earlier this year, that's why we moved here, but we're over all that now. Honestly.'

It was her job, Damien had said, too much pressure. No wonder she'd taken those pills. Best thing was to hand in her notice, move away. He said it so many times that she accepted it as truth, like she did with so many things. There was little room for doubt in her mind and she dared not let it in.

'I can see it on you,' Mary said.

'See what?'

Mary glanced down, and Sara became conscious of the tails of the red nail tracks above her right wrist, barely visible beyond the ends of her sleeve. She tugged at her cuffs, pulled them down.

'The fear of him,' Mary said.

Sara shook her head. 'No, I'm not—'

'You're afeart of him, I know. But you've no call to be. Men like that, they're weak. That's why they're always thran, always angry. Because they've nothing in them but the hate they have for their own selves.'

'It's . . . I'm not . . .'

'Why did you come here to me?' Mary asked, her features wide open, nothing hidden.

Sara stumbled over her words before she told the truth. 'I don't know. I just wanted to see if you were all right.'

'You came looking for something.' Mary reached out and took Sara's hand. 'I can't give it to you if I don't know what it is.'

Sara's tongue deserted her. Only Mary's words could fill the space between them.

'You've been close to death, haven't you? I can see it. It always leaves a mark. I have it too. Can you see it on me?'

Sara looked up from their joined hands and into her eyes.

'Yes,' she said, her voice no more than a breath.

'They'll come for you.'

'Who?'

'The children. They'll find you.'

'What children?' Sara asked. 'There aren't any children at the house.'

Mary's eyes sparked and flamed. 'Aye, there are. They're hiding. Waiting for me. Waiting for you.'

'Where?' Sara asked.

'In the walls where you can't see them. In the corners and in the floors.'

Sara pictured dark red stains on stone, a fleeting movement in a doorway, a girl with ribbons in her hands. She pulled her hand away from Mary's, wrapped her arms around herself. 'But the fire,' she said. 'The house was a shell when we—'

'The house doesn't matter,' Mary said. 'It never mattered. It's the land. Those children, they're like the trees all around and the grass in the fields. Those men planted the children there, like seeds. They're in the ground and they'll always be there. They've always been there. Like me. Always.'

23

Esther

Esther's shoulder ached from dragging the girl behind her, but still she giggled like it was a game of chase, like they weren't running for their lives, like Tam wasn't coming for them. The sun hung low over the fields on the other side of the river, burning the water with orange fire. She glimpsed it through the gaps in the hedgerow, a steep bank running down to the shallow edge. Warm on her skin as she ran, her ill-fitting boots hammering on the lane's rough surface, Mary skipping along, her soles barely touching the ground.

'Run,' Esther said between snatches of air. 'Run.'

She knew the main road lay in this direction, perhaps half a mile, maybe more. If they could reach that, they might be safe. They might flag down a car, find another house. Glancing back, she saw they had made it not quite a hundred yards from the driveway. Up ahead, there was a bend in the lane. She focused on that, as if getting out of sight of the house could save them.

An engine barked into life somewhere back there. Esther looked back once more and saw the police car swing out of the driveway, accelerate towards them.

'No,' she said.

The river, she thought. Tam can't drive through the river.

Up ahead, the hedgerow thinned. She pulled Mary towards the edge of the lane, hearing the car's engine roar behind them. Branches and thorns pulled at her clothes as she dived through, scratched at her face and hands. Mary cried out as Esther dragged her through behind her. The car's brakes shrieked as its tyres grabbed at the lane's coarse surface.

Esther's feet seemed to disappear from beneath her, and for a moment, she was free of the earth, flying. Then the ground rose up to slam into her chest, knocking the breath from her lungs, and her legs were up above her head, and the sky beyond them, and then her hip hit the bank. She landed on the muddy shore of the river, her shoulder jarred against the stones and wet earth.

Somewhere above, Mary called her name, and Esther struggled to her knees, then her feet. She reached up and took hold of Mary's hand, pulled her down over the grass and weeds and stones and to the river's edge. The sound of a car door opening up above.

'Come on,' she said, her feet splashing into the shallows.

Mary resisted, pulling back, her eyes wide and staring at the moving water.

'We have to go,' Esther said. 'You'll die if we don't go now. We'll both die.'

'I can't swim,' Mary said.

'You don't have to,' Esther said. 'I'll keep hold of you, I promise.'

The girl turned her terrified eyes to Esther's. 'What about Mummy Joy? Mummy Noreen?'

Esther grabbed Mary's shoulders. 'We'll come back for them. I promise, I'll get us away from here, I'll keep you safe, then we'll come back for them. And we'll take them to the seaside, I swear on my soul, we'll all go to the beach together, I promise. Mary, I swear on my life, we'll come back. Now come on.'

Mary allowed herself to be pulled to the river's edge. Esther waded into the water, felt the cold of it climb her calves and her thighs as it deepened, felt the current pull her away from the house. She fought to stay upright. A cry escaped her as the water reached her groin, the cold reaching into the very core of her, deep into her gut, into her bones. She cried out again. Looking back, Mary clung to her hand, the water up past her belly, creeping up to her chest. Her eyes and mouth wide with the shock of it, and Esther knew how it felt as her body threatened to rebel against the cold.

Movement at the top of the bank. She looked up, saw Tam pushing his way through the hedge, the rifle in one hand. He knelt on the grass, raised the gun, the butt against his shoulder, sighted along its length.

'No,' she said, 'no, no.'

Esther turned to the far bank, saw only that, felt only Mary's hand in hers. Nothing else. Nothing else in the whole wide world. No cold, no current trying to drag her feet from under her. Only the other side. Nothing—

She heard thunder, and something punched her hard in the middle of her back. The bullet tore along the surface of the water in front of her. He missed, she thought. The bullet missed and hit the water. Thank the Lord Jesus, he missed.

Then she looked down and saw the scarlet ribbons flaring from her belly, the water blurring red, pieces of her dress floating. Pieces of her.

Cold now. So cold. Her arms and legs are stone. Ice. She can't feel the rocks and silt on the bottom. Only the cold. It is everything.

She floats, sees the dimming sky, the great white streaks of high cloud.

Water laps at her neck, the sound of it filling her ears, touching her cheeks.

She sees Mary, looking down at her.

Mary's hand still in hers.

Hold on.

Hold—

24
Mary

I FELT THE BULLET HIT HER. Go into her and out of her again. I felt it through her hand. I mind she stood for a moment, terrible still, and then she leaned back in the water like she wanted to swim there. And she floated, the river pulling her away from me. But I helt onto her. I don't know for why, but I knew I had to keep a holt of her. Even when the water lifted me off my feet, I couldn't let her go.

My toes hardly touched the bottom, but I pushed agin the stones, pushed and pushed until I could stand. I pulled on Esther's hand, brought her close to me, and I could see her eyes. And she was looking back at me. She was still there. And I felt a happiness in me like I never felt before. I thought, they can save her. They have bandages and medicines for the cattle, they can use them on her, and they can save her. So I pulled her towards the bank, but it was awful hard, the river trying to pull agin me, pulling her away.

Daddy Tam came to the edge of the bank, his feet splashing in the water, and he hunkered down and reached out for me.

Says he, Bring her to me.

I tried hard as I could but every time I took a step closer, the water pushed me further away. I reached and I reached, my arm and my fingers stretching as hard as I could, so hard it hurt, but I couldn't do it. Daddy Tam lifted the rifle and helt it by the thick end. He reached it out to me so I could grab the thin end, where the bullet come from. It was hard in my hand, and hot. I mind there was still a lick of smoke coming from it.

He pulled me in until I could stand and walk, still dragging Esther behind me. He took her hand from mine and pushed me onto the bank, then he gave a big pull and she came up onto the grass beside me. I stayed down on my knees, coughing and shivering. Esther stared up at the sky, not blinking at all. I put my hand on her cheek and I looked down into her eyes and knew then she couldn't see me. She couldn't see anything at all. And I saw the hole in her belly, and I saw the inside of her, and I realised there was no saving her. No bandage nor medicine would fix her.

I let an awful howl out of me for now I was out of the water I felt the cold biting into me, eating my fingers and my toes. And for her, I howled and cried for Esther, for she was my sister, even though I'd only known her a lock of days. She was my sister, the only one I ever had, and now she was gone. All because of him.

Jesus, says Daddy Tam, Jesus Christ.

I looked up at him and he had water in his eyes. He must have seen the hate in me. It was so big and so hot there couldn't be any hiding it. Not from anyone.

He guldered at me, It was her own fault! No one made her run away. Both of you did it. It's your fault as much as hers. No one made you do it.

I nearly shouted back at him, telt him to shut his stupid, dirty auld mouth, but before I could, he lifted the rifle to his shoulder and aimed it at me.

Says he, I should've done this long ago.

I mind he was awful still and calm all of a sudden. I know rightly he was going to do it. It wasn't something he'd just took a notion of. He'd had it in his head to do it already.

There was times before that when I might've thought it'd be all right to die. I'd be away from that place, at least. But now the rifle was pointing at my head and I'd seen what it did to Esther, I didn't want that. I wanted to live.

He worked a lever or a bolt on the side of the rifle, back and down, up and forwards. I ducked my head down, put my hands over it as if they could stop the bullet. The grass was wet agin my face and it went in my mouth as I begged him, No, no, no, please don't.

I begged and I waited for the bullet.

But it didn't come. Daddy George came. I heard him shout from up the bank, Don't!

It needs doing, says Daddy Tam.

You shoot that child, says Daddy George, I'll shoot you.

Will you, now?

Aye, I will.

I lifted my head and looked up.

Daddy Tam still pointed the rifle at me, and up at the top of the bank, there was Daddy George. He had the policeman's gun in his hand and he aimed it at Daddy Tam. I near telt him to shoot, to blow that auld bastard's brains all over the water, but I helt my whisht.

Says Daddy Tam, I shoot this child, you shoot me, then our da kills you.

Not if I do him first, says Daddy George.

He pulled something on the policeman's gun with his thumb, something that went click. It's called the hammer. I know that now. That seemed to rattle Daddy Tam, for the rifle quivered in his hands.

You haven't the balls, says Daddy Tam.

Says Daddy George, Is that what you think?

That's what I know, says Daddy Tam. You were always a weakling. Da should've done you like he done the others, done you like a runt.

There was a crack, then, and the pistol jumped in Daddy George's hand. Daddy Tam ducked and said a bad word as the bullet cut the water.

Daddy George aimed again. Says he, That was a warning. I won't give you another.

Daddy Tam said more bad words, then he lowered the rifle. Says he to me, Get up to that road before I split your head open.

I got to my feet and I near fell back down for my legs was quivering. I got myself steady, and I looked down at Esther, and she looked up at the sky, darker now, still seeing nothing. Except heaven, maybe. I hoped so.

Go on, says Daddy Tam.

I climbed up the bank and Daddy George took my hand, pulled me up the last of the way. Straight back to the house, says he, heading down the bank to Daddy Tam. Don't make us come after you.

I walked past the car, me dripping water and shivering and my teeth chattering, and back along the lane. I heard them both behind me huffing and puffing, and I knew what they were doing. They were carrying Esther, what was left of her, up the bank. I heard Daddy Tam cursing and Daddy George telling him to settle himself. I looked back once and I saw them put her in the boot of the car like she was nothing but a sack of auld rags. I didn't look again, even when the car's engine started up and it turned and came along the lane. Daddy Tam didn't look at me as he drove past and through the gateway. I heard Daddy George's footsteps behind me and I kept walking till I reached the house.

Daddy George came through the door after me, his big hand on my shoulder, guiding me inside. In the kitchen, Daddy Tam stood at one side and Daddy Ivan at the other. The bathtub full of water still stood there between the sink and the stove as if someone had a use for it. Daddy Ivan had a face on him, and I knew Daddy Tam had telt him what happened. The policeman lay in the corner, his uniform half pulled off him, blood on his face. His hands tied together with twine. He looked at me, and I could tell by his eyes, he knew what was coming.

Daddy Tam pointed at him and, says he, Your fault. All of this is your fault.

The policeman shook his head and tried to say something. But Daddy Tam lit into him then, more anger on him than I'd ever seen before, and Daddy Tam was an angry man. They were all angry men, all three of them. But this was different. This came from deep inside him somewhere, all of his hatred roaring out of him like floodwater.

191

Daddy George pushed me to the cellar door, saying, Go, go, go.

He opened it, pushed me through, and I near cowped down the stairs. Mummy Joy came up and took a holt of me, brought me down to her bed, and pulled me under the blankets, even though I was soaking them through. She wrapped her arms around my head, covering my ears and my eyes, but I could still hear.

I heard all of it. The screaming. Those wet sounds like meat being butchered. They went on and on long after the screaming was just whimpering and on and on still until we heard him gurgling when they drownt him in the bathtub.

We helt each other in the dark and heard it all.

25

Sara

FORTY-FIVE MINUTES AFTER LEAVING THE care home, Sara walked onto the lane that led to the house. It felt good to be out, to walk so far, giving her heart something to do other than worry. Her thighs and lower back buzzed with the exertion, and she relished the sensation.

The hedgerow stood to her left, the steep bank beyond, and the river down below. She glanced through the gaps as she passed. The river churned murky brown and grey without the evening sun to cast gold on its surface. Sara looked for a girl, still and watchful in the water, but saw no one. Had seen no one. She was sure of that now.

Checking her phone, she saw it had gone three. Damien wouldn't be home till after five, she thought, so it would be her and Tony in the house. Antonio, to give him his real name. She thought it a beautiful name and if it were hers, she would use it always. Perhaps she would tell him so.

Sara felt heat rise on her neck and cheeks. A foolish reaction to a foolish want. She was a married woman with no use for girlish fancies. But still, she hoped he would be there when she got back. She hoped he would have time for a cup of tea.

'Stop it,' she whispered, words that had become too familiar over the last day or so.

When Sara entered through the gateway to the house, onto the drive, she saw Tony's van still parked in front. She felt a peal of joy, but she tamped it down. The air cooled as she walked beneath the thick and wandering branches of the ash trees. She remembered Mary's words, the seeds planted here. Sara paused, unable to move forward.

Walking on graves.

She could not banish the image, not now. The house, the grounds, the outbuildings, old and demolished, rebuilt and new. Built on graves. Mary had said the children would find her. The idea crawled across her back, held her in place, refused to let her move.

The front door opened, and Tony stepped out, his toolbox in hand. He walked towards the van, unaware of her presence, and opened the rear doors. Once he'd placed the toolbox inside, he turned and saw her in the shadow of the ashes. He stood still, watching her for a moment, as if she might be an illusion. Then he approached, concern on his face.

'You all right?' he asked.

Sara could not find a truthful answer.

The crease in his brow deepened as he drew closer. 'Sara? Are you okay?'

What do I want from him? The question formed in her mind, and again, the answer glimmered beyond her reach.

'Yes,' she said, finding her tongue. 'I'm a bit out of breath, that's all.'

He nodded but looked unconvinced.

'Come on in,' he said. 'I'll get you a cup of tea.'

It occurred to her that she should have been the one inviting him in, but she had no real objection. She followed him along the driveway and into the house. As she stepped inside, crossing the threshold, she felt herself an intruder. These floors and walls and doors were not hers, no matter how much money had changed hands.

Tony filled the kettle at the sink as Sara took a stool at the island. She placed her hands on the granite top, felt the cool creep between the bones of her fingers. Her life seemed to have drifted into an orbit around this structure, this gathering of wood and stone.

'So, what happened?' Tony asked. 'What did she say?'

Sara turned her gaze to the floor, near the Aga, the dark red stains on the flagstones. She thought of children, lost in the dark. And of the movement she'd caught in the corner of her eye. She looked to the back hall, saw nothing there but shadows. A steaming mug appeared on the worktop, stirring her from the trance that had taken her. She turned her head, saw Tony standing close.

'When they were renovating, did they find anything here?' she asked.

Tony took the stool next to hers. 'Like what?'

'I don't know,' she said. 'Anything.'

He shook his head, leaned his elbows on the worktop. 'Not as far as I know. Not that they would tell the likes of me, anyway. I'm not part of Francie's crew. They just bring me in to do the dirty work, really, but . . .'

His eyes became distant.

'But?' Sara asked.

'There was one day,' he said. 'I didn't think anything of it at the time, I just did what I was told.'

She turned to face him. 'What?'

'This one day, it would've been late in the job, but I was working down in the basement and all of a sudden, we were all told to go home. It happens sometimes, like if there's a gas leak, or if someone breaks open a water main, everyone on-site is told to go home. I assumed it was something like that, but . . .'

Tony shifted on his stool.

'When I think about it, they were nervous. The site manager and his boys. They called Francie, he went in to take a look, and then we were all sent home. He looked rattled when he came out. It was a Thursday, I remember that. They paid us for the last couple of hours of the day, and the Friday, then we came back on the Monday and nothing more was said about it.'

'Where did Francie look?' Sara asked.

'Where the extension is now,' Tony said. 'It used to be a stable block, I think, or maybe an old milking shed. They were digging up the concrete floors. I thought at the time they'd maybe dug up some old archaeological stuff. You know, like old coins or pottery or something. Site managers hate that. If they find some old stuff from a thousand years ago, they're supposed to down tools until a proper dig can happen. A lot of times, a project like this, they'll find some old bits and pieces and not let on, just dig over it so the job doesn't get held up. That's what I thought it was at the time. Either way, Francie told everyone to get out, and you don't argue with a man like him.'

'A man like him?' she echoed.

Tony opened his mouth, but he found no words, as if he knew he'd said too much. Sara could see him scrambling for an answer. Eventually, he took a swig of tea and set the mug back on the worktop.

'I need to get on,' he said, standing.

'Tell me,' Sara said.

'Tell you what?'

'What you mean by a man like him.'

Tony held his hands out, a gesture of surrender. 'Look, I'm sorry, I've no business saying anything about him. Just forget it, all right?'

'I want to know.'

'He's your father-in-law. I'm not going to say anything against him.'

'Please,' she said, reaching out to him, taking hold of his wrist. 'I want to know.'

Tony looked down at her hand. She pulled it away as if it burned. Heat crept across her cheeks once more, and her neck, down her chest. She reached for her tea, took a sip.

'You know who he is,' he said. 'You know what he's been involved in.'

'He did some time in prison,' Sara said, putting the mug down. 'Damien told me. Possession of explosives or something like that. Damien says he was wrongly convicted, that he didn't know the explosives were on his property.'

Tony laughed, caught himself, cleared his throat. 'If that's what Damien told you, then I'm not going to contradict him. It's none of my business.'

'I want to know. I *need* to know.'

'If Damien knew I said anything.' Tony shook his head and turned his gaze to the floor. 'If Francie knew.'

'I won't tell them.'

He looked up at her, and away, fighting himself.

'Tell me,' Sara said.

He leaned his head to one side, exhaled, gave in.

'Francie Keane wasn't the boy who hid the explosives,' Tony said. 'It was always some other poor bastard did that for him, whether they wanted to or not. It's before I was born, but one time my father was told to hide guns under his floorboards. He wasn't given any choice in it. It was Francie Keane who knocked his door and took him for a drive around the estate so he could tell him what's what. Either my da hid the guns or Francie would have his knees.'

His words quickened as he spoke, anger driving them.

'I don't know how Francie got caught with explosives, my guess is he was about to hand them over to someone, but he wasn't the boy who hid them. He was the boy told someone else to hide them, or they'd be dealt with. He was the boy said whose car those explosives wound up under. A cop, or a part-time soldier, or some tradesman who did odd jobs around a police station because he needed the work. They drive off in the car some morning and meet an incline, that tilts the mercury, and bang!'

He slapped the worktop, made Sara flinch.

'Maybe they die or maybe they live the rest of their life with no legs. If they're lucky, their children weren't in the car with them when the bomb went off. Francie would never have planted a bomb himself, he was always too smart, but he told plenty of young fellas where to put them. Young fellas who wound up in jail, or died, or lost their arms when the bomb went off too soon, but Francie made sure he kept his distance. I don't know if he ever shot anyone, but I know he said who got shot.'

He placed his hands flat on the worktop, leaned on them.

'Look, I wouldn't have taken the job here only I needed the work. Francie Keane scares the shit out of me. You wanted to know what I think of him, who he is, well, that's what I think of him, that's who he is.'

He glared at her while his anger burned like a Roman candle.

'I'm sorry,' Sara said.

Tony gave a brittle, crackling laugh, then the anger burned out, left him like a soul leaves a corpse.

'What for?' he asked. 'You didn't do anything. I'm sorry. Like I said, I've no business talking about your father-in-law. I should finish up my work.'

He turned to leave once more, but Sara's question would not wait.

'What about Damien?'

Tony stopped and turned back to face her. 'Don't ask me that,' he said.

'Is he like his father?'

Tony's eyes grew distant, staring somewhere miles beyond the walls of the kitchen.

'I went to school with him. We all knew who he was, who his father was. We were all afraid of him. You know, before the cancer got him, my da told me if you grow up to be a better man than your father, then you've done all right. Damien isn't a better man than his father.'

A heavy blanket of silence hung between them for a moment before she said, 'Thank you.'

'S'all right,' he said. 'I've said too much. I trust you to keep it between us.'

'Of course,' she said, meaning it.

Tony reached into his back pocket and produced a worn and tattered wallet. He took a business card from its folds, placed it on the worktop.

'If you ever need anything,' he said. 'Doesn't matter what time it is.'

'Thank you.' She took the card and slipped it into her pocket.

He bowed his head like a footman and turned away.

Sara watched him go, wishing he wouldn't.

26
Mary

I GOT TERRIBLE SICK. THAT NIGHT, I was awful cold, I couldn't stop shivering. Mummy Joy dried me out and wrapped me up in all the blankets we had, but the cold had got down deep inside of me. The guts of me was cold, I could feel the chill in my heart. I shook and trimbled till I thought my bones would come loose and I'd fall apart. And the coughing, terrible coughing, like something was clawing and tearing the lungs out of me. After a while, I went to sleep, but it wasn't like any other sleep I'd ever had. Like when dreams fill your head. This wasn't the same. With this sleep, the real world was inside my head, and the dreams were outside of me, all around.

Bad dreams.

There was pillars of fire. I saw them devour everything and everybody. I felt the heat of them, burning the flesh off my bones. They ate Mummy Joy and Mummy Noreen, turned them to ashes. I mind screaming, soul afeart they would eat me too.

I saw Esther in the fire. The flames didn't touch her. They couldn't. She walked straight through them and she didn't burn. Maybe it was because she was dripping wet from the water. I saw red ribbons in her hands, and she was holding them to her belly. She was lost, I could tell. Just wandering, wild afeart. I called out to her, and she turned her head to me, but she couldn't see me.

She wasn't all alone there. There was others. Children, I don't know how many. All ages. I could see them and they could see me. Sometimes they came close, other times they stayed away. But they were always there. They were always, always watching.

I don't mind much about them lock of days, when I had the fever, but when I came out the other side, the children were still there. They had followed me out.

27

Joy

J OY TURKINGTON WATCHED AS MARY sank into the
fever, a bundle of skinny arms and legs and sweat and fire.
It had started as shivers, coming in waves, as if an angry
sea raged through the child. Then the coughing, deep and
hacking, and Joy wondered how the force of them didn't break
wee Mary open. When Mary's eyes darkened and narrowed,
Joy touched her forehead, and her hand recoiled from the heat.

'My God,' she said, 'she's burning.'

Noreen came to her side and placed the palm of her good
hand, the one whose fingers weren't broken, on Mary's skin.
First her head, then down beneath the nightdress they'd
changed her into, feeling her chest. She said nothing, but Joy
could see it on her face.

'What is it?' Joy asked.

'I don't know,' Noreen said, 'but we need to get her cooled
down.'

She and Joy pulled the bedclothes aside, then Mary's nightdress. Noreen fetched the washbowl and soaked a rag in water
from the jug. She pressed it against Mary's forehead, her cheeks,
her chest, her belly, leaving droplets to glisten in the lamplight.

Fear took hold of Joy, a different kind of fear, one that coiled around her stomach, tightening like a serpent.

'Will she die?' she asked.

'No,' Noreen said. 'No, she bloody won't.'

She was a hard one, Noreen, always had been, but she had kept Joy alive all these years. Twice she had stopped her ending it. Once when she found Joy with a bed sheet looped around her neck, ready to jump from the upstairs landing. She had grabbed her, held her, fought her, until Joy gave up trying. The second time, Joy had been stabbing at her own wrist trying to find the vein. Noreen had entered the room at the moment Joy brought the blade to her throat and she seized her wrist, pulled it away, slammed her hand against the edge of the sink until the knife fell in among the dishes and the blood.

Noreen Weaver possessed a fierce will to live, a stubborn, spiteful drive to outlast the men who had held them in this house for more than a decade. She had outlived the third woman who had been here when Joy had first arrived, and four of the five children who had been born here in that time, and now this girl from the outside. Joy would have been dead these many years if not for Noreen. Sometimes, in the cold and wakeful hours of the night, Joy hated her for it.

They each kept watch as Mary's fever deepened, as her coughing grew more ragged, as the tremors spread out from her centre to her fingers and toes, her teeth chattering. Noreen said she wouldn't die, but Joy didn't believe her. She had said Matthew wouldn't die, no bloody way would he die, and yet he had perished in Noreen's embrace, like a candle flame blown out. A real live boy one moment, an armful of rags and skin the next.

Noreen had cried hard for Matthew, and Joy had too, and Joy had done Noreen's share of the work for a few days, just as Noreen had done for Joy when her last baby had died still tethered to her, still slick with her blood.

As the first promises of daylight showed in the gaps around the door at the top of the stairs, Mary began to scream. Awful screams, like the howling of the damned. Joy pressed her hands to her ears, but Mary's voice cut through, a blade piercing Joy's skull. Stop, stop, stop, she whispered to herself, feeling the spreading cracks in her mind.

Noreen took hold of her wrists, pulled her hands away from her ears.

'We have to get help,' she said.

'They won't help her,' Joy said. 'They'll let her die.'

'We'll see about that,' Noreen said, getting to her feet.

She climbed the stairs to the door and hammered it so hard with her fist that it rattled and shook in its frame. The noise seemed to free Mary from whatever torment held her, and she fell silent, staring up at Noreen with wild eyes.

'Mary,' Joy said.

'The children,' Mary said, then her eyelids fluttered and closed.

Noreen slammed her fist against the door again, over and over, and shouted, 'Hey! Hey! Hey!'

Soon, a hammering came from the other side.

'Whisht, now, quit that.'

Ivan's voice, firm and scolding, but not angry. Not yet.

'The child's sick,' Noreen said. 'She needs help.'

A pause, then, 'Go on back from the door.'

Noreen descended the steps, halted near the bottom. The padlock rattled, the bolt clattered, and the door opened inward.

Ivan stood there, blocking the light, his braces slung over his undershirt, his belly spilling over the top of his trousers. He peered down into the cellar at Mary's wretched form.

'Hm,' he said. 'You two, go on into the corner and don't move from it till I tell you.'

Joy did as she was told, backing into the corner as far as she could, arms wrapped around herself. Noreen followed, keeping her eyes on Ivan as he came down the stairs.

'She needs medicine,' Noreen said.

'Whisht, now.'

He approached Mary's bed. She stared up at him, unseeing, her breath coming in quick, shallow rasps. He reached down and placed his palm against her forehead, then her neck, her chest.

'Hm,' he said, then turned back towards the stairs.

'You have medicine for the cattle,' Noreen said. 'You can give her some of that. She'll die if you don't.'

Ivan didn't pause as he mounted the stairs, offered no reply.

Joy spoke, her voice cracking. 'If she dies, I die.'

He climbed up to the door, stepped through, and locked it behind him.

* * *

Joy lay on the bed next to Mary, thinking of ways to die. All she needed was a bed sheet and something to tie it to. The method wasn't the problem. The problem was Noreen, and her bloody stubborn will. Noreen would not let her go, she knew that. So, if Mary died, Joy would have to seek out a quiet place where she could not be saved.

A thought entered her mind, an idea that had appeared there before, always fleeting, always chased away for the wicked thing

206

it was. But now it lingered, black and foul. Joy moved her hand to Mary's throat, felt the heat and the sweat, felt the quickened pulse. All she had to do was squeeze; the child was so weak, there'd be no fight in her. Just a little pressure, just for a wee while. Then it would be over for her, and Joy could pull the sweat-soaked sheet from the bed and tie the knot that would take her away from this place. Let Noreen try and stop her. Just let her try.

Joy did not squeeze, though the idea remained like a poisoned wound. She buried her face between Mary's shoulder and cheek, and she wept, grieving for them both.

She didn't know Tam stood over her until he spoke.

'Get away till I get a look at her,' he said.

He smelled of drink. It tainted the air around them. She kept her gaze away from him as she slid off the bed and went to the corner where Noreen already stood. Noreen took her hand, pressed Joy's fingers between hers. Joy wiped tears from her cheeks with the back of her free hand, sniffed, and exhaled, the air fluttering from her chest.

Tam came to Mary's side and touched her forehead. He leaned down, one hand on the thin mattress, and turned her face towards his. With his thick fingers, he prised open one eye, then the other, peering into them, his tongue clicking behind his teeth. Finally, he stood upright and shoved his hands down into his pockets. He didn't look at them as he spoke.

'Pneumonia, I'd say.'

'Give her medicine,' Noreen said. 'She'll die if you don't.'

'She'll probably die if I do,' he said. 'Maybe the best thing for her.'

Those words cut Joy deep, even as she remembered her hand at the girl's neck, the wicked idea taunting her.

'No,' Joy said, her voice welling deep in her throat. 'She has to live. Give her the medicine. Let her live. Please.'

His shoulders rose and fell once as he breathed in and out, an impatient breath, weary.

'Whether she lives or dies is nothing to do with me. If it was, I'd get it over with. No point making a cratur suffer, whether it's got two legs or four.'

Joy went to speak, to curse him, to call him the foulest names she knew, but Noreen squeezed her hand, hissed through her teeth. Ivan might have forgiven her curses, but Tam would not. Tam would beat the life from her where she stood. He might do them all, the three of them, kill them stone dead and put them in the ground with Esther and the policeman.

And would that be so bad? All she had to do was scream at him, call him the fucking bastard that he was, and wait for his hard right hand.

Noreen knew her thoughts and grabbed her wrist, squeezed so hard the pain cut through to her right mind. Joy looked down at the sodden wood floor, clenched her teeth together hard enough to bring an ache to her jaw, hard enough to cause the blood to thrum in her ears and pulse behind her eyes.

'She'll hardly make it through the night,' Tam said, as if it were a blessing, then he went to the stairs, climbed and locked the door behind him.

Joy felt her legs melt away and Noreen's arms around her, guiding her to the bed while she whispered about prayer and the mercy of Jesus.

28

Sara

SARA WATCHED THROUGH THE WINDOW as Tony's van exited onto the lane. She paused there for a moment, looking at the empty space left behind. Then she went through the back hall to the extension. The walls were freshly plastered, windows and patio doors glazed, but the floor was bare concrete. Materials and tools lay scattered about, ready for the underfloor heating to be installed and covered with tiles that were being shipped from Italy. Sara picked her way through lengths of piping, bags of some kind of cement, careful of her footing. The ground floor was open plan, an expansive reception room with a central open fireplace that would create a border between the living and dining areas, with a staircase at the far end. Above, a gallery landing provided access to what would be the master and two spare bedrooms. Through the patio doors, she could see the yard, its stretch of stony earth waiting to be landscaped.

Sara made her way to the centre of what would some day be the dining area and looked down at the concrete. Smooth and fresh, it had been laid just days before they arrived. And what lay beneath? What had they found here? Whatever it was, had they left it in place or taken it away? She imagined packed earth and stone, and children, trapped there, looking up, reaching for the light.

I know how they feel, she thought.

Her life, her marriage, bound so tight around her that she couldn't move. She thought of Amanda, and the warning she had given, and Sara wished for that time back, so that she could listen. What if instead of taking those pills, she had simply walked through the door, called Amanda, and asked for shelter? Where would she be now?

Not here, not hundreds of miles from the people she had once called friends. A clean break, Damien had said, a new start. Away from all the pressures of her job and the malevolent influence of Amanda and the others. I want to keep you safe, he'd said on her first night home from the hospital, his chest against her back, his lips on her neck. His words so soft, soothing the burn of shame she felt for taking those pills. But she understood what he really wanted now. The distance he'd placed between her and everyone she had once cared for, and those who had cared for her.

A wash of loneliness came in, the crushing weight of it almost pushing her to the floor. She turned away from it, blocked it out. It would do her no good. Isolation was his weapon and she would not use it against herself.

Outside, the light dimmed, heavy raindrops smacking the glass. Sara shivered as the temperature dropped, and she no longer wanted to be in this room. She returned through the back hall and stepped one foot into the kitchen, freezing in the shadow of the doorway.

Damien stood at the island, shrugging off his rain-damped jacket as he studied the stack of old newspapers on the island's worktop. He lifted the one on top, a *Belfast Telegraph*, and read the headlines. A sigh escaped him as he slumped against the island.

'Fuck's sake,' he whispered, loud enough for her to hear. He read the piece, his forefinger tracing the words, his breath deepening with his anger.

Sara cursed herself for not hiding them away. She remained locked in place, unable to move for fear of alerting him to her presence but knowing that she must. She went to speak, her inhalation giving her away. His gaze shot from the page to her. He stared, unmoving, unreadable. She breathed out but no words followed.

When she could stand the silence no longer, she said, 'You're home.'

Stupid, stupid words, her tongue betraying her guilt.

Guilt? What for? She had done nothing wrong, had she?

'Yeah,' he said, a smile splitting his face, an ill fit that went no further than his lips. 'I finished up early.' He looked down at the newspaper. 'What's this?'

With terrible effort, Sara took another step into the kitchen. 'I was just reading up about the house.'

'Where'd you get these?' he asked.

Sara scrambled for a lie but could find nothing. As one part of her mind searched, another part told her the longer she stood in silence, the worse it would be. She had no choice but to tell the truth.

'Tony brought them,' she said, as if it didn't matter at all.

'The spark?'

'Yes. He told me his grandfather collected old newspapers, they were still in his mother's attic. So he dug these out. You can ask him.'

Damien cracked a joyless smile and said, 'Don't you worry, I'll ask him all right. And what exactly did you find out from these?'

Sara took another step closer. 'About the family,' she said. 'Not a family, exactly, but there were three men and two women, and Mary, she was just a little girl when—'

'When one of the men lost his head and killed everyone then himself,' Damien said. 'That's what you found out.'

'I don't know if it was as simple as that, no one really—'

'It's history,' he said. 'Sixty years ago. What are you dredging all this up for? What good could it do you? Why do you think this place was so cheap? They died. That's the end of it.'

'They died,' Sara said, her anger rising in spite of her fear. 'That's right. All but one of them died in this room. How am I supposed to feel about that?'

'You don't have to feel a single fucking thing about it.' His eyes flashed, his teeth bared. 'You didn't know them. They weren't *your* family. What difference does it make to you how they died, what room it was in? It's gone, it's in the past.'

'Mary isn't,' Sara said, already fearing his response. 'They were her family. She thinks this is still her home.'

Damien came so close she had to lean back. His words dotted her face with spittle.

'It's not. It's ours. Do you even know how lucky we are? Are you such a spoilt wee princess that you can't see how good we have it? This house, all this land, and no mortgage, no debt hanging over us? My father found this place for us, did all the dealing, did all the work renovating it. And you're pissing and moaning about something that happened more than thirty years before you were born.'

'It matters,' she said. 'I don't care how long ago they died. It still matters. We don't belong here. It's not our—'

'Shut up!'

His voice boomed in her ears, between the walls, through the house. She took an involuntary step back.

'Shut your mouth,' he said, his voice retreating low into his throat. 'Everything my father did for us, everything he did for you, even after you took those pills, and you throw it in my face. What an ungrateful wee bitch you are.'

'Don't call me that,' she said.

'I'll call you what I want. I'll call you what you are. And you listen to me, if I think you're going bad again, I will have you committed. Don't you think I won't.'

The threat stung. She remembered the three days she'd spent in an Early Intervention Unit, a separate building on the hospital grounds, with the alcoholics and the drug addicts, all the people who could no longer function. For three days, she was one of them, one of the wasted people, and the idea of going back scared her more than anything she could imagine.

But she would not be cowed.

'What did he find here?' she asked.

The words seemed to hit Damien like a punch to the belly, took his balance so he rocked back on his heels.

'What?' he asked.

'When they were working on the extension,' she said, 'they found something. Under the concrete floor of the old stable block. They called Francie in. What did he find there?'

Damien placed both his hands on the worktop, shook his head like she made no sense at all.

'I don't know what the fuck you're talking about.'

'What did they find?' she asked, moving closer, even if it put her within his reach. 'They called your father, closed the site down. It must have been something. What did they find?'

He gave her his gaze, full and hard and hateful. 'Why don't you tell me?'

Sara had the feeling of a line being drawn, of stepping across it, passing over a threshold from which they would never return. She should back down, be quiet, accept his word.

Instead, she said, 'They found remains, didn't they? I don't know what. Bones, I suppose. That's all there could be after all these years. Mary told me, they planted them like seeds. Is that what they found? Did they find the children?'

Damien held her stare as he slowly shook his head.

'And they called Francie,' Sara said. 'They called your father and he came and he looked and he saw the remains, but they didn't do anything, did they? They didn't call the police because it would've messed everything up. There would've been an investigation, more digging, and the site would've had to close. So they said nothing.'

'Stop talking,' Damien said, his forefinger raised. 'Shut your mouth right now and don't you say another word.'

'Did they take the remains somewhere else?' Sara asked, closing the space between them. 'Or did they just dig over them?'

'Shut up.'

'I suppose it would make more sense just to dig over them, bury them deeper. Is that what happened? Are we walking on graves?'

Damien glared at her for a moment, breathing hard, before he gathered up the bundle of newspapers and carried them to the sink. He dropped them in and opened a drawer, then another, and a third before he found what he wanted: a box of kitchen matches.

'Don't,' Sara said. 'They're not ours.'

He struck a match, held it over the sink filled with old paper.

'Don't,' she said again, crossing the kitchen to him, reaching for his hand.

He dropped the match, but the fall extinguished it. As he fished another from the box, Sara took hold of his wrist. He pulled his hand away, back, then swung it up, hard and fast.

The back of his hand connected with her jaw, the impact staggering her. She took three steps back before the room tilted, spilling her to the floor. Her vision tunnelled and sparked. She saw the matchbox fall, matches spilling.

Damien stood over her, his arms at his sides, his shoulders rising and falling.

'I . . .' He shook his head. 'I shouldn't have done that. I'm sorry. But you shouldn't have grabbed me like that.'

Sara got to her knees, then to her feet. She tasted blood and knew she had bitten the inside of her cheek. The room swayed, but she held her footing, went to the hall.

'Love, stop, come on,' Damien called after her as she opened the front door.

She walked along the drive to the lane, ignoring the rain, turned towards the village as her walk sped to a jog, kept running until she heard an engine behind her, tyres on rough road. Looking behind, to the bend in the lane, she could see no sign. She made for the hedgerow, forced her way through despite the scratching and tearing at her skin and clothes. On the other side, at the top of the riverbank, she crouched down and watched as Damien's BMW passed.

When it had gone, and she could no longer hear its engine, she stood upright. She glanced down at the river. Light reflected on its surface, pocked by raindrops.

The girl looked back, unmoved by the current, scarlet ribbons clutched to her belly.

Sara looked away, closed her eyes.

When she looked back, the girl had gone.

Had never been there.

29
Joy

JOY HAD FALLEN INTO A shallow and greasy sleep when she was woken by raised voices above. Her first instinct was to reach for Mary, but she found the space beside her empty. She sat upright, disoriented, searching the room. Mary lay on the next bed, Noreen crouched at her side, dabbing her forehead with a wet cloth. The child's breath came in thin, rattling wheezes. Joy went to ask after her, but another round of shouting from above drowned her out.

'They've been at it a good while now,' Noreen said. 'Tam's drunk, fighting the both of them.'

It had been some time since Tam had been drinking. Weeks, maybe months, it was hard to tell. Time here passed in days and seasons, nothing in between. When Tam started on the drink, there was no stopping him. His temper was foul enough when he was sober; with drink on him, he was pure wicked. Even his brother and his father trod carefully around him.

'What are they fighting about?' Joy asked.

'The child, I think.' Noreen pressed the cloth against Mary's chest. 'George wants them to help her. Tam wants to let her die.'

Heavy feet shook dirt from the ceiling above, bellowing voices, furniture pushed around the living room then moving to the kitchen. A clatter and a thud, and Joy pictured the table upended, a chair cowped. Then the entire world seemed to shake with the impact of bodies on the floor. Joy and Noreen both flinched. Roaring from above, two voices cursing, a third telling them to stop.

'They're killing each other,' Joy said.

'I hope they do,' Noreen said. 'Let one kill the other till they're all dead. That'd do me all right.'

The bodies rolled across the floor, like thunder across the sky. Joy put her hands to her ears. She did not like noise. The sound of raised voices, the banging of doors. They sparked dread in her. She found herself rocking back and forth and wondered how long she'd been doing it. Noreen watched, and Joy felt ashamed, forced herself to be still.

'They'll wear themselves out,' Noreen said, 'or the da will get the belt off.'

As if conjured by her words, there came the sound everyone in the house feared: leather on flesh. Even from down here they could hear it, the slap, followed by a cry far higher than a grown man should make. Then again, and again, and a fourth time.

Ivan's voice, now, cutting through everything, telling them to stop, stop, stop or he'd whip the skin off their backs.

Joy knew what the leather felt like. The sting and the heat of it on her shoulders, her buttocks, her thighs. How the pain lingered like it had been stitched into her skin. Of all the torments of this house, Ivan and his belt were the worst of them. The brothers were as likely to get it as the women, and somewhere inside, Joy was glad they got it now. She was glad of their pain, for they deserved every bloody bit of it.

Quiet fell over the house, sudden and heavy, the wretched rattle of Mary's chest the only sound. Joy and Noreen looked to each other, both questioning. They each flinched at the sound of the padlock being undone, the bolt sliding, the door opening. Neither of them dared to turn their heads and look.

'I want to see her,' George said.

Joy heard the steps creak under his weight. He was as large as his brother, but more fat than meat. His breath sounded like it was hard come by, juddering in and out of him. Joy felt the bulk of him through the wooden boards beneath her feet, and she wondered when he had last come down here. Years, she thought.

He came to the foot of the bed, and Joy dared to glance at him. His thinning red hair stood in clumps over his pink scalp. His lower lip was swollen and bloody, and his right cheek had puffed up. Half the buttons had been torn from his shirt, revealing the stained vest underneath.

George stood entirely still but for the rise and fall of his chest, staring down at the child. Joy searched his face for any sign of emotion, but apart from his wounds, it was as blank as ever, his lower lip drooping.

She inhaled, ready to speak, and the sound of her breath startled him, as if he hadn't known she was there. He looked down at her, and she felt naked. She stared back for a moment as she sought her tongue.

'Please help her,' she said.

He looked back to Mary, reached down, touched her bare foot. Joy felt the urge to slap his hand away, but she swallowed it.

'You have medicine for the cattle,' she said. 'Give her some.'

'There's penicillin,' he said. 'I don't know if it'll do her any good.'

'You can try.'

He fell silent, his fingers still resting on Mary's toes.

There was a forbidden thing Joy wanted to say. Something that was never mentioned, not in this house, not between these walls. She had never said it aloud, barely even thought it. But now, she had no choice.

'She's your daughter,' she said.

He pulled his hand away from Mary's foot, brought his fingers to his chest, cast his gaze down to the floor.

'Don't say that. You're not allowed to say it.'

'It's the truth.'

He formed his right hand into a fist, raised it over her. But she knew he would not strike her. He didn't have the fury left in him.

'Get her the medicine,' she said. 'Please.'

George lowered his fist, turned, and climbed the stairs.

* * *

He returned some time later carrying a tray. Noreen went to the corner without being asked, but Joy remained where she was, on the bed next to Mary's. George set the tray beside her. On it there sat two bottles, one labelled penicillin, the other white spirit. Alongside them, a clean cloth, and a syringe with a vicious-looking needle. He opened the bottle of white spirit, tipped some onto the cloth, then wiped the rubber cap on the bottle of medicine. Then he pierced the cap with the needle and drew some of the liquid into the syringe. Joy hadn't had an injection since she was a child, but she knew this needle was thicker than any that had ever pierced her skin.

'I boiled it in water to sterilise it,' George said. 'I had to guess her weight to measure the dose, but I think it's about right. Turn her over.'

Joy hesitated, then did as she was told, rolling Mary onto her stomach.

'Pull that up,' he said, indicating Mary's nightdress.

He dabbed more white spirit onto the cloth, wiped a patch of skin on Mary's buttock. Joy looked away as he plunged the needle into the muscle. Mary emitted a low groan.

'There,' he said. 'Now we have to wait and see.'

He returned the items to the tray and went to lift it. Joy placed her hand on his forearm. He turned his head to her, shock in his eyes.

'Thank you,' she said.

He did not answer.

30
Mary

I WAS STANDING ON A BEACH. I'd never seen one before, and I never have since. Not till now. But I was there, on the sand. The farm was behind me. The house and the barns and the old stables and the fields on the hills. When I looked over my shoulder, I could see Mummy Joy and Mummy Noreen in the windows. I don't mind if they was watching me or not, but I could see them.

The sea was afore me. It didn't make any sound. I wouldn't know what noise the sea would make, but I thought I should hear something. Away in the distance, I could see all the other countries. I could see America and France and Africa and England, all those places, far away between the sea and the sky.

Esther stood in the water. It came up to her middle. She helt red ribbons in her hands, up agin her belly. She was saying something to me and even though I could hear nothing, I knew what it was. Come in, she was telling me, come into the water. And I felt it on my bare toes, the sea, just lapping at them like a kitten. I mind it was warm and blue and I wanted to dive in and swim in it. I didn't know how to swim, I still don't, but that didn't matter. The water would carry me to her.

But something stopped me going in. I knew if I went into that water, if I let it swallow me up, then I would never come out again. I looked back at the farm and I remembered that I hated thon place even though it was the only place I knew. I turned back to the water where Esther stood, and I saw she wasn't alone. The children were with her, and they were watching me, and they wanted me to come to them. They all did, them and Esther, and I wanted to go to them so much I could feel it pulling like there was a string tied to the heart of me. But I knew I'd stay there forever if I took another step.

I opened my mouth to say I couldn't go with them into the sea, but no sound came out of my mouth, only air, like there was no voice in my throat. There was a wee boy, maybe five or six years old, he looked awful familiar, like I'd known him before. The water was near up to his chin, and he helt his hand out to me. Maybe I should have taken it. Things might have been better for everyone if I had. If I'd gone into that water, into the sea, and stayed there with them.

But I didn't. I turned away from them and walked back towards the farm. The sand under my feet turned to muck and grass and then the concrete of the yard.

And the children followed me.

* * *

It was terrible dark when I woke, and terrible cold. I was wild afeart. I wondered if I'd died and if this was hell, and if hell wasn't a lake of fire but a cold and black place where you could see nothing but what was inside your own head. I must have cried out loud because straightaway I felt a hand on my arm, and I knew whose hand it was. I heard her reaching around in the dark for something, and then a match striking, and the lamp came on, and there was Mummy Joy leaning over me.

Ah, wee pet, says she, I thought you would die.

And she gathered me up in her arms and helt me awful tight, too tight, near crushing me, but I had no strength to get free of her. So I let her crush me and I was glad of it as she rocked me.

I fell back into my sleep near straightaway, but before I did, I saw them in the shadows, the children, watching.

* * *

For days, I came and went between one world and the other, and many's a time I couldn't tell which was which, nor where I belonged. Esther lived in the dream place. I saw her there, but I could never speak to her, and she couldn't speak to me. But I could tell she was afeart, and she was lost. She wanted to go home but couldn't find her way.

The children came with me, from one world to the other and back again. At first they kept a distance from me, like they weren't sure of me, but after a while they came closer. Still none of them spake, but they watched.

That wee boy came closest of all, and I felt like I knew him, and he knew me. I thought of that memory I had of a boy that lived with me and the Mummies, and tried to mind that boy's face, to mind if he looked like this one. I tried but I couldn't. Memory is a liar; it tells you things that never were and forgets the things that were real.

What I do know is, he'd always been there. And the others. Always.

When I think about it now, I wonder, was that place always bad. Was the wickedness in the soil? Maybe it had always been there, even before the house. Maybe the wickedness seeped up through the soil, like the water did through the floorboards, and maybe it spread its wickedness to them men.

Maybe it's always been there. Maybe it's still there now.

* * *

After a few days, I was awake more than I was asleep. I could do no more than lift my head from the pillow, and I had a terrible cough that hurt every bit of me. But I was well enough that I could be left to myself while Mummy Joy and Mummy Noreen got on with their work upstairs. Once a day, Daddy George came down with a tray. He stuck me with a needle in my backside, and it was terrible sore, but he said it was what saved my life. If I was good and took the needle, I was allowed an apple or a plum, but only for them lock of days. I wasn't to get used to having good things like that.

When I was all alone, the children gathered around. They didn't speak, but I talked to them. I didn't have much of a voice, and sometimes I could hardly fit a word around the coughing, but I did it anyway.

There was half a dozen of them, sometimes more, sometimes less. All ages, from a wee tote who could barely walk, to a girl who was near my age. One time, she carried a baby, all covered in blood, and I screamed and screamed till Mummy Joy came down the stairs to see to me. I never saw that baby again. I think it was in the house somewhere, but they kept it hidden from me after that.

As the days went by, I got a wee bit stronger and the cough started to fade. Soon I was able to sit up in the bed, then stand on my own two feet for a wee bit. All the while, I talked to the children. I showed them the room, and my bed, and the wardrobe. I showed them the dollies I'd made from sticks and twine.

By the time I was fit to get back to work, I knew why the children had followed me back into my world: they needed someone to care for them. So that's what I did. I was their mummy now. So when Mummy Joy telt me we were going to try to get out of that place, I didn't know what to do.

31

Sara

S ARA CLIMBED INTO THE PASSENGER seat of Tony's
van. She had called him as she reached the edge of
Morganstown; he had suggested she wait in the forecourt of the small filling station that stood at one end of the
main street. A good choice, as it happened, because she was
able to stay behind a cage full of gas canisters, watching for
the van, ready to hide if she saw Damien's BMW.

'What happened?' Tony asked as she buckled her seat belt.

Without thinking, her hand went to her jaw, and she saw
the realisation in his face. It caused hot shame to break within
her.

'I just need somewhere to stay,' she said. 'Just for tonight.
I'm sorry to bring you into this, but I don't know anyone else
here.'

'I'm happy to do it,' he said, putting the van in gear and
pulling out of the forecourt. 'I'm not sure how my mother's
going to feel about it, mind you.'

They spoke little as Tony drove towards Lurgan, country
roads giving way to a stream of dual carriageways punctuated
by roundabouts and housing estates. The town itself was
jammed with vehicles, pavements lined with schoolchildren

waiting to cross at one of the never-ending sets of traffic lights. Graffiti on the walls as Tony cut through housing developments, three-letter acronyms, most of which Sara didn't recognise. Some streets with Union flags dragging from the lamp posts, red, white, and blue, others with Irish tricolours, green, white, and orange. Small houses clustered in rows, some well-tended, others going to ruin.

These were the streets she had seen on the news as she grew up, not the peaceful country lane where she now lived, but these dense gatherings of houses with barely room for Tony's van to navigate. It was these streets where she saw youths throwing bricks and petrol bombs at police in riot gear, children growing up in battlegrounds, raised to hate and be hated.

His mother's home was a three-bedroom redbrick in a cul-de-sac of near identical houses that faced a fenced-off railway track. She waited in her doorway, watching as Tony pulled up at the kerbside. A small woman of late middle-age, distrust in her gaze. She flicked ash from a cigarette and coughed into a tissue.

Sara followed Tony through the gate and along the path.

'Ma, this is Sara,' he said.

'You can call me Nuala,' the woman said, stubbing out the cigarette against the brickwork before tucking the butt into the packet. 'I don't need trouble brought to my door, but Antonio says you need help, so I'll not turn you away. You'll take some-thing to eat.'

It was an instruction, not a question, and thirty minutes later Sara sat at the table in Nuala's kitchen, a plate of chips, beans and fish fingers in front of both her and Tony. The sight and the smell brought a memory of her grandparents' home on a council estate back in England, a place her own mother seemed ashamed to come from. She ate in silence and gratitude, not realising how hungry she'd been until her plate was cleared. Sara insisted on doing the dishes, Tony drying, and once everything was put away, Nuala announced she was going to bed, leaving them both alone at the table.

'You want a beer?' Tony asked.

Sara almost refused before she realised she did indeed want one. A lot. He fetched two cans of Harp lager from the fridge, opened them both. Sitting down, he took a swallow straight from the can. Sara did likewise, the beer fizzing icy-cold on her tongue.

'What now?' Tony asked.

She thought about it for a moment before realising she had no answer to the question. 'I don't know,' she said.

'You could go back home to England,' he said. 'Have you still got family there?'

'My mother and a younger brother. Near Bath. We haven't spoken for a couple of years. Our relationship is . . . difficult, I suppose you could say. I could get a flight, but I've no cards to pay for it. Damien keeps control of the money.'

'I could book it for you. I haven't much, but I could cover that.'

'Thank you, but I think I should stay.'

'Why?'

'Because . . .'

She looked down at the table, the beer can held there between her hands. She had an answer, but it seemed foolish, and she didn't want to say it out loud.

'You can tell me,' Tony said.

She lifted her gaze to see him looking back, and she believed him.

'Because I feel like I'm needed here.'

'Who needs you?'

'Mary,' she said. 'The children.'

She could not hold his gaze as she waited for some scornful dismissal.

Instead, he said, 'If that's how you feel, then you have to go with it.'

Sara placed her hand on his forearm and squeezed it. It rested there a moment too long before he got up from the table. He drained the last of his lager.

'I don't know about you,' he said, 'but I'm having another one.'

* * *

A mild but pleasing beer buzz had helped Sara fall asleep in the spare room, curled on top of the covers, her cheek resting on her hands. The vibration of her phone woke her at close to two in the morning. She checked the display: Damien calling again. He had tried a few times around ten, then every thirty minutes until midnight. As she thumbed the red reject icon, she pictured him pacing the kitchen floor, one hand balled into a fist, the other pressing the phone to his ear. She thanked God she had disabled the location services, or Damien would have been at Tony's door by now. He would figure it out eventually, though.

Sara rolled onto her back and pulled the light duvet around herself. She had slept for more than three hours, probably the longest stretch she'd had in weeks. Maybe she could get some more before morning light crept through the blinds. Her mind had begun to drift when the phone vibrated again. She rejected the call. A minute or two later, another vibration, and this time it was a different caller: Francie Keane. She rejected his call, too, then powered off the phone.

As she fell back into sleep, she thought of lost children in the darkness, trapped between walls and floors, calling to her, asking her to help them. And a girl with scarlet ribbons.

She did not stir until Tony knocked on the spare room's door just before nine in the morning.

* * *

'Can you take me to see Mary at the care home?' Sara asked when she'd finished the breakfast of toast and cereal Tony had made for her. The cutlery rattled in the bowls and plates as a train passed along the track outside. His mother had gone to her job behind the counter of the small corner shop a few streets away.

'Again?' he asked. 'Why?'

Sara searched for a truthful answer. Eventually, she said, 'She needs me. And I owe her.'

'Owe her what?'

'She reminded me who I am. I know that doesn't really make any sense, but that's the best way I can put it. If she hadn't come to the door that morning, I'd still be scrubbing the floor, trying to wash those stains away.'

Tony stared at her, patient confusion on his face. Sara couldn't blame him. It made no more sense to her than it did to him.

'Can you take me?' she asked.

'Aye, why not?' he said. 'Not much point in me going to the house to work, I suppose, is there? When I don't show up, Damien will know you're here, but he'll work that out sooner or later.'

Sara could see the fear on him even as he tried to hide it by turning his gaze to the window overlooking the small back-yard. She understood the risk he was taking.

'Thank you,' she said.

* * *

Less than an hour later, the van pulled up once more in front of the care home. Margaret, the receptionist, recognised Sara as soon as she entered.

'Are you here to see Mary again?' she called from behind the desk.

'Yes, please, if that's all right.'

'Course it is,' Margaret said with a beaming smile. 'She was asking about you as soon as she got up this morning, saying you'd be coming by. Can you remember how to get to her room?'

'Yes, I think so,' Sara said, wondering how Mary knew she would come back. She thanked Margaret and climbed the stairs, remembering the doors she'd passed the day before, the turns and the corridors. A shower at Tony's house had freshened her, and the first proper food and sleep she'd had in days buoyed her, but she was conscious of wearing yesterday's clothes. Not that Mary would mind or even notice.

She found her waiting exactly where she'd been sitting the day before, by her open window, with the other chair already in place.

'Come on in,' Mary said, beckoning with both hands, a smile glowing on her face. 'Sit down. You'll take a cup of tea before we go. The girls will bring you a cup of tea and some biscuits if I ask them. They're awful good to me here.'

Mary's smile dimmed as she saw the confusion on Sara's face.

'Go where?' Sara asked as she sat.

Mary took Sara's hand in hers. 'To the seaside. To Portrush. Do you mind you said you'd take me?'

Sara considered telling the truth, that she had promised no such thing, but what was the point?

'Yes, I'll take you,' she said. 'But not today. I don't have a car.'

'But some day you'll take me,' Mary said, her smile brightening again.

'Of course I will. I just wanted to see how you were doing today, if you needed anything.'

'No, I don't need anything, except maybe to get out of here once in a wee while. And maybe to see the children. See that they're all right. Did they find you?'

Sara shook her head. 'No. But I think someone might have found them.'

The smile fell from Mary's lips. 'How?'

'When the people were working on the house, they dug up the floor of the old stable block. I'm not sure, but I think they found something. And I think they buried it again and built over the top of it.'

Mary turned her gaze to the window. 'They shouldn't have disturbed them. It'll do nobody any good at all.'

'Are there more?' Sara asked. She pictured the red stains on the kitchen floor. 'Are there any more in the house?'

'Aye,' Mary said. 'They're everywhere. Don't you worry, they'll find you when they're ready. When you're ready.'

'I should call the police. They should know if there were human remains found, no matter how old. Shouldn't they?'

'For why? Just so they can go tramping through the place digging up more floors? Sure, what good could that do?'

'I don't know,' Sara said. 'Some kind of justice, maybe.'

'Justice?' Mary looked back to her now, a thin smile on her lips. 'Them men who planted them children in the ground, they got their justice. Believe you me, they got what was coming to them.'

Sara hesitated before asking her next question, unsure if she really wanted the answer.

'Can you tell me about them? I read some newspaper stories, but I wondered, what actually happened in the house?'

Mary became silent, eyes distant, and Sara felt sure she'd lost her again. Then she spoke, her voice firm, her words final.

'I tried to tell them what happened, the doctors and the police and the judges, but sure, no one ever listened to me. Not a one of them ever paid a bit of mind to what I saw, what happened to me or the women, nor any of it. They all had their spake, but they'd no use for mine. They just wanted it all swept away, like yesterday's dirt.'

She leaned forward, her eyes sharp.

'I mind the way they looked at me in the hospital, then in the police station, then in the courthouse. Like I was some wild animal they'd found in a trap. They couldn't get rid of me quick enough, away to that home they put me in where they wouldn't have to look at me any more. No one cared tuppence for what I said then, and no one cares now.'

Mary got to her feet, unsteady, refusing Sara's outstretched hand for support. She limped towards her bed, her foot still tender from the cut.

'I care,' Sara said.

'I'm awful tired,' Mary said, hoisting herself up onto the bed. 'I'm going to take a wee sleep. But you can come again if you want to.'

'I will,' Sara said, standing and heading for the door.

'And here,' Mary called after her, 'you can still take me to Portrush, if you want to. I'd like to go to the seaside. I never did see the ocean.'

'Okay,' Sara said, unable to hold back a smile. 'Soon. I promise.'

32
Joy

FOR JOY, THE DAYS SETTLED back into their usual
grind, one much the same as the next, with Mary
improving a little with each that passed. Up early in
the morning, cleaning out the fires, lighting the stove, boiling
water so the men could have tea with their breakfast. In the
midst of it all, through the ashes and the grime, Joy saw a glint
of something she hadn't seen in such a long time. Maybe years.

Joy saw hope.

At first it seemed a foolish notion, and she dismissed it. But
as the days came and went, the idea of it grew bigger and
brighter, like something unearthed from the soil. So she kept
picking at it, revealing more and more of its shine.

One evening, as Mary slept, Joy spoke to Noreen as they
scraped the last crumbs out of the bowl of food that had been
sent down. The makeshift bandage and splint had been removed
from Noreen's fingers, and they had healed crooked, gnarled
like those of an arthritic old hag.

'You remember what she said?' Joy asked. 'About George?'

'What?' Noreen asked, but Joy knew she remembered.

'About using him. About him being the way out.'

Noreen was quiet for a moment, then she said, 'Don't.'

'But what if she's right?'

'She's not, though. There's no point in talking about it.'

'But what if she is?'

Sitting next to her on the bed, Joy felt Noreen stiffen as her patience thinned.

'Whatever you're thinking of, you better put it out of your head. It won't work. All you'll do is get us into trouble.'

'You don't know that,' Joy said, her own anger rising.

'Yes, I do.'

'You haven't even heard what I'm thinking of.'

Noreen leaned forward, rested her elbows on her knees, her hands over her eyes.

'Go on, then.'

Joy couldn't help but smile.

'It's like Mary said. George is the weakest of them. And he has a soft spot for me and Mary. We can use that.'

'How?'

'Let him think I'm sweet on him. See if I can put notions in his head.'

Noreen took her hands from her eyes, turned to look at Joy. 'What sort of notions?'

'That he could have a life away from the other two. Sure, Ivan and Tam treat him like dirt. They treat him near as bad as they treat us. Maybe I can put it into his head to leave and go out on his own and take me and Mary with him. That I'll be his wife and Mary will be his daughter. But a real wife and daughter, a real family, not like it is here.'

'And then what?' Noreen asked.

'Then we leave him. As soon as we're out of here, me and Mary can go to the police and tell them what's been going on.'

Noreen's laughter crackled like old leaves as she shook her head.

'Oh, you're an awful stupid wee girl.'

'Why?' Joy asked. 'Why am I stupid? Why wouldn't it work?'

'Because they'll never let him go. Even if you could talk him into it, Ivan and Tam would put a stop to it. They'd kill him before they'd let him go, you and the child along with him. Me too, probably.'

'Not if we keep it a secret,' Joy said. 'If we sneak away in the night, they wouldn't—'

'And what about me? They'd have me buried out in the fields before the day was over.'

'No, I'll get help, I'll tell the police to come and get you out.'

'I'd be dead long before you even called them. Sure, they'll come after you and George and the child. The two of them'll kill us all. Can you not get that into your head? We'll all be dead before you can set one foot out that door.'

'We have to try, for Mary's sake.'

'We have to live,' Noreen said. 'That's all that matters.'

Joy knew the words on her tongue were a mistake, but she spoke them anyway.

'You want to stay here, don't you?'

Noreen's eyes hardened. 'Don't you dare say that.'

'It's true,' Joy said, regretting each word as it left her mouth. 'You're too scared to go back to the world, so you'd rather stay here. You'll keep Mary and me locked up with you because you're too much of a coward to—'

Noreen slapped her hard. Joy felt the callouses of Noreen's palm on her cheek, her head rocking on her shoulders, followed by a floating sensation. She slipped from the bed and backed away across the damp floor. The urge to bite and tear at Noreen came on her strong, but then she saw Mary woken from her slumber, looking from one to the other, confused.

'It's all right, love, go back to sleep,' Noreen said.

'Aye, back to sleep,' Joy said, pulling the blankets up around the child.

Neither woman spoke again as they readied themselves for bed.

* * *

In the morning, Joy cleared the upstairs fireplaces, sweeping up the ashes and scooping them into the tin bucket. She was on her knees in George's room when he entered, looking for the shirt she'd ironed for him earlier. He slipped the braces off his round shoulders, pulled the shirt from the coat hanger on the door and burrowed his arms into the sleeves.

Joy sat back onto her haunches, her filthy hands in her lap, and waited in silence until his attention was on her.

'Thank you,' she said.

He paused doing up his buttons. 'What for?'

'For giving Mary the medicine. For saving her life.'

'Aye, well,' he said, turning away from her, moving towards the door.

'She's an awful good child.'

George hesitated on the threshold.

'She's so gentle and loving. So kind. So good-natured. There's no harm in her at all. Any father would be proud to have her as a daughter.'

'She doesn't have a father,' George said.

'You know that's not true.'

'Don't tell me what I know.'

He left her there, her knees in the ashes.

* * *

That night, as they settled down for bed, Joy lay with Mary, holding her close. She whispered to her as the child drifted in and out of slumber, told her about the outside, about cars and buses and villages and towns and cities. About dances and picture houses and music and books. She whispered promises to her that some day soon they would walk free of this place.

Soon, Joy said, very soon.

As Noreen extinguished the lamp, she caught Joy's gaze with her own. Joy would not look away until the darkness swallowed them all.

33

Mary

I FOUND ESTHER'S DRESS HANGING IN the old wardrobe, the one with no doors, just a rail inside. It was tucked away into the corner, like she'd hidden it there. I looked down, and there was her shoes in the bottom. The dress still had the smell of her on it, that good smell she had, clean like soap and flowers. The damp hadn't got to it yet. I lifted it down from the hanger and held the blue fabric up to my face and I breathed her in. Then I cried for her awful hard for she was my sister and I missed her.

A notion came on me then. The idea seemed a terrible sin, but now it was in my head I knew I'd never be rid of it. I looked up to the top of the stairs and listened. No one was in the kitchen, as far as I could tell. I pulled the dress on over my head, over the top of the nightie I had on me. Esther wasn't a tall girl, and she was slender, but her dress near drownt me. I could've fit into it twice. Even so, I didn't care. I ran my hands over the material, softer than anything I'd ever had on me. I turned in a circle and let the skirt of it flare out and I wished I had a mirror so I could see myself. But the children could see me. They watched from the corners and the dark places while I spun round and round till I was dizzy.

The floor was coarse and cold and damp on my bare feet. I went back to the wardrobe and took the shoes and slipped my feet into them. They were far too big for me, but they were awful light, you'd hardly have known they were there at all. They slapped on the floor as I walked circles around the room, letting Esther's smell rise up from the dress so I could breathe it in.

What are you doing?

Mummy Noreen at the top of the stairs. I took a buck lep at the sound of her voice, and I started trimbling, thinking I was in trouble.

She came down the stairs carrying some of our clothes that she'd washed. Says she, What are you at?

I'd no answer for her. All I could do was look at the floor.

Mummy Noreen put her hands on my shoulders. Says she, They must've forgot about this. They'd have burned it otherwise.

I looked up at that. The notion of putting the dress on a fire was a worse sin than me wearing it.

Take it off, says she, put it back where you got it. You can take it down to look at it now and again, but don't go wearing it. If Tam catches you with that on you, you know what he'll do.

I did know. My whole body went stiff at the notion of it.

As I took the dress off and hung it up, says Mummy Noreen, If you're fit to be dancing around down here, you're fit to do a bit of work up there.

* * *

I was terrible sad to leave the children and go upstairs. They could've come with me, surely, I wouldn't have minded, but they didn't like the light. They wanted to stay in the dark places, where they could hide.

When I went up there and got to work, it was the same as before, and it wasn't the same. I did the jobs I always did, but I was slow, and I got tired awful quick. Every once in a wee while I had to go and sit down, or maybe lie on the floor. Daddy Tam didn't like it, he said I was nothing other than a lazy wee shite, but Daddy George telt him, The child needs to rest. She shouldn't be working at all. Daddy Tam didn't like being telt anything, and not by Daddy George. They argued a lot, them days. They didn't get to hitting the other, but they weren't far off it.

Everyone was quiet around them. Daddy Tam was more cribb'd than ever. And he had a smell about him, a smell that was sour and sweet. Mummy Noreen said he was drinking, that's what the stink was. She warned me to say nothing to him, to keep out of his way, or he'd beat the tar out of me.

Things were different downstairs, too. Mummy Joy and Mummy Noreen weren't getting along so well. They always had their wee rows, always over stupid things, but this was more than that. Mummy Noreen was angry about something, and I didn't know what. Mummy Joy had done something on her, or said something, or hadn't done something, or whatever it was, but Mummy Noreen was wild annoyed with her. Even once, I got in her way, and she give me a clip round the ear. Not hard, not like Daddy Tam would hit me, but it hurt all the same. And here, didn't Mummy Joy lit on her, she had her by the throat. If Daddy Ivan hadn't come along, I don't know what would've happened.

One day, the sun was out, and Mummy Joy asked Daddy Ivan if I could peel the spuds out in the yard. The sunshine would do me good, she said, to get the warmth of it into my bones. I said nothing, but I hoped he'd say yes. And here, he did, and he carried a bucket of water and a stool out the back door for me, and I brought a bag of spuds and a knife, and I sat there in the sunshine peeling and singing to myself while the chickens pecked at the scraps.

After a while, I saw Daddy George come in through the back gate. I suppose he was done with his work for the day. He came slopping across the yard, his boots all mucked. I sat there, still peeling away, while he scraped his boots by the door. I could feel him looking at me. He stood there a lock of minutes, watching me work. A couple of times, he took a breath, like you would before you spake up, like he wanted to tell me something. But he never did. After a wee while, he went on inside.

I thought about it after. I wondered if he didn't know what to say, if he didn't have the words in his head. Then I realised, even if he knew what to say, maybe he just didn't know how to say it. How does a man like him, reared in a house like that, know how to talk to a child?

I took my time over them spuds because it was good to be out in the sun. By the time I'd dropped the last one into the bucket, the flesh of it all white and soapy, the sun had gotten low over the house. I dropped the knife into the water with the spuds, picked up the bucket and the stool, and carried them inside. The bucket was awful heavy, but I managed all right.

Daddy George was taking a cup of tea at the table in the kitchen. Mummy Joy must have made it for him, for she was fussing around the stove and the kettle when I set the bucket down next to her, the water splashing over the sides. I put the stool in the corner and waited a moment for one of them to tell me what to do. Neither of them did, so I went out into the hall, sat on the stairs for a wee while, to see how long I could get away with that.

From the kitchen, I heard Mummy Joy's voice, and it shocked me, for she never would talk free to the Daddies, not even Daddy George.

Says she, Imagine having a place of your own. With a family.

Daddy George said nothing.

Says she, Imagine if you had your own land, your own animals. Imagine if you had a wife of your own, all your own, and a child. Maybe a daughter.

Whisht now, says Daddy George. Go away on and get them upstairs windows cleaned.

She walked out into the hall, and she stopped when she seen me on the stairs. I thought maybe she would scold me for idling, but she didn't. She smiled and stepped around me and went away on upstairs. I got up on my feet and went to the kitchen door. I saw Daddy George in there, still at the table, still at his tea. But he wasn't drinking it. He was staring away off into some dream or other. He never knew I was there, watching.

* * *

When it was time to go to bed, I asked Mummy Joy if I could sleep in beside her. She lifted up her blanket for me, and I cuddled down into her, my back agin her belly. She wrapped her arm around me, the blanket around us both. I was awful tired and my eyes were hanging on me. I yawned, and I felt her nose and mouth at my neck.

Says I, Tell me about outside.

Says she, What do you want to know?

About the seaside, says I.

I could feel her smile agin my skin.

There's a place called Portrush, says she. We went there on our holidays. There's two beaches.

Says I, Two beaches?

I couldn't believe it.

Aye, says she, There's the East Strand and the West Strand. And in between them, there's the Arcadia Café. My mummy and daddy went to the tea dances in the upstairs there when we were on holiday. A band would play and a singer would sing, and all the people would dance.

I closed my eyes and I tried to imagine it, all of them, dancing.

Says she, If I was good, I was allowed a mineral. Like lemonade or cream soda. I liked orangeade the best. All fizzy on your tongue, and if the bottle was fresh, the bubbles would near burn you. We stayed in a guest house along the front, near the harbour, and in the mornings you'd get breakfast, oh, such a feed. Bacon and sausages and eggs, and potato bread, and soda farls, and fried mushrooms.

Mummy Noreen spake up from the other bed. Stop it, says she, you're making me hungry.

But Mummy Joy didn't stop, and I don't think Mummy Noreen really wanted her to.

We'd go to the beach, says Mummy Joy, and I'd paddle in the water and jump into the waves. Sometimes it was so cold I could hardly stand it, but my mummy near had to drag me out. I'd go climbing over the rocks, find the wee pools, looking for crabs and all sorts.

I'd heard of crabs. The way Mummy Joy described them to me, I pictured them like big spiders with hands.

In the evenings, says she, we'd maybe go to the restaurant in the big hotel, what was it called?

There's two, says Mummy Noreen, the Northern Counties and the Londonderry.

Whichever one, says Mummy Joy, we'd go for our tea. But you know what my favourite thing was? Going for fish and chips and sitting at the harbour and eating them out of yesterday's newspaper. Salt that would dry your mouth out and so much vinegar it'd take the breath from you.

Stop it, says Mummy Noreen, in a big moan.

Says I, I want to go there.

You will, says Mummy Joy. Some day soon, we'll get out of here, and I'll take you to Portrush, I promise. And you can go to the beach and get fish and chips, then we can go to Barry's Amusements and we can go on all the different rides, and then I'll take you to the dance and you can have all the lemonade you want.

Says I, Will we go with Daddy George?

Everything was quiet for a while, then says Mummy Joy, Time to go to sleep.

34

Sara

Tony stopped at a Tesco supermarket in Lurgan and bought sandwiches and drinks for them both. They ate in the van, and Sara was grateful for the silence. When they got back to his house, she would switch on her phone and try calling her mother. She still wasn't sure of her next steps, but she needed to hear her mother's voice. Knowing she had a home to return to, even if that didn't happen now, was something to which she could cling.

Should she call the police, tell them there were potentially bodies buried beneath the house? Mary's words lingered: what good would it do to disturb them? She knew Damien and his father had a scorching hatred for the police and calling them would hurt her husband and his family. But she would not do it out of spite.

Tony drained the last of his bottle of Coke and stowed their rubbish into a nearby litter bin before returning to the van and setting off.

'You know, you're welcome to stay as long as you want,' he said as they navigated the streets leading to his house.

'I'm not sure how your mother feels about it,' Sara said.

'Och, she's fine. She'd be lost without some drama going on.'

His smile was infectious, and Sara felt it on her own lips, like recognising an old friend. 'You don't strike me as the type to cause much drama,' she said.

'Me? Aye, well, I have my moments. Maybe not in your league, but still.'

She laughed even as she remembered swallowing pills and waking up in an A & E ward. Before she could dwell on the memory any further, Tony cursed, looking at his wing mirror.

'What's wrong?' Sara asked.

He didn't reply as he turned onto the road that ran parallel to the fenced-off railway track, the cul-de-sac where he lived a hundred yards ahead. She asked again as his gaze shifted from the mirror to the road and back again. When he held his silence, she leaned across until she could see into the passenger wing mirror.

Francie Keane's Range Rover, and behind it, Damien's BMW.

Tony cursed again. 'We can drive to the police station, see if they follow us there,' he said.

'No,' Sara said, feeling a weight drop low in her stomach. 'They've seen us. There's no point in running.'

As if in answer, Francie's car accelerated, passed the driver's side of the van, and pulled across the road, blocking it.

'Christ,' Tony said, braking hard enough to throw Sara forward, the seat belt gripping her chest.

She checked the mirror and saw that Damien's car blocked the way behind.

'You wait here,' Tony said as he shut off the engine, unbuckled his seat belt, and opened the driver's door.

'No,' Sara called after him, but it was too late.

Tony approached the Range Rover as Francie walked around from the driver's side. He raised a finger to point at Tony before he could speak.

'You mind your own business, boy,' Francie said, his voice booming.

Sara looked around for witnesses, anyone, but the van had stopped at a high wall that bordered the backyards of the houses. She turned in her seat, searching for windows with a view. Those that she saw were empty, no one watching. She looked in one wing mirror, then leaned across to the other, and saw Damien exiting his car, leaving the driver's door open.

'Can you not just let her alone for a few days?' Tony said, keeping a few feet between him and Francie, taking a step back when the other man got close. He kept his hands up, palms out, as if surrendering. 'Let her get her head together, like. Then see how she feels.'

Damien came to the van's passenger door, reached for the handle. Sara searched for a lock but couldn't find it. Too late, she grabbed the inner handle, used all her weight to hold it closed.

Tony jogged over, took hold of Damien's sleeve. Francie followed.

'Just a few days,' he said. 'Come on, just leave her alone for a few—'

'Get your fucking hand off me,' Damien said, pulling his arm away.

Tony reached for him once more. 'Come on, let her—'

Francie pushed Tony back and away, against the wall.

Tony kept his hands up. 'Here, there's no—'

Francie moved with such speed that Sara did not see him throw the punch, only saw Tony's head rock with the force of

255

it, the sound, like a hammer on meat, echoing off the gable walls of the houses. He staggered against the wall, his shoulder sliding along it for a few steps, his mouth open, blinking. Francie followed him, swung another fist, an uppercut to the jaw that lifted Tony off the ground. Sara cried out when she heard the crack of his head on the pavement.

'Stop,' she said, her voice lost in her chest.

Francie loomed over Tony, swung his boot into his flank. Tony didn't move, a pool of blood spreading from the back of his head. Francie kicked him again, and a third time.

'Stop!' Sara screamed.

The passenger door tore open, and Damien reached inside. She tried to slap his hands away, but one gripped her arm while the other snaked around to undo the seat belt. He pulled her down from the van as she screamed at Francie to stop, leave Tony alone, not to hurt him. She tried to resist as Damien dragged her towards his car, but he was too strong.

Sara called for help, but the words were lost in her sobs and the sound of Francie's boot against Tony's unconscious body. Damien opened the BMW's passenger door and bundled her inside. She tried to climb out, but he slammed the door, trapping her leg between it and the sill, the metalwork hacking into her shin. A cracked howl erupted from somewhere deep inside her, and he shoved her back inside before shutting the door. He ran around to the driver's side, climbed in, and started the engine.

As Damien turned the car, Sara snatched one glance at Tony, motionless on the ground save for a jerk each time Francie Keane's boot collided with his ribs.

*   *   *

Sara spent the journey back to their house – Mary's house – with her face buried in her hands, weeping, the tears slicking her palms. Every few minutes, Damien told her to shut up, quit her yapping, and she tried, but the sound of Tony's skull meeting the pavement kept ringing in her head.

When Damien pulled up in front of the house, he shut off the engine, removed his key from the ignition, and turned in the seat to face her.

'Look at me,' he said.

She kept her face hidden.

He seized her wrist, pulled her hand away, and said, 'Look at me.'

She raised her head and saw him staring back, dark rings beneath his glistening red eyes. His shoulders rose and fell with each furious breath. His voice trembled with his rage.

'This stops now,' he said. 'Whatever this is, whatever is going on in that fucked-up mind of yours, it's over. You've humiliated me in front of my father, in front of my mother, my whole family, and anyone else who hears you ran off with a fucking spark.'

'I didn't run—'

'Shut up,' Damien said. 'You don't say a word unless I tell you to. You understand?'

She did not answer.

'I'm angry,' he said. 'I was angry last night. I shouldn't have hit you, but I was angry. And I'm sorry. But I won't be made to look a cunt in front of my family. We'll get through this. I'll get you a counsellor or a therapist or whatever you need to help you get your head straight, but we'll get through it. This time next year, the house will be all done up, we'll maybe a have a kid. We'll be a family. But this . . .'

Sara recoiled as he jabbed his finger against her head.

'You have to get this sorted. And that wee shit Tony Rossi won't be coming anywhere near you or this house ever again.'

'Is he dead?' Sara asked, her voice no more than a papery whisper. 'Did Francie kill him?'

Damien looked straight-ahead, through the windscreen to the fledgling lawn and the trees. 'My da never killed anyone,' he said. 'Anyone who says he did is a fucking liar.'

'Tony's a good man,' Sara said. 'A decent man. He didn't do any—'

Damien snatched a handful of her hair and pulled her close, his nose almost touching hers. 'Shut your fucking mouth,' he said, the words forced through his teeth.

She felt his breath and spittle on her lips. Then he released her hair and sat back, slowly shaking his head as if he were dealing with a dim-witted child.

'There must have been witnesses,' she said. 'The houses all around. Someone must have seen.'

'An estate like that?' Damien said. 'No. Nobody there talks to the cops. No one saw anything. They never see anything.'

She wept once more and he sat quiet for a time, as if indulging her. Then he opened the driver's door and climbed out. He came around to the passenger side and reached in for her, his hands hard but gentle.

'Come on,' he said, easing her out of the car. 'When we get inside, you go and clean yourself up. You stink.'

She stood, her arms at her sides, her gaze on the gravel beneath her feet, while he unlocked the front door. He took her by the arm and guided her inside, the gloom of the hall closing around her. Two words appeared in her mind, shocking her.

I'm home, she thought.

*   *   *

They barely spoke as afternoon turned to evening, as dusk swallowed the last of the day's light. Once Sara had showered and changed her clothes, she searched the kitchen cupboards for something to dress the wound the car door had left on her shin. She eventually found an open first aid kit among the tools in the extension, and she taped gauze over the cut. That done, she went upstairs to their bed and tunnelled beneath the duvet, hiding there.

She listened to Damien wander the hall and the rooms, the landing, upstairs and downstairs, out into the extension, and back into the original structure of the house. His expensive shoes clicking on stone floors and bare wooden stairs, his phone beeping and chirping, text messages coming and going. He had taken her phone as soon as they entered the house, and she imagined him trawling through her call lists and text messages. Not that he'd find anything.

At one point, he knocked on the door, as if she could refuse him entry.

'Do you want anything to eat?' he asked.

Sara pushed back the duvet, faced the window, away from him. The darkness surprised her, and she supposed she must have slept at some point.

'No,' she said, even though it was a lie. She would not take food from his hand.

He left her, closing the door over, and she listened as he rattled through the kitchen cupboards searching for food and utensils. He bellowed a string of curses when something clattered to the floor. Eventually, she smelled something burning, followed by more curses and a stretch of silence.

A deeper darkness took her for some time, her slumber haunted by broken dreams of broken children between walls and beneath floors, until she jerked awake with the image of a girl wading through a river, scarlet ribbons spilling from her belly.

As the bedroom reassembled around her, as the world found its axis, she felt Damien's chest against her back, his arm wrapped around hers.

'You're awake,' he said.

She closed her eyes.

'I'm sorry,' he said, his voice quiet like a creeping thief. 'About what happened last night. About what happened today. All of it. Things are going to get better. I promise. Maybe I'll get some counselling too. My da was in prison for half of my childhood. That must've left some marks on me. If you grew up where I did, you'd understand. We sorted things out with our fists. That's just the way it was. But I can change. I swear to God, it'll get better.'

Sara didn't have the will to argue, to throw his lies back at him, so she lay still and silent within his embrace. As time passed, his breathing steadied and deepened, eventually turning into a grating snore.

Go, she thought. Get out now.

She eased out from beneath the weight of his arm, slipping the duvet away from her body, and lowered her feet to the floor. She stood and looked down at him. He still wore his jacket. It crossed her mind to reach inside the pocket, looking for the phone he'd taken from her earlier, but she couldn't risk it. Instead, she took quiet steps around the bed, towards the open door, and the darkness beyond. As she reached the threshold, Damien's phone trilled and jerked him awake. He cried out and shot upright on the bed, his wide eyes darting around the room. Sara froze, watching him over her shoulder.

'You stay there,' he said, his voice hoarse. He reached into his pocket, removed the phone, checked the screen as he straightened. 'Fuck,' he said, then cleared his throat as he brought the phone to his ear. 'Yeah? What's happening?'

He listened for a moment, then got to his feet. He pushed past Sara, heading for the stairs. She followed him down, her bare feet padding on the steps.

'Fuck,' he said. 'So is he going to . . .?'

Sara stopped halfway down the stairs, her legs unable to support her as her mind completed the sentence with the worst imaginable words. She slumped onto a step, holding the banister to save her from falling.

'Fuck,' Damien said. 'Yeah, I'll be there in twenty minutes. We'll figure something out . . . Yeah . . . Not at the house, no. Where?'

He listened as he turned to Sara, but he was unable to meet her eyes.

'All right. Twenty minutes. See you there.'

He hung up, stared at his phone for a moment.

'Fuck,' he said.

'Did he die?' Sara asked.

Damien didn't answer. Instead, he said, 'Don't even think about leaving this house. The windows are all locked, and I'll lock this door when I go. Best thing you can do is go back to bed. Get some sleep. It'll be better in the morning.'

He turned his key in the front door, closed it behind him, locked it. She listened to the car's engine cough into life, then recede into the distance until the silent darkness of the house swallowed her.

Sara remained on the step for an immeasurable time, her shoulder and head resting against the banister. She might have dozed for a while, she must have, because a dream crept into her waking.

In that dream, she saw a small boy, ragged clothes and bare feet, standing in the doorway to the kitchen. But she didn't see him. Not really. He was no more than a folding of shadows, an impression of a boy, a confluence of light and darkness.

But yet, he was there, in the doorway at the foot of the stairs, looking up at her.

I'm awake, she thought. I'm not dreaming.

Still, he stared.

Sara's breath froze in her chest.

This shadow-boy, this small disturbance of light, stepped into the kitchen, his eyes never leaving hers until he was out of sight.

Sara stood and followed.

35
Joy

J OY WAITED WITH THE OTHERS, each at the foot of her own bed, to be allowed upstairs to prepare breakfast for the men. Mary's chest still rattled with coughing fits, but she was almost back to the girl Joy knew. Noreen stood with her arms wrapped around herself, nails pulling at the sleeves of her dress.

'What are you going to say to him today?' Noreen asked.

Joy kept her silence.

'What are you going to do? I know you're working on him. And if I can see it, so can Ivan and Tam. They won't let you away with it. They'll —'

'Shut up,' Joy said.

'They'll put a stop to it. You wait and see. Just keep me out of it.'

'I said, shut your mouth.'

Before either of them could speak again, the door at the top of the stairs opened, Ivan's stout silhouette blocking the light.

'Come on,' he called down to them.

Noreen went first, looking back over her shoulder at Joy, a warning in her eyes. Joy followed, taking Mary by the hand. Upstairs, they set about their appointed tasks. Mary cleared out the ashes from the stove first, then Joy got it alight, Noreen heating water in the kettle and fetching eggs from the larder.

When the men had been fed, and had finished their mugs of tea, George sat back in his chair and scratched at his chin.

'I need a shave,' he said, standing. As he went to the door to the hall, he spoke to Joy. 'Bring me up some hot water.'

Joy filled a pot at the sink and brought it to the stove. Noreen came to her side, went to whisper something, but Joy stepped away. Ivan watched from the table as he filled his pipe. He said nothing. When Joy left the kitchen a few minutes later, holding the pot of steaming water, she felt both their gazes on her back.

She found George in his bedroom, standing at the dressing table below the window, a bar of soap, a towel, his shaving brush and his razor set out in a row. He grunted what might have been a thank you as she set the pot in front of him. She should have left him then, but instead she stepped back and watched as he took the soap in one hand, the shaving brush in the other, and began to create a thick lather with the water. He brushed the lather onto his face, working the bristles into his stubble, bending over so he could see himself in the mirror. Then he took the razor and scraped at his cheek, turning his face in the light.

'Here,' Joy said, taking the wooden chair from the corner and setting it behind him. 'Sit yourself.'

He did as she said, and she took the razor from his hand. She placed a finger under his chin and tilted his head back. The bare skin left behind by the blade was clean and pink like a baby's.

'You know, I used to have a sister,' George said.

The surprise of his speaking, and what he said, made Joy pause the blade mid-stroke. 'Did you?'

'Aye,' he said, his eyes distant. 'She was a couple of years older than Tam. She was an awful nice girl.'

'What was her name?'

'Eva,' he said.

'What happened to her?'

'She ran away. At least, that's what Da told us. It wasn't long after our mother died. A few weeks, maybe. We came down to breakfast and she wasn't there. Da told us she'd run off in the night. She was an awful nice girl.'

Joy said nothing, continuing to scrape the blade across his skin. She sensed he had more to tell her, but it was some time before George spoke again.

'There's a place for sale.'

'Oh, aye? Where?'

'Waringstown. It's not half the size of this place. But it's big enough. Good fields. Good grazing. There's a milking shed and all. I could raise cows for dairy instead of beef. It's harder work, but still.'

'Can you afford it?' she asked.

'Aye. Well, I haven't got the money myself. Da puts all our money away for us, me and Tam's. I'll have to ask him for it.'

Joy pulled the blade down from his jawline, feeling the resistance of the coarse hairs on his throat. 'Can you not just take it?'

'It's Da's bank account. He'd have to take the money out and give it to me.'

'What if he says no?'

'He can't,' George said, his voice thinning with uncertainty. 'It's my money. He's just been saving it up for me.'

'Aye,' Joy said. She rinsed the blade in the water then brought it back to his throat. 'It's your money. He can't keep it from you. Sure, that would be like stealing it from you. He wouldn't steal money from his own son, would he?'

'No. No, he wouldn't. Not my da. That doesn't matter yet, anyway. I have to make an offer on the place and see if they'll accept it. No point talking about getting the money till I've made a deal.'

'When are you going to do that?'

'Today,' he said, as if the decision had been made in that moment. 'I'll take the car and go and see about it today. The estate agent's in Portadown. I'll go over and see them today. Aye, that's what I'll do.'

'That's a good idea,' Joy said, 'but, here.'

'What?'

'Maybe don't say to your da or your brother about it just yet. No point in saying anything till you've got a deal, is there?'

'Aye, I think you're right,' he said. 'I'll say nothing. Not yet, anyway.'

'Aye,' she said. 'Not yet.'

As she drew the blade down his rounded cheek, he reached up and took her wrist. The blade left bright red beads on his skin.

'Listen,' he said, 'if it works out. If I can make a deal and I get it all sorted.'

'Aye?'

'You'll come with me, won't you? You and the child?'

'Aye,' Joy said, smiling, her voice gentle. 'We'll come with you.'

* * *

Joy ironed his good Sunday shirt for him, and his tie, and she brushed the hairs and dandruff from his suit jacket. Ivan watched from the kitchen table as she did so, drawing on his pipe, the smoke billowing around him. Noreen watched too, flitting between her tasks. When the clothes were presentable, Joy brought them upstairs to George, and she helped him dress, making sure the shirt was properly tucked in, his tie straight, his jacket smooth. Then she polished his good shoes at the kitchen table, a decent pair of brown leather brogues. Ivan remained watchful, shrouded in pipe smoke.

When George came downstairs, his sock soles padding on the floor, his father eyed him up and down.

'What's all this?' Ivan asked.

'Nothing,' George said, his cheeks turning a brighter pink. 'I'm just heading out for a wee while. I've a few messages to do.'

'What messages?'

George fingered the seams of his trousers. 'Just some messages. I'll be heading to Portadown, so I'll take the car.'

'Will you, now?' Ivan sat back in his chair, his eyes narrowing. 'What if I need the car?'

'Do you?' George asked, alarm on his face.

'No, not that I know of. Have you got your work done?'

'I'll be back by one. I'll get everything done this afternoon, don't worry.'

'You'd better. Tam's got enough to do without having your share.'

George's voice hardened, his shoulders rising. 'I'll get it done, I said.'

'Aye, well, just see you do.'

George sat down, and Joy knelt at his feet, slipped his shoes on, tied the laces. He stood and flexed his hands, shuffled his feet.

'I'm away, then,' he said.

'Righto,' Ivan said.

George stood for another moment, shifting his balance onto his toes then back onto his heels, then he headed to the front door. Joy remained on her knees as she listened to the key in the lock, the door opening and closing, locking again.

She looked up from the floor and saw Ivan staring back at her.

'Have you work to do down there?' he asked, smoke puffing between his lips.

Joy shook her head and got to her feet. She gathered up the shoe polish and brush and brought them to the cupboard, suppressing a smile as she did so.

36
Mary

I DIDN'T KNOW FOR WHY AT the time, but Mummy Joy
was all of a flutter that morning. Like she'd got lighter
somehow, like her feet weren't touching the floor. Not
Mummy Noreen, though. She had a face on her, scowling at
the rest of us like we were up to divilment.

When Daddy George came back from wherever he'd been,
I was peeling carrots at the sink. He came into the kitchen,
undoing his tie. I wondered why he was wearing his good
Sunday clothes when it wasn't a Sunday. I supposed at the
time he'd maybe gone to church by his own self, without the
other Daddies.

Says Daddy Ivan, Well, did you get your messages done?

Aye, says Daddy George, and he said no more even though
anyone could see he was busting with something to tell.

Daddy Tam came in from the yard then, and he telt me to
get him a bowl of water for to wash his hands. He smelled of
the cattle, and of sweat, but also that sour-and-sweet smell.
What Mummy Noreen telt me was the smell of drink.

He looked at Daddy George and he laughed. I couldn't mind
a time I'd ever heard him laugh before, and the sound of it
put the fear in me, so I went back to the sink and the peeling.

Says he, What're you all dolled up for? Are you away to a dance or something?

Daddy George's face went pure red, and says he, I had some messages to do, that's all.

Daddy Tam looked at Daddy Ivan and, says he, Is that right? Messages?

Aye, says Daddy Ivan, that's what he telt me, anyway.

Daddy Ivan was like that. His face was always like a white-washed wall. Nothing there to tell you what was in his head. But his eyes. He was always watching. Always. There was nothing in thon house he didn't see. Nothing he didn't know. Mummy Joy should've minded that.

Says Daddy Tam, What messages needed your Sunday best, eh?

That's my business, says Daddy George.

Daddy Tam laughed again, slapping his fat thighs. Daddy George's face went even redder than it was already.

Oh, your business, says Daddy Tam, laughing away. Look at you, the big man doing big business. What business were you doing?

Daddy George pulled his tie off and shoved it in his pocket. Says he, I've my own life, you know. There's more things in the world than this farm.

That set Daddy Tam off laughing again. I daren't have looked up from peeling the carrots, but I wondered if Daddy Ivan smirked then, because Daddy George roared at the both of them.

Aye, says he, go on and laugh at me. Just you go on. But you'll not keep me locked up here like you do them girls. I'm not your slave. I'm not your cattle.

His voice sounded like there was tears behind it.

Calm yourself, says Daddy Ivan. There's no call to be thran.

Don't tell me to calm myself, says Daddy George. From the corner of my eye I saw him point at Daddy Tam. Says he, Tell him to keep his mouth shut. Tell him to stop running me down and laughing at me because I'm sick of it, you hear me? I'm sick of the both of yous treating me like I'm a fool, because I'm not. And if I say I've got business to do, then that's all you need to know about it, right?

Says Daddy Tam, If I treat you like a fool, it's because you *are* a fool. You always was a fool and you always will be.

And here, didn't Daddy George let a gulder out of him, and he lifted the pot full of carrot peelings, and he threw it at Daddy Tam's head. Daddy Tam put his hand up, and that pot clattered off his wrist, and he let a yelp out of him. Carrot peelings everywhere and the pot bouncing and clanging off the floor. Then Daddy Tam runs at Daddy George like a bull, head first. The two of them slammed into the side of the sink and threw me out of the way. I went skittering across the floor, trying to get to the corner, to where it was safe.

Daddy Ivan got up from his chair then, and I saw the face on him, and I saw him pull his belt from his waist, and I crawled under the table. I heard him lash at the both of them, and the two of them squealing like pigs. I looked out from under the table, between the chair legs, and I saw Mummy Joy come running, stopping in the doorway.

Then I saw something I never thought I'd see as long as I lived. Even now, dear knows how many years later, I still don't really believe I saw it.

Daddy Tam lay cowering on the floor, his arms up around his head, and Daddy George stood with his back to the sink.

I saw Daddy Ivan pull his arm back, thon belt of his cracking like a whip, and he swung it at Daddy George, and here, didn't Daddy George lift his hand up above his head and catch the belt in the air? He did, I saw him. And he grabbed a holt of it, and he turned his hand so the belt wrapped around it, and he yanked it right out of Daddy Ivan's hand.

I mind Mummy Joy in the doorway, her gasping, her hand going to her mouth, her eyes all big and wide. Even Daddy Tam, down on the floor, his eyes were near sticking out of his head. He skittered away backwards until he bumped into the wall.

It went terrible quiet for a while, nobody saying anything, but the men breathing hard. All staring one at the other. Then Daddy George raised his hand, the belt hanging from it, the buckle dangling there. I mind the one thought I had in my head was, if he strikes Daddy Ivan, that'll be the end of him. That'll be the end of everything.

But then something else happened, and it near shocked me more than him taking thon belt. Here, didn't Mummy Joy spake up?

Don't, says she, and she stepped into the room, slow like the kitchen was full of sleeping animals that would ate her if she woke them. And she reached up and she took a holt of the belt, but Daddy George didn't let it go. So she put her other hand on his shoulder, and she came between him and Daddy Ivan, and she looked Daddy George right in the eye, and spake low and quiet to him.

Give it back, says she.

And he let her take it from his hand, and she gave it over to Daddy Ivan, turning her eyes to the floor as he took it off her. He wrapped the buckle end around his fist, and he swung it terrible hard at her. She dropped her arm down to try and save herself, but the belt cut around her wrist and her thigh and to the backs of her legs.

I mind the way she howled. I could hear the pain. She fell to the floor in a heap, curling around herself. Daddy George stood still and his face, oh, his face, so much hate and anger in him. But he wouldn't fight. He knew what Mummy Joy had telt him by taking thon belt out of his hand. But I could see the rage on him like it was burning the heart of him.

As Mummy Joy crawled away, crying, Daddy Ivan spake up.

Says he, Have yous no work to do? What are yous all lying around for? Do yous think this farm runs itself? Do yous think I'm going to do it all for yous?

Before I knew what he was doing, he turned and he reached under the table for me, and he dragged me out by my hair, up onto my feet, and I let a squeal out of me as he let me go. He kicked me hard in the backside and I went stumbling to the door and I went over the top of Mummy Joy, the two of us landing there in a heap.

We gathered each other up, got to our feet, and helped each other across the hall and into the living room. Mummy Joy fell into one of the armchairs, me on top of her, and she helt me awful tight. It was a while before either of us noticed Mummy Noreen was in the corner, a wet rag in her hand, a bucket at her feet.

Says she, You see what you're doing? Do you see how this is going to go? For the love of God, can you not see?

It's too late, says Mummy Joy, there's no stopping it now.

And she was right.

37

Sara

S ARA STEPPED THROUGH THE DOORWAY into the darkness of the kitchen, the stone floor cool on her bare soles. She waited while her vision adjusted to the dimness, the night beginning its surrender to dawn. Her gaze travelled the room, searching for the boy she hadn't seen. She found him, the impression of him, the layering of shadow, over by the old fireplace where the cooker now stood. His head bowed, he stared at the floor.

She knew what he stared at.

Slowly, she crossed the room to him, to the place where the red stains lingered on the stone. She could no longer see him, the shadows dispersed, but she could feel him, watching her as she knelt down. The stone slabs were smooth against her skin as she ran her fingertips across the surface, the grouting rough. She could barely see the stains in the blue dimness, but she could feel the change in texture.

In the floors, Mary had said.

Sara placed her hand flat on the stone and closed her eyes. She felt the cold hardness, and the sand and earth beneath, but what else? She opened her eyes, admonishing herself for such foolishness. There had been no boy, simply a trick the darkness played on her exhausted mind. Nothing more.

A movement snagged her attention, at the other end of the kitchen, the doorway leading to the back hall. She turned her head, saw a child, a small girl, little more than a toddler.

Shadows and light, that's all. Nothing there, Sara told herself. Nothing there but shadows and light.

But the child stared back.

Sara pushed herself up onto her knees.

'What do you want?' she said, her voice cracking.

The child stepped back into the darkness, became one with it, but Sara knew she remained there, waiting. Sara got to her feet, used the island for support as she walked to the rear of the kitchen, seeking the child in the dark corners of the back hall. She stepped through, saw the child slip into the extension, keeping to the dim pools as the first hints of light crept through the glass of the patio doors. Following, careful where she placed her feet, she searched the shadows for the girl, found her crouching by a row of cement bags, propped against the wall. On top of them, a large chisel, and a mallet.

Sara looked at them for a time, one idea chasing another through her mind, until she understood. She went to the bags, lifted the chisel in her left hand, felt the heft of it. This was not the tool of a woodworker, not made for carving and shaping. It was heavy, and its blade was wide and stout. This was made for breaking concrete and splitting stone. A masonry chisel, she thought it was called. She lifted the mallet in her right hand, and it was heavier still.

A good blow from the chisel would shatter the glass of the patio doors and set her free. And then what? She could walk to the village and get help. Maybe knock on the door of Buchanan's Grocers, just like Mary had done sixty years or so before.

She realised then that the small girl, or the shadow of her, no longer crouched by the cement bags. Sara turned in a circle, searching for her. She found the girl in the doorway leading into the back hall, and the kitchen beyond. The shadow-child stared back at her for a moment, then retreated.

Sara followed, entering the hall, seeing the child merge into the light and shade of the kitchen. And the boy there, over by the fireplace, guarding the stains, waiting for her. She entered the kitchen, its deep blue turning to grey as the birds outside awoke and began their morning songs.

In the half-light, the stains appeared quite black against the deep grey of the stone. Sara knelt down beside them, let the chisel and mallet drop to the floor. She felt their weight through her knees as they impacted the surface. Her fingers traced the rough grout between the flagstones, her nails scratching at the coarse borders.

She raised her head, looking for the boy, but he was no longer here beside her. There, in the fuller darkness of the back hall, she saw him and the little girl, the suggestion of them in the shadows. And more, others, their forms less distinct, but present nonetheless. She turned her head to see the door out to the hall, to the foot of the stairs and the front door. The shadows moved, took shape, dissolved, reformed. More children, watching.

I should fear them, Sara thought. But she did not.

They'll find you, Mary had said.

Sara lifted the chisel in her left hand, the mallet in her right, and placed the cutting edge on the grouting between the flagstones. She lifted the mallet and struck the head of the chisel with all her strength. The sound hit her ears hard, made her wince. She did it again, and again, and the chisel's blade sank between the stones.

By the time she had worked her way around the first stone, splitting the grouting, dawn light soaked the kitchen. Her shoulder and back ached, along with her knees, and blisters had begun to form on her palms. She brought the chisel back to the starting point and hammered down between the stones once more. It took less effort than before, and as it deepened, she tilted the chisel away so its blade worked underneath the stone, raising it a fraction. She hammered it in further, lifting the stone a little at a time, until there was just enough room to slip her fingers underneath.

Sara shuffled around to the other side of the stone, ignoring the shrieking pain from her knees and back. She wedged her fingers under the stone and pulled it up and towards herself. The weight was less than she'd expected, but heavy enough to pull a grunt from deep in her chest. She moved aside and let the stone fall away, cracking as it hit the floor. A square of bare sand now lay exposed, dark and damp to the touch, with a deep red stain to one corner. She explored the sand with her fingers, compacted and dense, then lifted the chisel and mallet once more.

The next few stones were easier, some smaller than the first, some larger, the grouting giving way with less force. As sunlight crept over the kitchen, she worked, chipping and lifting, until she had cleared perhaps three feet squared of hard-packed sand, flagstones scattered around, some whole, some fractured. The red stain at the centre, brighter now, like a butterfly trapped in the grains.

Sara leaned back on her heels and stifled a cry at the pain that erupted in her back and shoulders, the burning sting of the blisters on her palms. She looked around, to the doorways to the back and front halls, and saw nothing but the empty spaces there. Part of her better mind tried to tell her there had been nothing there at all, never had been, but she knew now that wasn't true.

She returned her attention to the sand and the red stain. Coarse to her touch, gritty beneath her fingernails as she dug at the surface. Too compacted to do more than scratch. She reached for the chisel, gripped the shaft in both stinging hands, and stabbed at the sand, dragged the blade through it, moving it away in clumps and drifts. Perhaps two inches of packed sand and pebbles, broken up by the chisel, then scooped away by her hands. The idea crossed her mind to go to the extension, see if she could find a spade or a shovel, but she knew if she got up off her knees now, she might not be able to get down again, so she kept digging until she found dark, damp earth. She stabbed at the ground, dragged the chisel across it, dislodging earth and stone, dug with her hands, clearing away a shallow crater, piling sand and dirt all around her.

As Sara's fingers delved into the earth, they found something smooth and hard. She stopped, breathless, staring down into the small hollow, and she saw yellowy white through the deep brown. Her fingernails scrabbled through the dirt, pulling it aside, exposing more, an inch of it now, and something else, a ridge bordering a rounded hollow. She stopped, staring at what she'd unearthed, knowing what she saw, even as her mind fought against it.

An eye socket.

'My God,' she whispered.

Despite her every instinct not to, she reached down and touched it, the bony ridge, the smooth surface of the brow.

'I'm sorry,' she said.

A shadow fell across the bone, across her outstretched hand.

'What have you done?' Damien asked.

38

Joy

JOY GOT ON WITH SWEEPING the floors, despite the pain. Every time she moved, the welts that had been left on her skin by the belt rubbed against the fabric of her clothing. But she had known worse pain, and she could tolerate this now that she had a scrap of hope to cling to. The logical part of her mind knew that Noreen was right, that this would not go the way she planned, but the hopeful part had grown bigger, brighter, louder, until it eclipsed all else. When she looked ahead, all she could see was walking out of this place, Mary's hand in hers, George taking them away.

And then what?

She didn't know. It didn't matter. As soon as she was free of this house, she could do anything she wanted. George was too weak to hold her. He wouldn't know what she'd done to him until it was too late. Another part of her pitied him, knew this would destroy him. But when she thought of all the times she'd had to bathe for him before being taken to his room and the stinking, sweating weight of him on top of her, his clumsy, fumbling hands, the foul breath from his drooping lip, when she remembered that, then the pity washed away to leave only hate.

Joy avoided him as the day ground on into evening, but she kept Mary close, finding ways the child could help her, giving her menial tasks, like carrying the dustpan outside for emptying or dusting the surfaces. They spoke little, which was not unusual when they were upstairs, but a heavier silence hung over the house today, as if the very walls were ashamed of what had happened.

Ivan wandered from room to room, watching, watching, watching, his eyes small and dark and quick. She felt them on her when he passed, the welts beneath her dress singing out at his presence.

Noreen watched too. Several times, she tried to take Joy aside, get her on her own, but Joy resisted. She knew what Noreen would say, and she had no desire to hear it. But as the darkness slipped in from outside, the oil lamps doing little to hold it back, Noreen trapped her on the stairs.

'I won't help you,' Noreen whispered. 'All right, I can't stop you, but I'll not help you.'

'You do what you want,' Joy said, louder than she should.

'Aye, I will.' Noreen's voice rose as she spoke. 'I'll live. You get yourself and thon child killed. But you won't take me with you.'

They glared at each other for a moment before Joy pushed past Noreen and down the stairs to the living room. She closed the door behind her and pressed her back against it, her arms folded across her chest. Her curses resonated in the room.

The sloshing of liquid in a bottle startled her, and she let out a cry, as if she'd been touched by a cold hand. She searched the room for the source of the sound. There, in the far corner, where the light from the fireplace could not quite reach him,

Tam sat on the floor with a bottle of whiskey resting on his knee. He brought it to his lips and took a swallow, grunted as it went down. His thick tongue appeared from between his lips and retreated again.

'What're you at, girl?' he said, the words lumpen in his mouth. 'What're you sneaking around like a mouse for?'

He pointed the neck of the bottle at her.

'I see you,' he said in a sing-song voice through a lopsided smile. 'I see you.'

* * *

Down below, when they'd eaten the scraps that Ivan had allowed them and extinguished the lamp, they went to bed. Mary crawled in with Joy, as had become her habit of late. Every night, as she wrapped her arms around her daughter and pulled her in close, she marvelled at how little there was of her. How small and thin. And every night it caused a bell of sadness to ring inside her.

Tonight, as Joy and Mary spoke to each other in the dark, Noreen remained silent. Joy could feel her there on the other bed, watching and listening, anger festering in her. But she didn't care. Let Noreen lose herself to this place. Joy had Mary, and that was all that mattered.

'When we go away from here,' Mary said, 'will the children come with us?'

Joy felt a crackle behind her eyes. 'What children?' she asked.

'The other children who live here with us.'

'What children?' Joy asked again.

Behind her, in the dark, she knew that Noreen held her breath.

'There,' Mary said, 'and there.'

283

Although she could not see, Joy felt Mary's arm move, pointing into the black corners of the room.

'Who are they?' Joy asked, though somehow, she knew the answer.

'They live down here with us,' Mary said. 'When I got terrible sick and I had the fever, I found them in that place. And when I came back, they came with me. But they've always been here.'

In the light of day, Joy might have told Mary to quit her auld nonsense, but here, in the darkest mile of the night, she knew Mary spoke the truth. And it did not frighten her.

Noreen spoke up, her low voice startling Joy. 'Is there a wee boy with them?' she asked.

'You mean the boy I remember?' Mary said. 'The boy who used to be here and then he wasn't?'

'Matthew,' Noreen said. 'His name was Matthew.'

'Aye,' Mary said. 'Matthew's with them.'

Joy felt something crack inside her as she heard Noreen's mournful sob, and she wrapped her arms tight around Mary, her legs too, and she wanted to swallow the girl whole, absorb her, pull her into herself. She buried her face in Mary's hair.

'When we go,' Mary said, 'will they come with us? I need to look after them. Can they come too?'

'No,' Joy said, 'they can't. They can never leave. This is where they belong.'

*   *   *

By morning, as she made her toilet, as she washed and dressed, as she set about her tasks, Joy had put the conversation out of her mind. As she swept ashes from the living-room fireplace, she did not think of children watching from the corners. As she gathered wood from the yard, she did not concern herself with dark eyes in pale faces. She had never seen them from the corner of her eye, not ever, no quick movements that made her turn her head only to find nothing but folded shadows. And if she had ever seen such things, she would never admit it, not even to herself.

All she cared about now was the phone call that George was going to make later that morning. After breakfast, he was going to walk into the village and use the telephone box on the main street to call the estate agent in Portadown. Little else entered her mind apart from the children, whom she banished as quickly as they appeared.

As she and Noreen gathered dishes from the table, George stood and informed his father and brother that he was heading into Morganstown on foot to follow up on yesterday's messages. He wouldn't be very long.

'You needn't be,' Ivan said. 'I want them cattle moved up into the top field. They've grazed the bottom field bare.'

'Aye, I'll get it done,' George said.

He didn't look at Joy as he fetched his coat from the back hall and walked out to the front. As Joy piled dishes in the sink, she watched him shuffle along the drive to the gate and the lane beyond. She felt a small spark inside, knowing that when he returned, he might have news that would change everything.

'You have to stop it.'

Joy turned to Noreen's voice, then looked around the room. Ivan and Tam had left them alone in the kitchen. She turned back to the sink, and the dishes soaking there.

'I told you, there's no stopping it.'

Noreen put her hand on Joy's arm. Her voice trembled.

'Please, Joy, please stop it. They won't let him go and they'll kill you for putting the notion in his head.'

'I have to try,' Joy said. 'For me and Mary.'

'They'll kill her too. And me. They'll kill us all.'

Joy said, 'It's done. That's all there is to it.'

Noreen came in close, hissing, 'Then *I'll* stop it.'

Joy turned to her, their eyes inches apart. 'What?'

'I'll tell Ivan. You're a bloody fool if you think he doesn't see it anyway, but I'll tell him, and I'll make sure he knows I had no part in this. You get yourself killed, get the child killed, but not me, right? Not bloody me.'

'You wouldn't,' Joy said.

'Wouldn't I?'

Noreen turned to go, heading for the back hall, but Joy grabbed her wrist.

'Don't,' Joy said.

Noreen tried to jerk her wrist away. 'Let go.'

'You'll say nothing to anyone.'

'Or what?'

Joy shoved Noreen into the wall with one hand and reached into the sink with the other. Her fingers found the wooden handle of the knife, and she pulled it from the water. She threw her weight at Noreen, pinned her against the wall with her forearm, brought the blade to her throat, light reflecting on the underside of Noreen's chin.

'You say anything and I'll kill you myself,' Joy said. 'I'll cut your throat if you try and stop me.'

Small hands reached up and gripped Joy's arm. She looked down, saw Mary looking back at her.

'Look,' Mary said, 'she's bleeding.'

Joy turned her gaze back to Noreen and the blade beneath her chin. She saw the thin trickle of red on the metal, blood melding with dishwater before it dripped onto her fingers. And the fear in Noreen's eyes.

'Just keep your mouth shut,' Joy said.

She took the blade away and allowed Noreen to spill to the floor.

39

Mary

FTER A WHILE, MUMMY NOREEN gathered herself up and disappeared away off somewhere with a tea towel pressed agin her throat. Mummy Joy stood at the sink, staring out the window, saying nothing. The house came over terrible quiet then, and after it was all over, after they were all dead, I took the notion it had been taking a breath, holding it, ready for what was to come.

But right then, in that moment, I no more knew what was coming than I knew the number of hairs on my head. I still had the notion things were going to be all right. Wee fool that I was.

I mind I looked down and I saw drops of blood on the floor, in the corner, where Mummy Joy had Mummy Noreen up agin the wall. Says I to myself, I better get that cleaned up afore Daddy Tam or Daddy Ivan sees it. If they sees it, they'll bate the hides off all of us. There was still hot water in the pot on the stove, so I poured some into a bucket, fetched the hand brush, and got down on my hands and knees and scrubbed.

Here, didn't I scrub the whole kitchen floor, as clean as it had ever been? I've no notion how long it took, but Mummy Joy never moved from the window in all that time. I was glad Daddy Ivan nor Daddy Tam never came back, because she would've got a hiding just for standing there, her two arms the same length.

Then, all of a sudden, she spake up.

He's back, says she.

I never lifted my head, just kept on at the scrubbing. But I listened, and I watched from the corner of my eye. Daddy George let himself in and locked the front door behind him. He came into the kitchen, and Mummy Joy turned away from the window. He put a big paper bag full of food on the counter next to the sink.

Says he, Where is everyone?

Tam's out in the fields, says she, and I think Ivan's in the yard.

Says he, What about Noreen?

Never worry about her, says Mummy Joy. Well, what happened? What did they say?

And here, Daddy George started to giggle and titter, and so did Mummy Joy.

Says she, Did they take the offer? Is it done?

Aye, says he, they took it. The place in Waringstown is mine just as soon as I hand over the money. You know what that means?

Aye, says Mummy Joy, I do.

He telt her anyway. Says he, It means we'll have a place of our own. It means we can be a real family.

I could feel his happiness from all the way across the kitchen. It glowed out of him like light from a lamp. It touched everything. It made me dizzy in the head. Even though I knew it was all a lie, even though I knew it would never ever happen, it felt like a real and good thing, just for a wee moment.

He took her in his arms, and she looked awful small in them, like he could crush her, just ball her up like a piece of paper.

And she hugged him back, even if she couldn't reach all the way around him. I wanted to giggle too, and I had to put my hand over my mouth to keep it in.

And then I saw when he tried to kiss her, she pulled away, turned her face and only gave him her cheek. I knew then it was false. I knew it all along, but I knew then most of all and I felt sad for him, even though he didn't deserve it. I felt sad for myself too. I knew I'd never have a father, not a real one, nor a real mother nor a family. I mind the notion came into my head, what a thing it must be, to have that. A family and a home where no one's afeart of anything.

Then I heard Daddy Ivan's boots tramping up to the back door, and says I, He's coming, and Daddy George and Mummy Joy near leapt apart from each other before he walked in the kitchen.

He stopped there in the doorway to the back hall, looking from one to the other of us, those wee eyes of his hunting for secrets.

And he found them in the end, like I knew he would.

There was never any secrets from him.

*   *   *

We worked through the day, doing what we had to do, but Mummy Joy never settled herself. I had to do half her work for her, she was that busy fiddling and footering. I had the same nerves in my belly, but I knew one of us had to get things done or we'd all be in trouble. Mummy Noreen did her share too, even if it was with one hand, her other holding a flannel to her throat. If the Daddies noticed the blood on her dress, they never let on themselves.

It was getting late in the day when Daddy George took Mummy Joy aside, and says he, Why don't you cook the tea for everyone? I bought a gammon in the village there, and new potatoes and some parsnips. Cook it fancy, make it special, maybe use some of the honey from the larder. Put everyone in the right form. And then it'll be a celebration, won't it?

Aye, says Mummy Joy, a celebration.

She didn't sound sure of it.

Says I, Can I help?

Daddy George smiled down at me, and says he, Aye, why not?

So we set about it, Mummy Joy getting the gammon ready, boiling it with carrots and onions in the big pot, me peeling the parsnips and more carrots. We were wondering what to do with them, should we mash them or just boil them?

Mummy Noreen appeared behind us, and says she, Roast them in the honey, along with the gammon. I saw that in a book one time, when I was at the library to stay out of the cold. I used to like looking at the cookery books.

Aye, says Mummy Joy, we'll do that.

She clapped her hands and tittered and we all took into it, laughing and chittering like I'd never ever known us do before. And I had that feeling again, like everything was going to be all right, like I was going to be free of thon house.

I should've known it would never let me go.

* * *

Before the men sat down for their tea, Daddy George spake up.

Says he, The girls have worked awful hard on this feed. Maybe they could take a plate down with them while it's hot instead of waiting for the scraps?

Daddy Ivan gave him a terrible hard look. Daddy Tam just sat there with a dirty wee smile on his face, his eyes all red from the drink.

Go on, says Daddy George, just this once. Sure, there's plenty for everyone.

Daddy Ivan let a grumble out of him, then, says he, Aye, all right, just this once.

He nodded at Mummy Noreen to make the plate up, and she took the biggest one she could find from the sideboard and she piled the food up so high I was afeart she would spill it all over the floor. We took it downstairs, and I still remember the smell of it, steaming hot. I can't mind a single other time I had hot food down there. The three of us dug in with our fingers and all the fighting and thran was forgotten about while we ate. I'd never tasted food cooked in honey before that, and I can still now mind the sweetness of it on my tongue.

The Mummies let me clean the plate, running my fingers round it, getting the last wee scraps. Then I lifted it to my mouth and I licked it till it was shining. I was so busy with that I didn't hear the noise from upstairs. The first thing I noticed was the Mummies had gone terrible still and quiet. When I lifted my mouth from the plate, I heard the voices up there, thundering.

It was Daddy George, mostly. Shouting at the other two. Daddy Ivan's voice was calm. Daddy Tam was laughing, the hoots of him over everything else. I couldn't make out all the words, but I heard Daddy George telling them he wasn't the eejit they thought he was, they always treated him like he was stupid, but he wasn't, he knew things too. They never let him have anything for himself, he was shouting, why would they never let him do what he wanted to do?

And Daddy Tam laughing harder and harder, and that must've hurt Daddy George more than anything, for that's when there came the big crash, a bang first that shook the dust from the ceiling, then cups and plates smashing, cutlery clattering above us.

Mummy Noreen put her hands over her ears and put her head down to her knees. Mummy Joy stared straight ahead of her, and I could see she was trembling. I reached over and took her hand and she squeezed mine so hard I was afeart she would crush my bones to pieces.

There came a terrible thumping and rumbling from up above and I knew Daddy George and Daddy Tam were bating each other up there and any moment Daddy Ivan would have the belt off him and swinging. Right enough, I heard the snap of it, and them men squealing.

Then it got awful quiet and all I could hear was my own heart jumping and kicking like it wanted loose from my chest. Mummy Joy squeezed my hand harder still and I would've cried for her to stop if I'd had any voice left in me at all.

I don't know how much time went by. Like I said, I haven't a great notion of time, I can hardly tell a minute from an hour, but right then it felt like it stretched out forever and ever until time wasn't a real thing a person could even reckon.

Then the door at the top of the stairs opened. I was the only one dared turn her head to see. For a moment, I couldn't tell who it was, he was nothing but a black animal eating up all the light from around him.

Then he spake up, his voice all broken with anger, and I knew who it was.

The three of yous, says Daddy Ivan, get up here now.

40

Sara

SARA TURNED HER HEAD, SAW him standing over her, horror on his face.

'What the fuck have you done?' Damien asked.

'What about Tony?' she asked. 'Is he alive? Please tell me.'

Damien took a step back and said, 'Get up.'

She looked back to the exposed skull, most of it still hidden in the earth. 'They're everywhere,' she said. 'Mary told me. In the walls and the floors. And you knew. You knew what they found there in the extension. You knew there were others and you did nothing. Said nothing.'

'Get up,' he repeated.

'We've been walking over their bones,' Sara said. 'All these children. You knew, your father knew, and you didn't care. How could you imagine living here with—'

He reached down, grabbed a handful of her hair, hoisted her upright. 'Get the fuck up!'

Sara howled at the pain, her back and shoulders, her knees, her scalp.

'Look what you did,' Damien said, his breath hot against her ear. 'After everything my father gave us. After everything you've put me through. Look what you fucking did.'

He threw her to the floor, sent her sprawling through the scattered earth and sand, across the displaced and broken flagstones. She scrambled up onto her knees, but he was on her, grabbing her hair again. From the corner of her vision, she saw him raise his free hand, form it into a fist, ready to bring it down on her.

Her fingers found something long and hard, a handle, the mallet. Without thought, she swung it up behind her head, and it met his fist. Through the shaft, she felt bone break, and he gasped, an agonised inhalation, then he whined. He rolled back onto his haunches, still astride her legs, clutching his now misshapen hand to his chest.

'You fucking b—'

His words were cut off by the mallet connecting with his chin. His head spun, twisting his neck as he fell against the island, knocking a stool to the floor. He searched for her with dim eyes. A string of blood and white fragments spilled from his lower lip as he coughed. She saw the disrupted line of his jaw and knew she'd broken it.

Somehow, as she backed away, he got his feet under him and stood upright. He coughed once more, spraying blood and teeth across the floor, and reached down with his one good hand to seize the chisel.

Sara got to her hands and knees, tried to crawl away, but he stood on her ankle, ground his sole into her flesh and bone. He lifted the chisel by its shaft, its blade pointing down, ready to stab at her.

She saw the hate in his eyes, and she did not hesitate.

Sara swung the mallet with the very last of her strength, the force of it buckling his knee, and now he screamed as his leg gave way. He collapsed against the island, tried to cling on, but he slipped, his head striking the worktop as he fell.

Sara scrambled to the far side of the kitchen, to the door leading to the back hall, and pressed her back against the frame. She watched as he lay on his back, mumbling and gurgling, his arms moving as if they weighed more than his body could hold. He tried to lift his head, but his neck couldn't support it.

She didn't know how much time passed as she huddled against the door frame, but eventually she realised she had to move, had to get out. Keeping her gaze on Damien, she struggled to her feet, fighting against the pain that coursed through her body, her back and shoulders, her knees. She crossed to him and used one hand to support herself on the island as she bent down, every bone in her body seeming to protest at the effort. Damien's eyes darted around for a moment before focusing on her. He tried to say something, but it drowned in his throat.

Sara reached into the pocket of his jacket, found two phones, his and hers. She took them, set them aside, then dug her fingers into the pocket of his jeans, retrieved the keys for the house and his car before gathering everything together and bringing them to the worktop by the sink. There, she took the time to wash her hands and her face, then wiped down her clothes with a wet cloth. Then she took the phones and the keys, found her shoes by the door, slipped them on, and let herself out of the house. She locked the front door behind her, ignoring Damien's attempts to shout something.

She had never driven Damien's new BMW, so it took a moment to work out how to get it started, how the automatic gearbox worked. That done, she manoeuvred it along the driveway and onto the lane beyond. She had driven as far as the village before the adrenalin drained away and the tremors and tears came flooding in.

* * *

Sara sat in the parked car on Morganstown's Main Street, the BMW's engine idling, until the car's display said it had gone eight in the morning. The people of Morganstown were already going about their business, heading to their jobs in Lurgan, Portadown and Lisburn, stopping for petrol and coffee at the filling station at the end of the village. In the rear-view mirror, at the corner behind her, she saw Mr Buchanan laying his wares outside his shop.

Exhaustion chased the receding tremors, but she would not give in to it. She had things to do. The pair of phones lay on the passenger seat beside her. She lifted Damien's first, but she didn't know his passcode. Of course. Sara opened the driver's window and tossed it onto the road. Her own phone had only a few per cent charge left. To her surprise, Damien hadn't thought to erase her recent calls. There, Tony's number. She hesitated for a moment, then touched it with her thumb. The display changed and a dial tone sounded. She brought the phone to her ear.

A click, then silence, save for a distorted quivering breath.

'Hello?' Sara said.

'Who is this?'

A woman's voice, soaked in pain and sorrow.

'Mrs Rossi? This is Sara Keane.'

A pause, then, 'What do you want?'

'I wanted to know about Tony,' she said. 'Is he all right?'

A shuddering exhalation. 'Is he all right? Oh, dear God, is he all right?'

'I'm sorry, I—'

'Antonio's in surgery,' Mrs Rossi said. 'He has three broken ribs and a punctured lung. He has swelling on his brain. They have to open up his head so they can drain it.'

Sara closed her eyes.

'My boy's lying in the Royal Victoria Hospital with his head split open because of you. He might never be right again. You did this. You brought this to my door and I will never forgive you.'

'I'm sorry.'

'Don't,' Mrs Rossi said, spitting the word. 'Don't you bloody dare say sorry to me. And you listen. The people around here, they won't say anything to the police, but I bloody will. I don't care what Francie Keane threatens me with, I don't care if he has me killed, I will see him in jail for what he done to my Antonio. Him and that bastard son of his. Don't you come near my boy ever again.'

She hung up.

Sara cursed, and a fresh wave of tears came. When they'd passed, she lifted the phone once more and dialled 112. The operator asked her which service, and she said police. A man came on the line, his voice rough and weary.

'What's your emergency?' he asked.

She gave him her name and the address of the house.

'There's a man locked inside,' she said. 'He's injured. Broken jaw and hand, maybe his knee too. And he hit his head.'

'I'll need to put you through to the ambulance service. Just hold—'

'No,' Sara said. 'There are human remains in the floor. You'll find them in the kitchen. But there are others, in the extension, and more that haven't been found. You have to look for them.'

A pause, then, 'Listen, where are you now?'

Sara hung up and tossed her phone onto the road. It landed next to Damien's, glass fragments scattering. She put the car in gear and moved off.

She had one more thing to do.

41

Joy

JOY REMAINED AT THE CENTRE of the kitchen while Noreen and Mary were told to stand in opposite corners, faces to the walls, backs to the room. The table had been overturned, food and fragments of plates and cups scattered across the floor. One chair remained upright, and Ivan placed it in front of Joy before sitting himself down. He held the belt loose in his hands. Tam was nowhere to be seen, but George stood at the sink, his hair standing on end, his lip bloodied, his shirt tails pulled out. He did not look at Joy.

Ivan watched her for what seemed like eternity, his brow creasing over his small eyes. The room was silent save for Noreen's breath cutting the air. Joy felt a queasy calm covering her own fear like a blanket. She knew how quickly, how easily, that calm could be stripped away, and she knew she had to hold onto it no matter what happened.

For Mary, she thought. You'll get through this for Mary.

Ivan cleared his throat and, in a smooth and easy voice, he asked, 'So, what's been going on?'

Joy shook her head. 'Nothing,' she said.

Ivan wrapped one end of the belt around his right fist and let the buckle fall to the floor. Joy couldn't keep herself from wincing at the harsh jangle it made on the stone.

'Don't lie to me,' he said. 'You'll only make it worse.'

'I don't know what you mean,' Joy said, feeling a fray at the edges of the calm.

'Don't lie. What's been going on?'

'Nothing, I swear to God.'

The corners of his mouth turned down. 'Don't you dare call on the Lord to help you in a lie. For the last time, what's been going—'

'I had nothing to do with it,' Noreen said, turning from the corner. The words came tripping from her mouth, one stumbling over the next. 'I promise, I tried to stop it, I told her not to do it, but she wouldn't listen to me. I had no—'

'Shut up!' Ivan sprang to his feet and crossed the room to Noreen with a speed that belied his size and age. 'Get back in that corner.'

He shoved her into the space where the walls met, put his free hand to the back of her head and pushed her face hard into the gap.

'Don't you say another word till you're spoken to.'

Ivan turned back to Joy, walked behind her, trailing the belt buckle across the floor. Joy realised her bladder needed release.

'Please, I want the toilet,' she said.

'You can hold it,' Ivan said. 'Look at that boy there.'

George lifted his chin from his chest. He could not hold Joy's gaze.

'You promised that boy you'd make a home with him, and he believed you. He's a fool, but I'm not. Now tell him the truth.'

Joy swallowed, kept her eyes on George, and said, 'That *is* the truth. I'm going to make a home with him and be his wife. We're going to be a family. Him and me and wee Mary.'

A smile broke on George's face, blood dripping down his chin. 'See? I told you.'

'Shut your stupid mouth,' Ivan said.

The smile fell from George's lips. Ivan stepped up close behind Joy, and she felt his breath on her ear.

'Tell him the truth. Tell him what was going to happen the minute he took you and the child out of here.'

Joy shook her head, felt the sharpening ache of her bladder. 'He's buying that farm in Waringstown. Mary and me are going to live there with him. We're going to be a family. Please, can I go to the toilet?'

'Tell him the truth.'

'That is the truth. I promise. Can I go to the—'

'Tell him the truth. Tell him you'd leave him before you even set foot in that place, and you'd take the child with you.'

'No,' Joy said, 'I wouldn't, I promise.'

'Tell him!'

'No, I swear to—'

She heard the belt crack the air, felt it wrap around her buttocks, the buckle digging into her thigh. As her knees betrayed her, so did her bladder, and she fell to the floor as urine trickled down her legs.

'Tell him! Tell him!'

'No!' Her scream ripped at her throat.

He swiped the belt across her back once, twice, three times, and the pain flooded her mind like a red river.

'Tell him the truth!'

Joy turned her face up to look at him. 'I swear to God I—'

She saw his fist swing down at her, the leather wrapped around it, and there was nothing in the world she could do to stop it.

A thunderclap exploded in her head. Something tore in her neck and her vision was swamped with black constellations. She did not see the fist coming a second time, but she felt another blast of thunder and hard things on her tongue that might have been teeth. The universe narrowed and funnelled as something hot flowed into her eyes. She tried to say something, anything to stop it all, even the truth, because he was right, she could tell him that, yes, he was right, but her mouth was full of blood and teeth and she didn't have the words to say it and—

He struck her a third time, his fist connecting with the rear of her skull and then her cheek hit the floor and something cracked there and the pain became everything in the whole wide world. She knew then that she would die, and she wanted that if it would mean an end to this, and she was ready, but then something miraculous happened.

From the floor, her one open eye saw George charge into his father like a train, screaming as he went. He pushed him into the wall, and the two of them wrestled there for a moment before spinning across the room to the far side and Ivan cried out as George backed him into the stove. George freed himself from Ivan's grip, then swung his fist at his father, and again, and again, and over and over as Ivan wrapped his arms around his head to fend off the blows.

Joy lifted her head from the floor and she wanted to say kill him, kill him, but her tongue would not obey.

Ivan fell to the floor, curling himself up into a ball under the rain of clenched fists and booted feet. At last, George stopped, gasping for breath. Joy pushed herself up onto her knees and coughed out a mouthful of blood and teeth that splattered and spread on the floor.

'Don't you touch her again,' George said between breaths. 'You lay a finger on her again and I'll kill you. She's coming with me and she's going to be my wife. You're going to give me my money so I can buy that farm, and I'm going to be a real man with a real family and you can't stop me. You hear me, you auld bastard? She's going to be my wife.'

Joy heard a metallic snick-snick from the doorway to the hall, and she turned her head towards it. Through the blood and the black stars she saw Tam there, his rifle raised, and she stared down its black throat.

'Who, her?' he said.

She heard George scream, No! and she saw a fiery explosion and then she was falling, falling, falling down into the dark.

42
Mary

I FELT THE AIR MOVE WITH the shot and then my ears was full of this whistling and rushing noise. Mummy Noreen screamed an awful scream, the sound of it rising up and out of her, and she screamed again and again, and she didn't stop. I dropped down into the corner, my back agin the wall, my hands over my ears, making myself small. I thought if I made myself small enough, no one would see me there.

Daddy George let out a roar and I watched as it died in him, and it turned to this terrible cry, like a dog with a broken back.

Daddy Tam lowered the rifle. Ach, says he to Daddy George, quit your yapping.

Daddy George quit his crying all right, he near choked on it, but then he threw himself at Daddy Tam and Daddy Tam couldn't get thon rifle back up quick enough. Daddy George slammed into him like a hammer and the two of them bounced off the wall and onto the floor. The rifle clattered away across the stone and I could have reached out and took it if the notion had entered my head. Daddy Ivan got up on his knees and guldered at them to stop, but there was no stopping them, the two of them rolling and punching and kicking the other. I mind seeing Daddy George bite Daddy Tam on the neck, growling like an animal, and Daddy Tam squealing, then Daddy George was on top of him and he made his fists into a ball and he pounded them into Daddy Tam's jaw I don't know how many times. Then he got a holt of Daddy Tam's hair and he pulled his head up and drove it down into the floor over and over again until Daddy Tam went all loose. All the time, Mummy Noreen was still screaming, and Daddy Ivan was still shouting at them to stop.

Daddy George sat astride him for a lock of seconds, his chest heaving and blood dripping from his mouth, then he crawled off him and over to the rifle. He took a holt of it and pushed himself up onto his feet. He pulled the bolt back and a brass shell came out of it and jangled on the floor, then he pushed the bolt back again.

At the same time, Daddy Tam gathered himself and he got up onto his knees. He looked up, blinking at Daddy George like he didn't understand what his eyes telt him. Then he let a laugh out of him that turned into a cough that I thought would rip him in two.

Says he, You haven't got the nerve, boy.

He got himself up straight on his feet, and I saw his clothes was all covered in blood, and I knew it was Mummy Joy's blood as much as his, and my mouth filled with sick and I swallowed it.

You were always a weakling, says he to Daddy George. A weakling and a fool. You see what that got you? A bloody idiot, that's what you—

He took a step towards Daddy George, and I felt that air move again as Daddy George pulled the trigger, and that ringing in my ears, and it punched a hole in Daddy Tam's belly. I mind the shock on his face when he looked down and saw the hole in him. Then he staggered back agin the wall, into the spattering of his own blood there.

Says Daddy Ivan, Oh, no, no. And he got himself up on his feet, but not quick enough to stop Daddy George pulling that bolt back and pushing it forward and pulling the trigger again. This time, it was Daddy Tam's chest that opened and he let out this long sigh and then he fell to the floor and he didn't move again until Daddy George put another bullet into him, and one more, and then there was no more bullets left.

Quiet now. Mummy Noreen's screaming had died away to nothing and all I heard was that terrible ringing and whistling in my ears. Daddy George stood over Daddy Tam and the kitchen was filled with smoke and I could smell it, the blood, and the dirty stinking things that came away from Daddy Tam as he lay dying.

Says Daddy Ivan, What did you do? Oh, Jesus, son, what did you do?

Daddy George's face went loose like his soul had left him. Then he lifted thon rifle by the thin end and swung the thick end at Daddy Ivan's head. It sounded near as loud as the rifle shot, and Daddy Ivan's head fell to the side like his neck had come loose. Daddy George swung the rifle again, and Daddy Ivan's head swung the other way and he stood there for a moment before he fell into a heap on the floor.

I mind his eyes looking right at me as he lay there, blood pumping from the rip in his scalp, and I could see the yellowy white of his skull. I don't know if he could see me or if his mind had left him already. Then Daddy George swung the rifle down on his head like he was hammering a nail into the floor and I had to close my eyes, but I heard it, that hard sound getting softer every time he swung the gun down, Daddy George grunting and crying as he did it over and over.

I opened my eyes when it stopped and Daddy Ivan was still looking straight at me, but his head was the wrong shape now, and I knew he could see nothing but the hell he was damned to.

Daddy George let go of the rifle and it clattered on the floor. He stood there for a moment with his arms hanging at his sides, then he went over to the sideboard where the good plates was kept and he reached up to the top of it and he lifted down the pistol that had belonged to the policeman. He pulled back the hammer with his thumb and put the pistol to his head. He squeezed his eyes shut and tears ran down through the blood on his cheeks.

I heard a cry from the corner, and I turned my head and saw Mummy Noreen push herself away from the wall, running for the door, and she slipped in the blood and came down hard. She got her feet under her again and she threw herself at the door.

I didn't see Daddy George aim the gun at her, but I heard the crack it made, and I saw the hole blown in the middle of Mummy Noreen's back, between her shoulder blades, and she made this moaning sound as she fell across the threshold.

I looked back to Daddy George, and him at me. He stood there crying like a hurt child, the pistol in his hand, the smoke pouring from its snout. Then he turned the gun to aim at me and I knew for sure I was going to die. And I didn't mind at all.

But I didn't die. He let a whine out of him and he put the pistol back to his own head. He stood there crying, shaking, his finger on the trigger. Then his hands dropped down to his sides and the pistol slipped from his hand and rattled on the floor. He looked at me, and I saw all the shame and the pain in him and I wanted to tell him it was all right, it was all over now. But I said nothing, and he turned and he walked to the door and stepped over Mummy Noreen's body on the threshold. I heard his footsteps on the stairs, the steps creaking under the weight of him, then the floorboards of his bedroom above.

I stayed there, crouched in the corner, for what felt like a terrible long time, and it was so quiet. The smoke scratched at my throat and my eyes and the smell sickened my stomach, and I think it was that got me to move: the dirty stink of it all. I stood up and pushed myself away from the wall.

There was no thought in my head about what I was going to do, but I reached down and I picked the pistol up off the floor. It was all slick and slippery in my hand. I took care not to stand in Mummy Joy's blood as I went to the door, for I thought that would be a terrible sin.

I stepped over Mummy Noreen's legs and went to the bottom of the stairs. From up above, I could hear Daddy George weeping, an awful desperate sound. I started climbing the stairs and I heard him clearer as I reached the top. His bedroom door was open and even though his lamp wasn't lit, I could see him in the darkness, sitting on the edge of his bed. He saw me watching and he dropped his head in shame. I walked along the landing and into his room, the pistol heavy and cold and wet in my hand.

He looked up at me again and I could see the tears glistening in his eyes and on his cheeks. Says he, I hid that gun in the kitchen. I thought if Da said no, I couldn't leave, I'd take that gun and do myself in. But they were right, you know. I am weak. And I'm stupid. I don't even have it in me to kill myself.

Says I, It's all right. You don't have to.

Just then, I don't know for why, I minded this one Sunday afternoon when Daddy George carried a calf out of the cowshed and into the yard. One of its back legs was broken and hanging from it all wrong. He laid it down on the concrete and called Daddy Ivan out, asked him to help it. Daddy Ivan went back into the kitchen and came out with the big knife in his hand. He opened the calf's throat and the blood poured out.

No call to let the cratur suffer, says he.

I minded that time, and I lifted the pistol up in both my hands and I put the snout of it agin Daddy George's forehead.

I thought of all the years I'd been there in thon room under the house, living in the damp and the dirt. All the years Mummy Joy and Mummy Noreen had been there. All the hidings they'd took, all the bruises they'd had, all the bloody lips and black eyes. I thought of the times they'd been called upstairs and I'd filled a bath for them before I was sent back down into the dark. I thought of the times Mummy Joy had come down the stairs, the shame and the tears on her face, the stink of him on her body.

I thought of all the times he could've let us go. All the times he could've turned a key and opened a door. All the times he could've saved us.

312

But he never did.

I put both my thumbs to the pistol's hammer and I pulled it back, just the way I'd seen him do it. It was awful hard to do, but I managed, and it clicked as it locked into place.

He breathed in and out, just the once.

I pulled the trigger.

43

Sara

WHEN SARA ARRIVED AT THE care home, Margaret at reception told her Mary was waiting for her. She let her gaze linger too long on the dirt on Sara's jeans and sleeves.

'I was gardening,' Sara said.

Margaret gave a forced smile and said, 'Mary's up in her room. You'll just need to show me some ID when you sign her out, all right?'

'Oh, sorry, I think I left my driving licence at home,' Sara said, the lie coming as easy as a breath.

Margaret waved the matter away. 'Och, sure, we know who you are.'

Sara thanked her and climbed the stairs. She found Mary in her room, sitting on the edge of her bed, dressed, with plain and stout shoes on her feet.

'Is it today?' Mary asked.

Sara couldn't keep the smile from her mouth, in spite of it all. 'Yes, it's today,' she said. 'I have the car outside.'

On the way out, as Sara signed the book, Mary lifted two apples and two bananas from the fruit bowl on the reception desk. Then Mary gave Margaret a long hug.

'You have a good day,' Margaret said.

'I will, don't you worry,' Mary said, stuffing the fruit into the pockets of her cardigan as she walked with Sara to the door.

In the car, while Mary hummed to herself, Sara spent several minutes figuring out the BMW's navigation system, and eventually she had a route to a car park overlooking one of Portrush's two beaches. A little over ninety minutes to get there, according to the satnav. Sara hoped that would be enough time. She knew the police would be searching for her, and for Damien's car. Please let there be enough time, she thought, a quiet prayer to no one.

On the journey, Mary talked about her days in the care home, how the staff were awful good to her, their names, what food they gave her. She talked about the cats she used to have out at The Ashes, six of them before the fire, all of them strays that she had adopted. And the chickens she kept, five hens and a rooster, and all the ways she knew how to cook an egg on the old wood-fired stove.

Sara listened and told Mary about herself. About the girl she used to be, the dreams she used to have, the woman she had wanted to be. How that woman had been stolen from her and she hadn't even realised until it was too late. But it wasn't too late, was it? Things were different now, and she would find that woman again, one way or another.

They reached the outskirts of Portrush before eleven, a golf course to one side of the road, sprawling caravan parks to the other. Sara missed the turn for the car park and had to drive in a circle to find her way back. The day was autumn-overcast and cool, and the town was quiet. She imagined it in the summer months, thronging with holidaymakers and day trippers.

At one point, she pulled up to a set of traffic lights at a tangled junction, a monument nearby, and a spired building made of red brick. All around them, ice cream shops, cafes. Ahead of them, Barry's Amusements, apparently closed. Sara imagined the screams of delight she might hear had it been open. To their right, past the smaller outdoor amusement park, a glimpse of the sea, blue-green, stretching away to the hazy horizon. Mary saw it and gasped, took hold of Sara's arm.

'Look,' she said. 'Look.'

A few minutes later, they had circled the town and pulled into the car park. The ocean came into view, stretching as far as Sara could see, north, east and west. The car park was nearly empty, and she was able to find a space at its far side, next to the path that skirted the beach. She shut off the engine and they sat in silence for a few moments before Mary spoke.

'Look at it,' she said, giggling while she wiped a tear from her cheek. 'Would you look at it.'

'Let's go,' Sara said, unbuckling the seat belt.

Her back and shoulders ached, worsened by the ninety-minute drive, and the blisters on her hands stung from the steering wheel. But she didn't care. It was worth the pain. She went around the car, opened the passenger door, and helped Mary out. They held hands as they walked down the gentle slope that led to the beach.

Mary looked down at her feet as the paved surface faded into sand and let out a laugh. They walked further, feet slipping as the ground shifted beneath them, down towards the water's edge, stopping where the sand remained dry. The water came in shallow waves, in and out, breathing like deepest sleep.

317

'Look,' Mary said, turning from east to west and back again. Rocks at either end of the long beach, saltwater carried by the wind to spray around them, small islands to the north, perhaps a mile offshore. Close to them, to the west, perched on top of the rocks, an old white-painted building with the word ARCADIA proud upon it in blue lettering. Gulls squabbled overhead. A few bodyboarders rode the waves. Further along the beach, an elderly man threw a stick for a yelping dog.

'Listen,' Mary said, closing her eyes.

Sara did the same, hearing the ocean rumble and sigh.

'I always wondered what it would sound like,' Mary said. She inhaled through her nose. 'Can you smell it?'

'Yes,' Sara said, 'I can.'

'Such a thing,' Mary said. 'You know, when I was a wee girl, I used to imagine if you stood on a beach, you could see the rest of the world. You could see England and France and America and Africa and all those places if you looked hard enough. But all you can see is the waves and the sky. And that's enough, isn't it?'

'Yes,' Sara said. 'It is.'

A movement on the water caught her eye, almost as far out as the islands. There, another. Black darts leaping from the distant waves and disappearing again.

Sara pointed. 'Look, did you see?'

'Aye,' Mary said with a giggle. 'Are they . . .?'

'Dolphins, I think,' Sara said.

Mary laughed and clutched Sara's hand to her breast, squeezed it hard. 'Thank you,' she said, breathless. 'I think I need to sit down now.'

Sara turned back towards the car park. 'Of course, we'll head—'

Mary sat herself down on the sand, shifting her rear to make herself comfortable. Sara lowered herself to join her, going slow to keep the pain to a minimum.

'Are you hungry?' Mary asked.

She reached into her pockets and pulled out the fruit she'd taken from the reception desk. Sara realised she was indeed hungry and gratefully accepted a banana and an apple. They ate in silence and watched the dolphins until they'd moved too far from the shore to be seen.

Sara glanced back over her shoulder, to the car, and wondered how long before the police found it. It was a valuable car, and she believed it had some sort of tracker device fitted. Only a matter of time before they would come for her, possibly arrest her for what she'd done to Damien. She would tell them everything, hold nothing back, and bear the consequences. But for now, there was nothing but the ocean, and Mary, leaning against her. Sara put her arm around her, felt her shiver.

'You're cold,' she said. 'We'll have to go soon.'

'I don't mind the cold,' Mary said. 'I never have. Tell me something.'

'What?' Sara asked.

'Can I ever go home again? To my house?'

'I don't know,' Sara said. 'I hope so. With everything that happened there, you still want to go back?'

'It's my home. It's the only one I ever had. And the children need me. Did they find you yet?'

'Yes,' Sara said, 'they did.'

'What about Esther?'

Sara pictured a girl with scarlet ribbons clutched to her belly.

'Yes,' she said. 'Her too.'

Mary nodded, seemed satisfied at that. 'I won't be here forever. They'll need you when I'm gone.'

'Who are they?' Sara asked.

'They're my brothers and sisters,' Mary said. 'All of them. And they're your brothers and sisters now, so I suppose that means you're my sister, too.'

She took Sara's free hand and squeezed it tight.

'Tell me what happened at the house,' Sara said. 'I want to know. When this is all over, I'll make sure I get the house. Damien can fight me for it in court and I'll tell them everything.'

Mary nodded along as if she knew what Sara was talking about.

'If I'm going to go back there when it's is all over, if I'm going to live there, then I need to know.'

Mary lifted a fistful of sand with her free hand, let it run through her fingers. She watched the grains fall and drift, wonder on her face.

'I never telt anyone,' she said. 'No one who'd listen, anyway.'

'I'm listening,' Sara said.

Mary looked out to sea, its greys and blues reflected in her glittering eyes.

'Maybe it's time,' she said.

Then she nodded, exhaled, a decision made.

'Aye, it's time.'

She took a long breath.

'Here, now, till I tell you . . .'

Acknowledgements

THIS HAS BEEN THE MOST difficult book of my career to date, and it wouldn't exist without the help of the people around me. I owe them my heartfelt gratitude.

As ever, my deepest thanks go to my agents, Nat Sobel and Judith Weber, and all at Sobel Weber Associates, and Caspian Dennis and all at Abner Stein Ltd. They have guided me through some of my most trying years as a writer.

Bronwen Hruska, Juliet Grames and Paul Oliver at Soho Press have shown patience and kindness far beyond that which could be expected of any publisher, as well as friendship, for which I am eternally thankful. And also Katherine Armstrong, who helped me get this book over the line, as well as Kate Parkin, Ben Willis, Ciara Corrigan and all at Bonnier Zaffre. And Victoria Woodside, whose sharp eye has saved me from multiple embarrassments.

The book *Regulating Sexuality: Women in Twentieth-Century Northern Ireland* by Dr Leanne McCormick was very helpful in providing a contextual backdrop for portions of this novel.

My life has been improved immeasurably over the last few years by my fellow Fun Lovin' Crime Writers: Mark Billingham,

Chris Brookmyre, Doug Johnstone, Val McDermid and Luca Veste. I hope to see them all on a stage very soon.

And my friends in the wider crime fiction community whose camaraderie has helped me want to keep trying.

Finally, Jo, Issy and Ezra, whom I don't deserve.

Reading Group Questions

1. Mary's chapters of the novel are written in a colloquial style – how did the language she used affect the reading experience for you?

2. Throughout the novel we get glimpses into Sara and Damien's past showing how their relationship developed to what it is today. What did you think of the ways in which the author showed Sara becoming trapped in a controlling relationship?

3. 'She never imagined, even after they married, that she would come to live in the place he never ever called Northern Ireland. Always the North, the North of Ireland, sometimes the Six Counties, but never Northern Ireland.' Why do you think the author chose to set this novel in Northern Ireland? How important was this setting to the story?

4. We learn Mary's story through the limited perspective of a child who doesn't fully understand what is happening around her. How did this affect your reading of the situation?

5. What do you think are the main themes of the novel? How does the author express those themes?

6. The ocean appears multiple times throughout the novel – Esther speaks about the seaside, Mary dreams of the sea, and the novel ends with Sara and Mary sitting on the beach and looking out over the water. What do you think the ocean represents to these characters?

7. What did you think of the ending of the novel? How do you feel about the way each of the characters' stories were resolved? Do you think any of them deserved a different ending?

8. Throughout the book, Sara and Mary form a connection. Why do you think the two women are so drawn to each other?

9. Did the plot unfold in the way that you expected? If not, which parts surprised you?

10. How do you think the children added to the story? Do you think Mary and Sara's paranormal experiences really happened?